After the Storm

By Sangeeta Bhargava

The World Beyond
After the Storm

a&b

After the Storm

SANGEETA BHARGAVA

Allison & Busby Limited
13 Charlotte Mews
London W1T 4EJ
www.allisonandbusby.com

First published in Great Britain by Allison & Busby in 2012.

A CIP catalogue record for this book is available from
the British Library.

First Edition

ISBN 978-0-7490-0944-1

Typeset in 11.5/16 pt Sabon by
Allison & Busby Ltd.

Paper used in this publication is from sustainably managed sources.
All of the wood used is procured from legal sources and is fully traceable.
The producing mill uses schemes such as ISO 14001
to monitor environmental impact.

Printed and bound by
CPI Group (UK) Ltd, Croydon, CR0 4YY

To Chotu

Chapter One

March. 1947. The year that would go down in history as the year India won its independence from colonial rule. But the speech Mili had just delivered had nothing to do with India's freedom or the British.

Mili joined her hands and said, 'Namaste,' as the hall burst into applause. She stepped off the podium and went outside. Taking a deep breath of the pine-scented air, she tightened her shawl about her. She had forgotten how crisp and cool Kishangarh was at this time of the year. She looked at the greenery and the unspoilt beauty all around, from her vantage point at the top of the hill. The pine, deodar and chinar trees, the still waters of the lake below, the Himalayas in the distance. She watched half a dozen mountain goats bleating their way down the hill, led by a couple of Kumaoni girls with peachy skin and cheeks as red as strawberries.

A young Bhutia lad was trudging up the hill. He was

bent double under the weight of the three pitaras he was carrying on his back. He reminded Mili of Badshah Dilawar Ali Khan Bahadur. She smiled. It had been a similar day in March, in the same town, when she first met him, oh so long ago. How long ago was it? Six years? Just six? It seemed more like twenty.

Mili stared at the chain of snow-covered mountains, the mighty Himalayas. They always reminded her of Ma's string of Hyderabadi pearls – sparkling, clear and smooth. If only life was like that.

She stood upright. Who was that talking to the gatekeeper? Raven? She shielded her eyes from the glare of the sun with her hand and looked more intently. Yes, it was him. A faint smile flickered across her face. Was that a hint of a pot belly, she wondered, her smile broadening into a grin. He had put up the lapels of his jacket to keep out the cold. It added to his charm – making him look casual and yet smart.

She started running down the gravel path. But by the time she reached the gate, he was gone. She looked down the hill in dismay, then turned to the gatekeeper. 'The English gentleman you were speaking to a moment ago?'

'Nothing important, memsahib. He only telling me give this note to Malvika Singh . . .'

Mili snatched the piece of paper from him. 'That's me. The note's for me.' Clutching it in her hand, she walked over to a deodar tree near the gate. Leaning against the tree, she began to read it. It didn't say much. Just that he was surprised to see her after all these years and would she care to join him for tea at his house that evening.

She stared at the note. A chiselled, lean face with hazel eyes stared back at her. Raven. He was laughing at her . . . now he was scolding her and Vicky . . . and now that his back was turned, Vicky was sticking out her tongue at him . . .

1941. Mohanagar. A lazy February afternoon. The palace slumbered while a wintry sun kept its vigil. Mili, however, was wide awake and stood looking out of her window. She watched with an amused smile as Vicky pulled herself up the low wall that surrounded the inner courtyard of the palace. Jumping to the ground with a thud, Vicky dusted her palms on her frock. Mili stood still. The sound had woken up one of the doorkeepers. She shook her head as he mumbled, 'Oh, Vicky baba,' and went back to sleep. Nice cushy job he had. All he had to do to earn his salary was to sleep at his post.

She turned her attention back to Vicky. She was looking around carefully. Then she scampered onto the veranda and threw a tiny pebble at Mili's window. Mili hid behind the golden drapes and urgently held her finger to her lip as Bhoomi began to giggle. As soon as Vicky leant against the windowpane and peered in, Mili swung it open.

'What th—' Vicky cried as she fell into the room. Mili burst out laughing. Bhoomi stood in a corner with the edge of her sari over her mouth to suppress her giggle.

'What the devil . . .' Vicky mumbled as she came towards Mili, hands on her hips. Mili tried to back off but Vicky had grabbed her shoulders. 'Mili,' she shouted as she shook her.

'Y-yes?' replied Mili, pretending to be frightened, a frown creasing her forehead.

'I've got admission in STH.'

'I know,' replied Mili, as Vicky loosened her grip.

'How'd you know?'

'Because . . .' Mili's bright eyes twinkled as she waved an envelope at her, 'I just got my admission letter as well.'

The two friends hugged each other excitedly, like fledglings that had just discovered they could fly.

'Such fun,' squealed Vicky, as she pushed back her thick-rimmed glasses from the tip of her nose. 'No more of this boring city. Where nothing ever happens . . .'

'And just think,' added Mili, fiddling with her hair that Bhoomi had plaited and tied neatly into rolls with blue ribbons, 'no more having to take Ma's permission for every little thing or Bauji's ifs and buts. Oh Vicky, I'm so thrilled.'

Vicky lifted her chin and looked down her nose at Mili. 'Princess Malvika Singh. Say thank you to Miss Victoria Nunes. If it wasn't for my illness, you—' She stopped speaking and gestured to Mili to look behind her. Mili turned around with a start and almost bumped into Ma.

Ma did not speak, merely nodded her head as Vicky and Bhoomi joined their hands and bowed. Mili shifted uncomfortably and began chewing her thumbnail as Ma turned to look at her. Nobody spoke. The only sound that could be heard was that of the tennis racquet hitting the ball, from the court adjoining the veranda. Must be Uday playing with that new friend of his.

'Is it true you've got admission to that school in Kishangarh?' Ma finally asked.

'Yes, Ma,' Mili replied, looking down.

'I'd better go,' muttered Vicky and started to climb out of the window.

'We do have doors, you know,' Ma said, a bemused look on her face. She had never been able to fathom Vicky's ways.

Vicky scratched her head and grinned foolishly before replying, 'Yes, of course. I forgot.'

Ma raised her hand. 'Stay and hear us out,' she said. She cleared her throat. 'Mili, we know we let you apply for admission to that school on Mrs Nunes' insistence and you have our permission to go. But your Bauji will need some convincing.'

'Please talk to him, Ma,' Mili said as she clutched her hand. 'You can do it.'

'Yes, Your Highness. He listens to you,' added Vicky.

'We'll see what we can do. But it won't be easy,' replied Ma, thinking hard.

'Can Mili come? With me? To see my mother?' Vicky asked. 'She'll be thrilled.'

Ma looked at Vicky and then at Mili, slightly perplexed. Mili grinned. Vicky's mind was like a racehorse, galloping from one thought to the next.

'Please, Ma? Can we go break the news to Mrs Nunes?' begged Mili.

'You know we don't like to send you to town these days because of the freedom movement. Not to mention the war . . .'

Mili looked at Ma with pleading, watery eyes. Ma hesitated for a moment, then shrugged her shoulders. 'All right, then,' she replied and turned to Bhoomi, who

11

had been standing quietly near the door all this while.

'Bhoomi, tell Tulsidas to take Princess Malvika and her friend to Mrs Nunes' clinic and to bring her back in two hours.'

'Yes, Your Highness,' answered Bhoomi as she joined her hands, bowed and backed out of the room to look for the chauffeur.

Mili grinned at Vicky, then hugged Ma. She always smelt of sandalwood – so pious and righteous that Mili found herself examining her conscience whenever she was in her presence. 'You're the best mother in all the land,' she whispered.

'Save those words for your father,' Ma replied as she left the room, her fragrance still lingering.

Mili walked over to her dressing table. She adjusted her blue silk dupatta and straightened the sapphire on her necklace, caressing its smooth surface as she did so.

'Isn't it tiresome? All this jewellery?' Vicky asked.

'Not at all,' Mili replied. 'I love it.'

Vicky stood behind her and grinned at their reflection in the gilt-edged mirror. 'Mummum will be pleased.'

Mili looked at her and smiled. Vicky had a plain, flat face and her huge glasses gave her an unnaturally solemn look. But the moment she grinned, her entire face lit up, her eyes laughing with such merriment that one couldn't help but smile back at her.

'Let's go. Ma will worry if we don't get back before dark,' said Mili, as she pulled Vicky towards the door.

Vicky looked at the clock that hung on the wall behind Mummum's desk. It had taken them twenty minutes to reach her clinic from the palace. She yawned as Mummum continued to talk into the telephone. She pulled a face at Mili, who sat primly and patiently beside her. How was it possible for someone to be so well behaved all the time? she wondered. She looked around at the bare walls. Why were hospitals and clinics always so boring? Wouldn't the patients get better faster if they had something cheerful to look at?

That's it. She couldn't sit still a minute longer. Her chair scraped noisily against the concrete floor as she got up. She walked over to the table that stood against the wall at the right-hand corner of the room. After scrutinising the bottles for a moment, she picked up one. Unscrewing the lid, she sniffed at it, screwed up her nose at the pungent smell and hastily slammed the lid. She opened another. 'Yuck, this smells like phenyl,' she muttered as she picked up a third. Umm, this didn't smell bad at all. And the syrup looked thick, like malt. She wondered if she could taste it. She looked at Mummum. She was still on the phone but was watching her from the corner of her eye and glared at her. Vicky pulled a face again, put the bottle back on the table, pushed back her glasses and went and sat down.

'Mummum, I've got admission!' Vicky had sprung to Mummum's side even before she had replaced the receiver on its cradle.

'Good heavens,' exclaimed Mummum. 'Is it true? Is it really true?' She hugged Vicky and kissed her hard, then embraced Mili. 'I always knew you'd be the one to do me proud. Those sisters of yours are useless.' She paused to look at her daughter's face and pat her hair. 'Mrs

Gomes,' she trumpeted to her secretary, 'my Victoria here has secured a place at the School for Tender Hearts in Kishangarh.'

Mrs Gomes looked up from her typing and hurried over to congratulate her. She shook Mummum's hand, then patted Vicky's head. 'Well done, Vicky,' she said.

'Victoria, Mrs Gomes, Victoria. You wouldn't call Queen Victoria "Vicky", now would you?'

Mrs Gomes licked her lips. Before she could reply, the other nurses and doctors had started filing into Mummum's cabin, having heard the news.

Vicky noticed the smug look on Mummum's plump face and smiled. Moments like this had been rare in her mother's life. Her family had severed all ties with her when she married Papa, as he was an Englishman. Relatives are cruel. They even regarded Papa's untimely death as divine justice and refused to accept her back into the fold. But Mummum was a proud woman. She faced life head-on. She worked hard to reach where she was now and Vicky was proud of her.

'Thank you, thank you,' Mummum's loud voice boomed for everyone to hear. 'And did you know STH Kishangarh is amongst the most acclaimed schools in this country? Until recently, ninety-five per cent of the students there were English.'

Vicky grinned as everyone exclaimed and congratulated her once again.

'Madam, this calls for a celebration, a par—' said Pankaj.

'Yes, why not?' Mummum cut in. 'And Pankaj, don't forget to invite Mr Chaddha. Let's see if I can persuade

14

him to change the second clause of the contract during the party.'

'Yes, ma'am.' With those words the staff dispersed and Mummum turned her attention to Mili. Taking her in her arms she exclaimed, 'I'm so happy, my child, that you're going to be there with my Victoria.'

Just then Tulsidas came into the room. He joined his hands and said, 'Beg pardon, ma'am, but I fear there be rumours of trouble brewing in town. Because of the arrest of them revolutionaries.'

'Good heavens, in that case . . . come on, girls,' Mummum said impatiently, shoving the two girls towards the door. 'You had better hurry. Oh, dear Lord, don't let my girls come to any harm.'

Vicky walked towards the car with Mili, then went back to give Mummum another hug. She grinned as Mummum frowned at her with feigned anger, lightly smacked her on the head and said, 'Off with you now.'

Vicky and Mili got into the Rolls-Royce. What trouble was that Tulsidas talking about? As far as Vicky could see, there was nothing unusual. It was evening. The bazaar through which they were now passing was as busy as it normally was at this time of the day. He had got Mummum all worked up for nothing.

Vicky looked out of the window. The sweet smell of jalebis wafted into the car and made her realise it was nearly time for supper. She looked longingly at the orange, syrupy sweets. The roadside vendor had piled the intricately curled jalebis one on top of the other to make a mini mountain. They beckoned to Vicky and she

15

was tempted to ask Tulsidas to stop the car. But no, Mili was not allowed to eat anything off the streets.

'Do you think we'll get jalebis? In Kishangarh?' she asked Mili, imagining herself biting into one and the orange syrup spilling over her tongue and gushing down her throat.

'You know, I was looking at some pictures of Kishangarh. And the winding road that ran down the mountain to the valley below looked just like a jalebi.'

Vicky rolled her eyes. Mili grinned and stuck out her tongue at her.

'Are you taking Bhoomi along? To Kishangarh?' Vicky asked, pushing back her glasses.

'Heavens, no. That would defeat the very purpose of my going there, wouldn't it? I want to stay there, with you, in the boarding school. See what life is like outside the palace.'

'But what if—' Vicky stopped abruptly as she realised the car had slowed down considerably, owing to a large crowd that had emerged out of nowhere. There were hordes of men clad in khadi kurtas, white pyjamas and white caps. Some of them were carrying banners and shouting slogans. Others waved the Congress tricoloured flag. Every so often they would raise their hands in the air and shout, 'Bharat Mata ki Jai. Down with imperialism. Release our comrades from prison. They're innocent.' There were even some women in the mob, dressed in starched cotton saris and shouting alongside the men.

'Close window, Your Highness,' said Tulsidas as he quickly rolled up his own.

Mili and Vicky hurriedly did the same. The car came

to a halt as the crowd closed in on them. Some of them were now shouting, 'Down with monarchy.'

Vicky looked at Mili. Her lips had gone dry and beads of perspiration were breaking out on her forehead.

'Oh no, oh no,' Mili exclaimed. 'What if they break the windscreen with their sticks?'

'Don't worry, Your Highness. They Indians, not Angrez. They not hurt children,' said Tulsidas as he rolled down his window a couple of inches.

'What in Lord Kishan's name are you doing? Getting all of us killed?' shrieked Mili.

Tulsidas rolled down his window another inch and stuck his head out. 'You wanting to hurt helpless schoolgirls? Indian girls? Shame on you. Back off.' With that he hastily rolled up the window again.

A few men stepped forward and peered into the car through the windows. 'They're Indians. Children,' said one, thumping the bonnet of the car. 'Let them pass.'

The throng parted to give way and the car crawled slowly out of the bazaar.

Mili was still shaking when they reached the palace. Vicky caressed her hand comfortingly.

'If Ma and Bauji come to know about this, they'll never let me go to Kishangarh,' Mili wailed.

'Driverji,' Vicky said to Tulsidas, 'please don't mention this incident to anyone. Least of all the King and Queen.'

'Not a word, Vicky baba,' said Tulsidas, putting a finger on his lips and shaking his head. 'What happen today go with me to my funeral pyre.'

Bhoomi came running down the palace stairs as Tulsidas held the car door open for Mili to step out.

'Princess, His Majesty wants to see you in his room right away,' she said.

'I'll be there in a minute,' said Mili. She looked at Vicky anxiously. 'Do you think he knows about the mob?' she asked.

Vicky gave her a small smile of reassurance. 'I'm sure he doesn't. And don't worry, it's over. The crowd's gone. You're safe.'

Mili nodded. Vicky waved out to her friend as the car pulled out of the driveway and made its way slowly to her home, just two blocks away.

The evening prayers had just been said and the smell of incense and camphor greeted Mili as she entered the palace and was ushered into Bauji's rooms. Bauji sat regally on the armchair that stood by the window. Everything about him was big and regal and sumptuous. His bedchamber was huge, the bed king-sized. The bed linen, the cushions, the drapes – they were all heavy, shimmery, velvety. Why, even the chandelier that was tinkling at her from the ceiling was the biggest in the whole palace. He himself was a large, formidable, swarthy man and Mili was a tad afraid of him. When angry, he looked like a rakshas. But when happy, and his belly shook with laughter, he reminded her of the elephant god Ganesh, the jolly, wise god. For Bauji was an extremely wise man too. He knew a lot. He had even gone to England for higher studies.

Ma was reclining on a sofa next to Bauji's armchair. Patting the sofa, she nodded at her. Mili sat down on the sofa tentatively. She looked at the huge rug spread before her. It was made out of the skin of twelve tigers. Or was it fifteen? Dadaji had apparently shot every one of them. She herself had been there for his last two tiger hunts, sitting behind him on the howdah, gorging on biscuits hidden under the seat for her by the servants. She had felt faint at the sight of all that blood oozing out of the tiger when Dadaji killed it. But not for a moment had she felt any fear. Well, at least not as afraid as she was of Bauji right now. *Oh Lord Kishan, my Kanha, please don't let the news of what happened in the marketplace this evening reach Bauji.* Else forget Kishangarh, he wouldn't even let her step out of the palace if he came to know about it.

Biting her thumbnail, she mumbled, 'You wanted to see me, Bauji?'

'We hear you want to go to a boarding school in Kishangarh?' Bauji asked. 'What's wrong with your present school?'

'Nothing, Bauji, it's just that Vicky's also going . . .'

'Why? The schools in Mohanagar are not good enough for her?'

'No, Bauji. She hasn't been keeping well. The doctor feels the mountain air will do her good.'

'Well, in that case she *must* go. But why do you need to tag along?'

'Your Majesty, they've been together since birth. How can we separate them now?' said Ma.

'Sumitra, what'll she do when she gets married?' asked Bauji. 'Take that girl along to her sasural as trousseau?'

Ma pushed back a lock of hair that had fallen over her forehead. 'Let her go. It'll be good for her. Be—'

19

She stopped speaking as a servant knocked and entered the room, bowed from the waist down, then placed a hookah at Bauji's feet. He again bowed and backed out of the room. Bauji put the pipe of the hookah in his mouth and sucked. It made a gurgling sound.

'You know we're quite liberal,' Bauji said after a while. 'We're sending her to the local school, unlike a lot of princesses who are taught at home by tutors. We don't even observe the purdah. But boarding school?'

Mili sniffed as a sweetish smell of tobacco filled the room.

'Times are changing, Your Majesty,' Ma was saying. 'The Congress is talking about democracy . . .'

'That congressman – Vallabh Patel. We don't like his views . . . If the English were to leave and these peasants and the low caste that Gandhi lovingly calls "Harijans" . . . Heaven forbid if they were to govern the nation. What would they know about how to rule a country?'

Mili looked at the rug again. Why did Ma and Bauji have to talk politics all the time? What did it have to do with her going to Kishangarh? Then she recalled the look on the faces of the men who had been shouting 'Down with monarchy' earlier that evening. She shuddered. They had looked menacing.

'That's why it's important to send Mili out in the real world,' Ma was saying. 'How long are we going to shield her?'

Bauji put the hookah back in his mouth and gazed into oblivion. 'No, Mili,' he finally said. 'We have given it much thought and we do not want you to go. Is that clear?'

'Yes, Bauji,' Mili replied in a muffled voice, as she darted from the room, blinded by tears, and flung herself across her bed.

How was she going to live without her soul sister? Bauji would never understand. Did he not wonder how two girls, so different in every way, could be such good friends? Didn't he realise it was because they were meant to be? Like Lord Kishan and Sudama. In fact they *were* Kishan and Sudama, in a previous life, she was pretty sure of that. Even Nani said so. And Nani never lied.

'Princess, dinner is served,' said Bhoomi, coming into the room and standing beside the bed, her head bowed as always.

'I don't want any,' snapped Mili, without bothering to turn around.

'Eat a little, Princess,' Bhoomi pleaded.

Mili swung around angrily and threw a pillow at Bhoomi. 'Did you not hear? Go away and leave me alone,' she snarled.

'Yes, Princess,' Bhoomi replied as she scuttled out of the room.

It was so unfair, Mili fumed. Why must she always listen to Bauji, even when he was being unreasonable? There had to be a way. There must be something she could do. Maybe she should run away. No one was going to keep her away from her friend. No one. Not even Bauji.

Chapter Two

Tucked away in a valley at the foothills of the Himalayas lay the town of Kishangarh. Raven could see the entire town from where he stood, atop a hill. Her beauty never ceased to mesmerise him. He watched her as she hid her face beneath a veil of mist. Closing his eyes, he breathed in her perfume – the crisp, fresh mountain air. He could hear the temple bells, which sounded like anklets on her feet. The setting sun cast a halo around her head just as the little cottages and thatched huts smiled shyly up at him. Nowhere else had he seen such untouched beauty.

Raven loved the hills, the Himalayas, the simple hill folk – the 'sons of Himalaya', as they liked to call themselves. But most of all, he loved Kishangarh. He was only six when Mother and he had moved here and it had been his home for the last twenty-two years; this was where he belonged. But Mother would disagree. For her, home would always be England. Raven leant against a deodar tree. He wondered what Wordsworth would have done if he had been to Kishangarh. He would have written an entire epic on its beauty, of that he was certain.

He looked over his shoulder at the sound of horses' hooves. A couple of uniformed policemen on chestnut-brown horses rode by. He watched the horses with longing until the descending mist swallowed them and he could see no more. The doctor had confirmed that morning that he would never ride again.

Discerning some movement in the playing fields of MP College, Raven hobbled over for a closer look. Some students were playing cricket. A lanky Sikh boy with an unkempt beard and moustache and a maroon turban on his head, clad in torn khadi pyjamas and kurta, was batting on ninety-four. A peach-faced English lad began taking his run-up. Interesting. Raven went over to a bench that stood at the edge of the field, put down his crutches and sat down to watch.

The peach-faced lad threw the ball. The Sikh batsman at the crease swung his bat and hit it. The ball flew into the air and was caught by the fielder at silly mid-on. All the English fielders shouted 'Out!' and raised a finger.

The batsman stood his ground. 'No, I'm not out. It was a no-ball.'

He was right. It was indeed a no-ball. The bowler strolled over to the batsman. Looking threateningly at the Sikh lad, he asked, 'So it was a no-ball, eh?' He tossed the ball high up in the air, then caught it himself. 'You darkies going to teach me how to play cricket?'

The other players had now gathered around the two lads confronting each other. Sensing trouble, Raven limped towards them.

The English lad caught the Sikh batsman by his collar and punched him hard. 'Cricket is not for uncouth boys like you. Go back to playing with your sticks and stones,' he shouted.

The Sikh lad was about to hit his assailant with his bat when Raven barked, 'Stop it,' in a clipped, authoritative tone. A hush fell on the field as everyone turned to look at him.

'Who the hell are you?' asked the Sikh batsman. 'Bloody gora. Hiding behind the tree and watching all the fun, were we?'

The other Indian batsman at the crease, the one clad in an ivory-coloured shirt and black trousers, touched the Sikh batsman's shoulder lightly. 'Let him be, Preeto,' he said, looking pitifully at Raven's crutches. 'Remember, we're not like these English. We don't lift a finger on a cripple.'

Raven looked aghast. The Sikh smiled scornfully at him, shrugged his friend's hand off his shoulder and spat on the ground. Then swinging his bat, he swaggered off the field, followed by the other Indian players.

Even though March heralded the arrival of spring, it was still cold in Kishangarh. Raven hobbled onto the veranda, sank into a cane chair and put the crutches on the floor. He rubbed his hands together, cupped them over his mouth, then rubbed them together again. He looked at his watch. It was almost ten o'clock. Miss

Perkins should be here any minute now.

He thought of the encounter between the English and the Indian students the previous day. Scenes like that were becoming more and more common now. Earlier, the Indians would cower and hang their heads or simply walk away in such situations. But now they stood their ground, thanks to the freedom movement that was gathering momentum throughout the country, under the helm of Gandhi and Nehru. But Raven had his doubts about the tactics they were using. How was it possible to overthrow a regime without a battle? Through mere non-cooperation? It simply did not make any sense.

Not that it mattered to him whether it was the English or the Indians who ruled the country. As long as he was allowed to teach, he did not care one way or the other. Not one bit.

Through the corner of his eye, he spotted someone in white coming up the hill. He got up clumsily to greet Miss Perkins, the principal of STH, as she stepped onto the veranda. She wore an immaculate white dress, made of the softest and finest synthetic cloth. It must have been imported from Rome, he was sure of that. She was a lean woman with thick, black, bushy eyebrows, which were straight rather than arched. If he were to be honest, she looked more like a man than a woman. He smiled inwardly. It must not be difficult for her to enforce discipline in the school. Her students must surely be afraid of her.

'You shouldn't have got up,' she said as she took her seat.

'Thank you for coming to my house to see me,' Raven said.

'Not at all. It is I who should be thanking you for helping us out at this moment of crisis.'

Raven shrugged his shoulders. 'It's not a big deal. I enjoy teaching. But do you not think it is irregular for a male teacher to be the dean of the girls' hostel?'

'It is indeed. But we are in a bit of a fix. The current dean and English teacher decided to leave India all of a sudden, just two days back. And with school reopening next week, we are in a bit of a quandary.'

'I see.'

'Yes, I'm afraid we're heavily understaffed at the moment. There is an exodus of Englishmen and women.' Miss Perkins paused and straightened the folds of her dress. 'India is no longer what it used to be, Mr . . . ?'

'Raven.'

'Mr Raven . . . ?'

'I have no surname.'

'I beg your pardon?'

'I have no father. What need do I have of a surname?' He watched as Miss Perkins lifted a single brow but chose not to say anything.

She cleared her throat. 'Y-yes, as I was saying, we are short-staffed. We've even had to open our doors to Indian and Anglo-Indian students. The only other option was to shut the school.'

'I will, however, be teaching at MP College as well. I've made a commitment to the college authorities.'

'I'm surprised. As one of the youngest professors in this country, I'd have thought you'd have no dearth of jobs. Then why choose a college for Indians?'

'Students are students. I was offered the job and I accepted.'

'It'll not be too much for you?'

'No. It's just one lecture a day. And as the school and college are next to each other . . .' Raven shrugged his shoulders. 'I'm sure I can manage that.' He looked up as Mother walked onto the veranda.

'You have met my mother?' he asked Miss Perkins by way of introduction.

'Yes, I think we have met once before at the school fair,' replied Miss Perkins, extending her hand to Mother.

After exchanging niceties, Mother turned her attention to Raven. 'Oh dear, you're sitting in a draught. It's so cold. Come inside.'

'I'm fine, Mother. Stop fussing.' He turned to Miss Perkins. 'Mother has become extra protective since my accident.'

He stopped speaking and listened, as the faint sound of slogans – 'Bharat Mata ki Jai. British leave India. Down with imperialism' – reached him. He could see a peaceful procession of khadi-clad revolutionaries marching down the dirt track below.

'When I see all this,' Miss Perkins was saying, 'I feel happy and secure for my girls that we've got a male staff member amidst us now.'

'Well, we, the English, thought we were building a haven here in Kishangarh – a home away from home,' Mother was saying. 'Alas, what we had run away from in the plains has followed us here as well.'

But Raven was not listening to either of the two. As

27

he watched the revolutionaries and heard them shout, different images and sounds began filling his head. Voices from the past; an order given – 'Fire!'; the sound of bullets being fired; agonised shrieks of pain. And then a stunned silence. Followed by an occasional crackling of flames and the smell of burning flesh.

Chapter Three

It was on a mild morning in March 1941, the year Mili turned seventeen and Vicky sixteen, that Mili found herself in Mohanagar railway station. She looked at Vicky, who was pushing her way through the throng with ease. She scurried to keep up with her friend, her two thick plaits, tied up around her ears like sausages, swinging to and fro. She was glad she was wearing her soft-soled dainty velvet shoes which did not make a sound as she walked. Like the padded soles of a tiger on the prowl. Unlike Vicky's ankle boots which were trictrocking noisily on the platform and drawing everyone's attention. If Mili's shoes made that racket, she would have died of embarrassment. But not Vicky. She simply grinned and strutted even more.

They had come early, the two of them, along with Uday and five servants. Reason – they were too excited. Ma could not take it any more and shooed them out of the palace.

'Princess, the train come in half an hour,' said Bhoomi as she dusted a bench. 'We wait here.'

Nodding, Mili sat down on the bench. She loved coming to the station. It had the feel of a funfair that never ended. The pheriwala selling colourful wooden toys, the thelewala selling an assortment of sweetmeats which drew more flies than customers, the chai waala selling cups of hot and sweetened tea. Mili had had a sip of that tea once. It was disgusting and smelt of kerosene oil.

'What now?' she mumbled as she saw a group of khadi-clad lads making their way down the station. 'These revolutionaries are everywhere. Such a nuisance.' But unlike the crowd that had surrounded their car last month, this mob was smaller and without any sticks, flags and banners. One of them was carrying a big wooden box with a slit down the middle of the lid.

Mili smiled nervously as Vicky looked at her. Vicky pressed her hand reassuringly. 'Relax. They're just asking for donations. They're not going to cause any trouble.'

Shouts of 'Vande Mataram, Bharat Mata ki Jai' now rent the air. The man carrying the donation box was giving an emotional recount of Bhagat Singh's martyrdom. 'Bhagat Singh,' he was saying to the crowd that had gathered around him, 'suffered untold torture, fasted for days and finally gave up his life. He was only twenty-three when he died. Only twenty-three. If a mere lad could do so much for his motherland, what I'm asking from you is very small.' He pointed to the wooden box. 'We are in dire need of funds to carry on our struggle against the British Raj. Please donate generously to help remove the shackles of slavery from our Hindustan. Jai Hind.'

'Jai Hind. Bharat Mata ki Jai,' the mob shouted in response. People started pouring money into the donation box. Mili grimaced as some women got emotional and began tearing off their jewellery and putting it in the box as well. As the revolutionaries came nearer, she hastily pulled her yellow dupatta over her head, hiding her gold earrings studded with rubies and diamonds as well as the matching necklace. She was not going to let anyone make her part with her precious jewellery.

Uday gave her a nudge. 'Boo-hoo, Bauji won't let me go to Kishangarh,' he mimicked. 'I thought you didn't get permission? Where you off to then?' he said, tweaking her plait.

'Stop teasing,' Mili pouted. 'He *did* refuse.'

She remembered how that had upset her. She hadn't eaten at all that day. In the evening she had been summoned to the garden by Bauji. He was having his afternoon tea with Mother. Mili went and stood beside the table, her hands behind her back, her chin tilted defiantly.

Bauji took a sip of his tea. Then he put down the cup on the table. He was taking his time. Mili looked around. The lawns were neatly trimmed, the rows of flowers straight. That's how Bauji liked his gardens – not a single blade of grass out of place. And that's how he wanted his daughter's life to be, Mili suspected. Regimented and orderly. That's how princesses were supposed to live.

'Sumitra tells me you haven't had your breakfast or lunch today,' Bauji said.

'What do you care? If you really cared, you'd understand how much it means to me to be with my friend,' Mili retorted.

'Now now, Mili, that's no way to speak to your father,' said Ma.

'I'm sorry,' Mili muttered. This was the first time she had dared speak to Bauji in that manner.

'So is this fasting to do with the fact that we did not give you permission to go gallivanting to the mountains?'

'She wants to go there to study, Your Majesty,' chided Ma.

Mili looked thankfully at Ma. She often thought it strange that she should address Bauji as "Your Majesty".

Ma spoke again. 'Why are you torturing the poor child? They have been friends ever since she was a baby, even before Vicky was born . . .'

'We were only thinking about her well-being, Sumitra. She is used to the comforts and luxuries of the palace. How will she manage on her own?' said Bauji.

'She'll learn,' replied Ma. 'Tomorrow, both the girls will get married. Proposals have already started coming for Mili. Then they will have to go their separate ways. But at least until then, let them be together.'

Bauji sighed and took another sip of his tea. 'All right, then, she can go,' he finally conceded.

'Oh thank you, Bauji,' said Mili, clapping her hands together. She looked at Ma gleefully.

Ma was smiling softly. She looked so petite whenever she was beside Bauji. He often teased her about her height. Mili had heard that when she was pregnant with Uday, Bauji would sigh and exclaim, 'What if all our children take after you and are stunted? That'll be the death of our dynasty.' But although Ma was small, she carried herself with such grace and quiet authority that she commanded the respect of everyone, including Bauji. Yes, even Bauji. For all his temper and arrogance, he was putty in Ma's hands. As she had just witnessed . . .

'I'm happy for you,' Uday was saying. Mili stared at him, then looked around the platform. The revolutionaries were leaving the station. She had been reminiscing and not heard a single word of what he had been saying. He was now raising his arm and exclaiming theatrically, 'Step out of the four walls of the palace, sister, and explore the world.'

'I think your palace has more than four walls,' Vicky said with a grin, pushing back her glasses.

Uday looked at Vicky. 'These glasses are good,' he said. 'You can see now.'

Vicky stuck out her tongue at him.

'But Uday, you have to admit – you're going to miss us,' Mili said. 'Who will cover up for me when I'm in trouble?'

'Yes, I suppose,' replied Uday. 'The palace will be quiet without your silly pranks and giggles.'

'If Bauji—' Mili stopped speaking as she noticed a lot of hustle and bustle on the platform. A minute later the train thundered into the station. She looked around at their luggage. Thank goodness they didn't have a mountain of it like they did whenever Ma was travelling with them. 'Ma, it'll be easier to put wheels under our palace than to get that lot into the train,' Uday used to joke.

She watched as the servants carried all the bags and suitcases into the train before getting into it herself, followed by Vicky. Calling out to Bhoomi, she asked her to open the window. Then peered out. A sudden hush seemed to have fallen. The crowd on the platform was parting and now stood on either side of the main entrance with heads bowed and hands joined respectfully. That could only mean one thing – Ma and Bauji had reached the station.

'Don't forget to write to us if you need anything,' said Ma as she patted her frail hand through the bars of the window. 'Bhoomi, did you remember to put the stationery in her trunk?'

'Yes, Your Highness,' Bhoomi replied.

'And the bottles of pickle are in the basket. Make sure they don't fall over,' Ma continued to fuss.

'Yes, Ma. Now stop worrying. Vicky will be there to take care of me.'

Ma looked at Vicky and smiled. 'We'd never send you off on your own. Imagine my little Mili going out into the big bad world all by herself. And did you pack your coat? Remember, it'll be cold up there.'

'Ma . . .' Mili began to protest.

Bauji had finished giving instructions to the servants and turned his attention to Mili. 'My child, take care of your health. Don't study too hard. See how it goes for three months. If you don't like the school, come back.'

'Yes, don't stay up too late and get dark circles. Then nobody will want to marry you,' added Ma.

'Ma . . .' Mili protested yet again, just as the whistle began to blow.

Bauji and Ma stepped back from the train and waved to her. Mili frowned as a woman bulldozed her way through the crowd. She was panting.

'Mummum,' exclaimed Vicky, 'I thought you'd never make it.'

'What a to-do, Victoria. I got caught in this meeting and then these people were taking out a procession on the road . . .'

Vicky put a loving hand on her mother's, through the bars of the window. 'I understand, Mummum. Don't explain. Just take care of yourself. And don't worry about me. I'll be fine.'

'I know, sweetheart. My brave poppet,' said Mrs Nunes.

Mili watched Mrs Nunes as she wiped her face with her handkerchief. Perspiration had made her make-up runny and her kohl smudged. She was now looking around, then joined her hands and said 'Namastey, Your Highness,' to her parents. Now she had turned back to Vicky and was asking, 'Where are your sisters?'

'Claudia was getting late for her rehearsal. And Michelle had an important class she couldn't miss,' said Vicky.

'Brats . . . all right, poppet, take care of yourself and Malvika,' said Mrs Nunes as the guard blew the whistle. She waved and blew a kiss to Vicky as the train began to chug slowly.

Mili and Vicky chatted late into the night. It was difficult to recall when exactly they had drifted off to sleep, but it was morning when they awoke and the train was pulling in at Shaampur station. If only Mili had known then that they would never take this train together again, she might have stayed up all night.

Mili straightened her crushed dupatta before alighting onto the platform. Vicky's Uncle George had sent his chauffeur to drive them up to Kishangarh. Mili nodded as the driver gave the two girls a friendly grin. He stepped aside to let them pass through the station gate and asked Bhoomi and the rest of the servants to follow him with the cases. Then it was time for goodbyes.

'The moment you need me, Princess, you tell, I come,' said Bhoomi.

'Yes, Bhoomi, I definitely will,' replied Mili holding her hands lightly. Then she smiled and waved to all the servants and got into the jeep. Once Mili and Vicky had been bundled inside, the vehicle made its way up the spindly road.

For miles around, Mili could see a chain of hills and mountains, covered with coniferous trees. They had been driving at a snail's pace for the last three hours. Sometimes the road slithered along like a long grey snake stretching right across the hills. At other times, it spun around a hill like a top, right up to the summit. And there were so many sharp turns and corners that Mili was left clutching her stomach and feeling very, very sick. Hey Lord Kishan, was this journey ever going to end?

Just then the road opened up to reveal a valley below. They were now in Kishangarh. As they reached the top of a hill, the jeep swerved around a bend and a mansion came into view. Engraved on the gatepost were the words 'School for Tender Hearts'.

'STH,' Vicky cheered loudly, as the driver hopped down to open the gate. Then he changed gear and took the jeep up the muddy track, right up to the main school building.

Mili and Vicky sprang out of the jeep as soon as the driver switched off the engine and let their gaze rove. The main school building was an elegant Victorian mansion, which sprawled leisurely over a vast expanse of land. It was late afternoon. Apart from the twitter of birds, peace and tranquillity reigned supreme. The air was fresh and smelt of pine. Not a speck of dust could be seen anywhere; nor mosquitoes, nor flies.

'Salaam, saab,' said a voice. Mili and Vicky turned around with a start. It was a short Bhutia lad in tattered clothes and a cap that had more holes than a sieve. 'Me, Badshah Dilawar Ali Khan Bahadur, the hostel errand boy,' he said.

Mili smiled.

Vicky looked at him and giggled. 'His name is longer than he himself is,' she whispered in Mili's ear.

Bahadur picked up two cases from the jeep and led the way to the girls' hostel, which was at the far end of the school. 'It is Sunday, no saab, so office closed. But you can see hostel warden.'

Nodding, Mili and Vicky followed him. The gravel crunched beneath their feet. Bahadur carried on speaking. 'Hostel constructed only two years back. Girls not wanting to stay away from home, that's why.'

Mili gave Bahadur a one-rupee note as baksheesh.

Bahadur gave her a crooked grin and raised his right hand in a sloppy salaam. He pointed towards a door on the ground floor, right next to the main entrance to the building. 'That be the warden's room.'

Biting her thumbnail, Mili looked at Vicky as she knocked on the formidable door and waited.

The warden looked them over as soon as she opened the door. 'What are your names?' she asked brusquely.

'I'm Victoria Nunes and this is Malvika Singh,' Vicky replied.

The warden opened a register. She looked up their details, then handed them the keys to their room and a typed sheet of paper.

'These are the rules of the hostel. I suggest you go through them very carefully. Now if you'll excuse me, I've work to do.'

With that, she closed the door. Mili and Vicky looked at one another, then shrugged their shoulders and began looking for their room. It was on the second floor. Mili looked around. There were some small holes in the wall. Screws must have been drilled into them. Perhaps to hang up pictures. There were three beds in the room; two in front of a large semicircular window and the third alongside the opposite wall.

'The other inmate – she hasn't yet arrived. Let's take those two beds, overlooking the window.'

'Yes, Vicky, let's . . .' said Mili as she drew aside the curtains with the big, red, flowery print. She threw the window open and gasped at what she saw. The entire town of Kishangarh was spread out on the opposite hill and around the lake in the valley below. It was a strange village-cum-town, this Kishangarh – with a scattering of cottages and huts playing hide-and-seek amidst the tall pine, deodar, chestnut and chinar trees.

Vicky began to unpack her cases.

'Oh, will we have to do this ourselves?'

'No, Bhoomi's going to come from Mohanagar to do it for you,' replied Vicky.

Scowling, Mili opened her bag and proceeded to empty it. After a while she tugged Vicky's sleeve. 'This is boring. Let's go and see if any of the other girls have arrived.'

Only a handful of girls were there. The rest would be arriving the following morning – the first day of term, they were told. As they strolled through the school grounds, they soon came upon the building where their classes were going to be held. It was an elephantine structure that had been freshly whitewashed. As the two of them sauntered towards the building, they perceived a man walking out of the library. He was on crutches.

Vicky brought her lips close to Mili's ear and whispered, 'Mili, did you notice? That poor fellow's disabled. But what's he doing? In a girls' school?'

Mili did not reply but stared at him as he ambled towards the entrance.

'Must be an errand boy. Like Bahadur,' Vicky concluded.

Mili looked at him carefully. He was now leaning casually against the wall and adjusting his crutches. He displayed a hint of annoyance at his handicap; like a tiger in a circus biting irritably at the shackles around its feet. No, he looked too arrogant to be a mere errand boy. She couldn't say what exactly it was about him – after all, he did not look very tall, he was lean and disabled, and yet he exuded an aura of command. Perhaps it was the way he stood there, with his chin thrust out and his lips curled sardonically – why, he could have been standing there without a stitch of cloth on, for all he cared . . .

But Vicky was pulling Mili towards the refectory, so she refrained from saying anything.

Chapter Four

Raven limped towards the English Department in MP College. He stopped near the fence surrounding the playing fields to catch his breath. He could see School of Tender Hearts' playground just a few feet below. The students were already seated by the time he reached the classroom. 'Good morning everyone,' he said and started taking the attendance. 'Jatin,' he called out.

'Present, sir,' the boy answered, his hand covering half his face.

Narrowing his eyes, Raven looked at him. He looked familiar. Why, he was the same Indian lad who had stopped the others from hitting him at the cricket ground last week. 'Thank you for sparing me the other day,' he said.

'Sir . . .' replied Jatin and he squirmed uneasily.

'So is it only cripples you don't lift your finger to or are there some more fortunate ones on your generous list?' asked Raven.

'I'm sorry, sir,' replied Jatin, head lowered. 'I didn't know you were a member of staff.'

'It's all right,' Raven said with a flick of his hand. He threw a piece of chalk at the Sikh lad who had been with Jatin that day. 'What did you say your name was?'

'Sir, Gurpreet.'

'Sir? Have you been knighted?' Raven asked with an amused smile.

'No, sir. Only Gurpreet, sir,' he replied, breaking out in a sweat.

'You play well,' said Raven. 'And you were right – it *was* a no-ball. But next time try to settle matters without coming to blows.'

'Yes, sir; thank you, sir,' Gurpreet replied.

Raven got up. Picking up a piece of chalk he said, 'There is a very important line in the play we're studying this term.' Turning his back to the class, he started writing on the blackboard: *This above all, to thine own self* . . . Drat, he should have never thought of writing on the board. Balancing oneself on crutches and writing at the same time was no mean feat.

He heard some shuffling but decided it would be easier to hobble around once he had finished writing. But when he did turn around, half the class was missing.

'I bet they're in Uncleji's Tuck Shop,' a student suggested.

'In that case,' Raven said to the class, 'please turn to page thirty-six and study the monologue. I will be back in fifteen minutes.'

So saying, he hobbled slowly towards the canteen.

* * *

Uncleji's Tuck Shop stood on the path that lay between STH and MP College and was a favourite haunt of students from the school as well as the college. It was run by Mr Kapoor, who was once the caretaker of STH but had now retired.

Sure enough, all his truant students were there. Raven leant against the door unobserved, as the smell of coffee and freshly baked cookies wafted towards him.

Gurpreet was speaking to the other students. 'Why were you wasting your time in class? You want to become actors? Or are you planning to set up a drama company? I'm telling you now. This Shakespeare and English literature are not going to get us anywhere. You will continue to remain slaves of these firangis all your life. What you need to do is join Guruji in his fight for independence.'

Raven continued to eavesdrop from the door.

Gurpreet paused to light a cigarette. He continued speaking. 'Have you any idea how powerful students can be? Students alone can bring down a government.' Then waving a sheet of paper he said, 'I want all of you to sign this petition . . .'

'Yesterday we got into trouble with Shrivastava Sir,' said Jatin.

'Why?' Gurpreet asked.

'We spent a lot of time making all those banners for Guruji and didn't manage to submit our home assignment on time,' Jatin replied.

Gurpreet said, 'Next time Shrivastava says anything—'

Raven straightened and a lopsided smile flickered across his face as Gurpreet noticed him standing at the door.

Clearing his throat Gurpreet mumbled, 'Umm . . . actually it's your fault. You should have finished the home assignment on time.'

'What are you saying, Preeto? How could we . . . ?' said Jatin.

Folding his arms, Raven looked sardonically at Gurpreet. 'Yes,' he said. 'Did you not tell Mr Shrivastava that Gurpreet had set all of you some other homework?'

Gurpreet shut his eyes and grimaced.

Turning his gaze to the rest of the students, Raven broke into a tirade. 'Is this what your parents have sent you to this college for? To let a fellow student lead you all astray?'

'Sir, I'm sorry,' Gurpreet said in a low voice.

'You are ready to trust your future in the hands of someone like Gurpreet?' Raven asked the students. 'Did you know he has failed twice in the same class?'

'Not twice, three times,' said Jatin.

Raven noticed Gurpreet dart an angry look at Jatin and mutter, 'Bloody marjaaneya, sucking up to a firangi. I'll see you later.'

Looking pointedly at him, Raven asked, 'Do you even know who this Guruji is and what he does for a living?'

'I said sorry . . .' Gurpreet said in an irritated tone.

Raven looked at him for a long moment, then turned back to the rest of the students. 'Go back to your classroom, all of you. And to make up for this lost time, I will take an extra class during the lunch break.'

The students grumbled and muttered in protest as they filed out of the tuck shop. Raven shook his head thoughtfully as he watched them leave. So now the

44

freedom movement had not only spread to a remote town like Kishangarh, but to its educational institutes as well. He thought of the Uprising of 1857. When the Indian sepoys had mutinied against the British. It had been one of the bloodiest mutinies ever witnessed by mankind. What would be the consequence of this movement? On the one hand was the Congress, demanding the British quit India, but it believed in the principle of non-violence. On the other hand were leaders like Subhash Chandra Bose who believed only war could gain India its independence. What would be the final outcome of all this? Would the Indians succeed in ousting the British this time?

Raven shrugged his shoulders. Not that it mattered. He did not care one way or the other, as long as his students did not bunk his class.

Raven looked up from his work. There it was again – yes, it was a knock. He looked at the clock. 12.45. Who could it be so late at night? He opened the door. It was Gurpreet and Jatin.

'Oh sorry, sir. We thought Sir O'Michael lives here,' said Gurpreet.

'He lives four houses down the block, on the left. But what's the matter?'

'Sir, we've got a test tomorrow and we've misplaced our notes,' said Jatin.

'He didn't make any notes. He was too busy watching the girls arriving at STH,' said Gurpreet with a grin.

Jatin kicked him.

'Perhaps I can help?' asked Raven.

'No no, sir, we wouldn't want to bother you,' replied Jatin.

'Now why would you say that?' asked Raven. 'Do you not like me? Or is it because you think I'm a cripple?'

'No, sir,' Jatin replied hastily, waving both his hands. 'It's just that you're new . . .'

'So because I'm new, you think I can't teach? You're casting a doubt on my abilities, young man.'

Jatin replied, 'No, sir . . . errr . . .' He nudged Gurpreet with his elbow and muttered, 'Why can't you say something?'

'Yes, sir; I agree, sir,' said Gurpreet.

Raven smiled as he saw Jatin rolling his eyes at Gurpreet's reply. He led them to the drawing room. Pointing to the sofa, he said, 'Why don't you two take a seat.'

'Thank you, sir,' they replied in unison.

Lowering himself awkwardly, Raven sat down heavily on the armchair. Something as simple as sitting down and getting up was a chore these days. But thankfully, not for too long. He was going to see the doctor tomorrow. He covered his legs with a blanket and let Jatin take the crutches from him and put them neatly beside the chair.

'Look,' he said, as he picked up his pipe from the table in front of him. 'You must not hold what happened at the tuck shop earlier today against me. What you do in your free time or after class is none of my business.' He put the bit of the pipe in his mouth and took it out again. 'But if you're going to disrupt my class, I will admonish you. Plain and simple as that.' He fiddled with the tobacco. The smell of tobacco was addictive. He felt

46

like lighting the pipe. But no. It was his policy never to smoke in front of his students. Or Mother. 'For me, my teaching and my students are important,' he continued. 'And my doors are always open for my students. You can come to me any time.' He paused to look at the clock and smiled at them. 'Even if it's the middle of the night.'

Gurpreet and Jatin grinned.

'So are you going to tell me?' Raven asked.

'Sir,' replied Jatin, 'in the grammar class yesterday, Sir O'Michael was—'

'Who are these people, Raven?' Mother asked as she came into the room. 'Don't they know you're not well and shouldn't be kept up so late?'

'They're my students, Mother,' said Raven.

'I don't care who they are. Finish whatever you're doing and go and rest.'

'Mother, stop fussing, please' said Raven, a slight irritation in his voice. When was Mother going to learn not to treat him as a little boy, especially in front of his students?

'I just came to say goodnight,' Mother grumbled as she straightened his blanket, threw an angry look at the two boys and left the room.

'Goodnight, Mother,' Raven called out as he smiled and shook his head. Mother found it difficult to trust anyone. She had not always been like that. It was after what happened with Father.

Wednesday. Evening. The last three days had taught Mili that everything at STH ran by the bell. Dinner was served at 7 p.m. sharp in the refectory. It was bigger than the dining room in the palace. There were rows and rows of tables with uncomfortable wooden chairs.

'I'm starving,' Vicky declared as the food arrived.

Mili looked at her plate – cutlets, boiled vegetables, mashed potatoes and bread pudding. That's it? No roti? No rice? What kind of dinner was this? She thought of the dinners served at home. The thick yellow kadi, the cottage cheese with peas, fried brinjal, cauliflower cooked with potatoes and cumin seeds, the colourful pulao and her favourite – tadka daal. She could almost smell the cumin seeds being roasted, the mustard seeds popping and the sizzling sound accompanied with rising smoke as lentils were added to the dry-roasted spices and butter ghee.

She glanced sideways at Vicky. She was wolfing down her food. She stole a look at the other hostellers. None of them were talking. All she could hear was the sound of cutlery. She looked at her plate in dismay. How was she expected to eat that? For the first time since she had left home, she felt homesick.

She took a bite of the cutlet. It was bland. It had no taste. The vegetables were the same. So were the potatoes. It was as though the cook had held them under a tap after he finished cooking, to wash off all the spices and flavours. She pushed it aside. Even Bhoomi wouldn't eat such food. She took a spoonful of the pudding. It was horrendous. True, there was a ration on sugar because of the war, but dessert with hardly any sugar in it? Who in Lord Kishan's name had hired the cook? In Mohanagar he wouldn't even get a job as the pets' cook. She pushed her chair back and got up.

Vicky looked at her. 'What happened?' she asked.

'I'm not hungry,' Mili replied. 'I'm going to our room.'

'I'll see you in ten minutes,' Vicky replied, stuffing herself.

How could she eat that? Mili wondered as she left the refectory.

She stood outside her room, looking at the little garden adjoining the hostel building. It was not tended. Some clothes lines with pegs stretched right across it. The grass was long, unruly. A potted plant had fallen over and the mud spilt out. She thought of the well-maintained gardens at the palace in Mohanagar. After all, they employed over sixty gardeners to take care of them.

'Salaam saab,' called Bahadur raising his right hand to his forehead. 'Enjoy food?'

'Enjoy?' Mili pulled a face. 'It was inedible.'

'Memsaab, when you don't like school food, go to Uncleji's Tuck Shop,' said Bahadur, pointing towards the main gate. 'I work there, morning, afternoon and sometimes Sunday.'

'But are we allowed to go there?' Mili asked.

'Yes, yes. It is just outside gate. Is part of school. Sometimes they serve hot food. And their sandwiches also nice.'

'Thanks, Bahadur. I'm sure I'll be one of their most frequent customers.' So saying, she went inside.

Just as she was getting into bed, a fair-haired, stocky girl entered their room. She had an exceptionally long nose but, overall, a pretty face. Until she opened her mouth. And her squeaky voice made you cringe.

'Hello, I'm Angel, your room-mate,' she said. 'I know I'm the last to arrive but I didn't think they'd make me share a room with natives,' she scowled.

Mili did not say anything but turned her gaze to Vicky who was glaring at their new room-mate over the rim of her glasses.

'We aren't delighted either, at having to share it with an Angrez,' said Vicky.

Angel looked up at the ceiling and said, 'And we've got the freakiest room in the hostel.'

'What d'you mean?' asked Vicky.

'This is the only room in the entire hostel that has one of those fan things on the ceiling,' replied Angel.

'Oh, I didn't even notice it. I wonder why?' said Mili.

'Maybe because it's always had inmates full of hot air,' laughed Angel.

Mili raised her eyebrows at Vicky. Vicky shrugged her shoulders as they watched Angel leave the room to fetch her luggage.

Mili looked at the fan again. Angel was right. Summers were cool and pleasant in Kishangarh. None of the houses there had fans. And definitely not ceiling fans. She wondered why this one had been installed. Maybe the room had been built for someone special. Or perhaps it was a mistake. She wasn't sure. But of one thing she was certain – she and Vicky were never going to be great friends with Angel.

Mili got into bed and rolled over on her side. Her stomach growled. She wondered if Vicky had heard it. But she was fast asleep. While she was wide awake. How was she ever going to fall asleep on an empty stomach?

And on a mattress that felt as hard and cold as the marble-topped dining table at home? She missed her soft eiderdown pillow and her white Rajasthani quilt with golden tassels. Next time she went home, she would remember to bring it along. It was one of her prized possessions. She had used it ever since she was two. It was soft and warm and whenever she snuggled into it she felt as though she had put her head on Ma's lap.

On the last night at the palace, Ma had come to her at bedtime, followed by Bhoomi, carrying a glass of milk.

'Ma, I'm not a kid any more,' Mili had protested.

Ma lovingly pulled her cheeks and said, 'Mili, let me fuss over you while I can. You will go away tomorrow. Then who am I going to spoil?'

'Ma, don't say such things. I'll get all mushy,' said Mili.

'Remember to have milk twice a day at the hostel as well,' said Ma. 'And don't start drinking tea or coffee like Vicky. Otherwise my fair and beautiful girl will become dark. Then how will we find a suitable boy for her?'

Tears rolled down Mili's cheeks. *Oh, Lord Kishan, you have no idea how much I'm missing Ma.* She buried her chin in the rough, scratchy blanket and tried to get some sleep.

A noise woke her up. It was the fan. It was whirring slowly. Then faster. And faster. The room began to turn icy cold as it rotated faster and faster. A cold chill ran down her back. Her teeth began to chatter and she shivered from the cold. And yet the fan continued to move faster. And faster. And then it fell on top of her. Her eyes flew open. She sat up. *Thank you, Lord*

Kishan, it was just a dream. She leant over and shook Vicky hard.

'What is it?' Vicky mumbled sleepily.

'The fan. It's weird. Scary. I think it's haunted.'

'Stop talking nonsense, Mili,' said Vicky, going back to sleep.

Mili lay back and looked at the fan again. There was definitely something sinister about it.

The next morning Mili sat on her bed, looking woefully at her bare arms. They had never been bare before. Not since she was a week old and Grandma had put two silver baby bracelets on her arms and silver anklets on her feet. She missed the way her bangles would clink each time she moved her hands. As for the drab school uniform, she almost gagged when she first saw it. Grey skirt, white blouse, grey cardigan and grey socks. And the thought that she had to wear it every single day had left her feeling quite desolate. Why, choosing what to wear and selecting jewellery to go with it used to be the high point of her day.

She tugged impatiently at Vicky. 'Get up, Vicky. It's Thursday. I want to go to the temple and ask Lord Kishan for his blessings.'

There was no response. Mili tugged at Vicki once more.

'Let me sleep,' mumbled Vicky. 'I'll see you in class.' And she buried her head under the blanket.

Mili threw a last look at Vicky as she left the room. She crossed the road with trepidation. Although there wasn't any traffic other than a few mountain goats, led by girls in long Gypsy skirts and ponchos, she was still scared. She had never ventured out alone before. Beads of perspiration covered her forehead as she came to a wooden bridge over a stream. It was held together by thick, strong ropes. Halfway across, she paused and looked around. She could see the temple now. Its mammoth roof, in the shape of an upturned cone, dominated the surroundings. The stream culminated in a waterfall just behind the temple. Its roar was deafening and Mili could barely hear the temple bells. And yet peace reigned supreme. Just Mother Nature, Mili and her god. So unlike the temples in Mohanagar – always noisy, crowded and squalid.

She remembered the time when she had gone to the Radha-Kishan temple with her cousins. She was thirteen then. Her aunts, uncles and cousins had come to Mohanagar for the summer holidays. She was about to run up the steps when Ma pulled her aside. 'You can't go inside the temple,' she hissed. 'You're menstruating.'

'So?' Mili said, hands on her hips.

'You are not allowed in the temple at this time of the month. Wait here near the steps till we get back.'

'What happened?' Chachi enquired. Ma whispered something in her ear. Chachi looked back at her and nodded.

Neelima, her nine-year-old cousin, tugged the edge of her mother's sari. 'Why isn't Mili coming?' she asked.

'You'll come to know in a couple of years,' her mother replied.

Mili lowered her eyes as Neelima looked at her

quizzically while the other children raced ahead to ring the temple bells.

She had stood there – at the bottom of the steps, alone, feeling like a sinner when she wasn't one, eyes brimming with tears and cheeks and ears red with embarrassment.

She now took a deep breath. The air was cool and fresh and she felt her spirits lifting with a new taste of freedom. No silly age-old custom was going to stop her communion with her god today. She took off her shoes and entered the spacious courtyard. A statue of baby Kishan in a crib, eating a ball of butter, stood in the centre of the courtyard. She shivered. The temple floor was made of white marble and felt like ice. She was glad the floor was clean and dry. How can one pray when one's feet are cold *and* wet?

At the entrance of the inner sanctum, she raised her right hand to ring the temple bell, when something stopped her. Ma, Chachi, Neelima – they were all looking at her and shaking their heads in disapproval. Mili pulled her hand down quickly. The smell of incense, camphor and dhoop emanated from the inner sanctum. She looked at the life-sized marble statue of Radha and Kishan. Lord Kishan was playing on his flute. The priest was ringing a bell with one hand and performing the arti with the other. She joined her hands and closed her eyes. The priest had seen her and was beckoning to her to come forward and accept the prasad. But she could not take a single step forward. As though her feet were bound in heavy chains.

She felt ashamed of herself. Would she never be able

to break free of these illogical beliefs and customs? She wished she was like Vicky – she always did as she wanted, without the slightest care.

Mili turned back and fled and did not stop running till she reached the gates of STH.

Vicky was waiting for her at the main entrance.

'What took you so long?' she hissed as the two of them sprinted towards their classroom.

'Whose class is it?' Mili asked, panting.

'English. Some Prof. Raven. He's a new teacher I'm told,' replied Vicky.

The two of them stole a glance at Prof. Raven from the door. He was buried in some papers and did not notice them. Mili and Vicky slunk to the back of the class and took their seats.

'Thank goodness. He didn't see us,' whispered Vicky.

Raven looked up. 'You two,' he said, pointing at them. 'Stand up, please.'

'Oh no,' Vicky groaned as she and Mili stood up.

'What are your names?' Raven asked.

'Victoria Nunes,' Vicky replied.

'Malvika Singh,' Mili said in a small voice.

'You're late,' chided Raven, waving a finger at them. 'Please don't make this a habit.'

'Yes, sir; sorry, sir,' said Mili and Vicky in unison.

As they sat down, Vicky asked Mili, 'What happened to your hair today? It looks like a sparrow's nest.'

'How should I know? I've never done it before. Bhoomi always did it for me,' replied Mili. She glared at Vicky as she giggled, then opened her book. She looked at Raven. He now stood in front of the class on the rostrum, his sleeves rolled up and his top button open. He was addressing the class. '. . . and what sets our school apart from the rest of the schools in the country are our excellent facilities – not only is our library stacked with copies of the latest edition, but it is also open all hours . . .'

Mili's mouth fell open as she realised something. She tugged at Vicky's sleeve and whispered, 'Vicky, he's the same handicapped man we saw the day we arrived . . . But today he's standing on his own two feet.'

'You're right,' replied Vicky. 'What the devil . . .'

Raven stopped speaking and looked at Vicky. 'Is there a problem?' he asked.

Vicky stood up. 'No, sir. We saw you on Sunday, on crutches, and thought . . . you . . .'

'That I was a cripple and, to your immense disappointment, I'm not?' said Raven.

'No, sir. I meant . . .' Vicky's voice trailed off.

'I was in an accident a few months back. One of my many injuries was a smashed knee. The plaster was cut some days back.'

'But, sir, the crutches?' said Mili.

'I had to use them for some days after the plaster had been removed,' replied Raven. 'Now, if your curiosity has been satisfied, shall we get back to our books?' He raised his eyebrows questioningly at Mili. 'You have already disrupted our class twice today.'

Mili looked down, her cheeks crimson. The entire class was looking at her. Without looking up she nodded her head and muttered, 'Yes, sir.' She felt humiliated and could feel her ears turn hot and scarlet. How dare he scold her in front of the whole class? She had never been admonished in front of everyone before. Not even by Bauji.

Chapter Five

That evening, after class, Gurpreet and Jatin scurried to Guruji's house, which lay in the valley, hidden by a clump of deodar trees. They stepped aside as four Bhutias carrying a doli huffed past.

'Did you hear, the British merchant ships have taken a heavy toll in the war?' said Gurpreet, looking at Jatin.

Jatin nodded. 'Yes, I read in the newspaper this morning.'

'I still don't understand Gandhi's stance of not attacking the enemy when they are embroiled in battle with another. They are our oppressors, after all. Whoever waits for the enemy to become strong and then attack? It's ridiculous.'

'Preeto, Bapu's thinking is beyond the comprehension of thickheaded sardars like you,' Jatin chuckled.

Gurpreet was about to box Jatin but they had reached Guruji's ramshackle cottage and Jatin was already knocking on the door. He ran a hand over his stubble and pulled a face at Jatin. A young lad dressed in a khadi kurta, pyjama and a waistcoat like himself answered the door.

'Is Guruji there?' Gurpreet asked.

'Yes,' answered the lad. 'In the prayer room.'

Gurpreet and Jatin entered the prayer room quietly, as the smell of dhoop, incense and roses greeted them. Guruji was seated on a sort of a rostrum which was covered with a white sheet. He held the holy Gita in his hands. In front of him was the statue of the Hindu god Krishna. A small earthen lamp flickered before the statue, throwing a warm yellow light on his face. Some thin carpets covered the floor of the rest of the room, which were in turn covered with white sheets. About thirty men and women were seated there, heads bowed, listening devoutly to every word that was being uttered.

Guruji was reading passages from the Gita. 'Don't worry about the fruit of your labour. Just keep working...' He paused and looked at his audience. 'And your work right now is to free your motherland from the yoke of the oppressive British Raj . . .' he continued.

Jatin took off his shoes and sat down at the back of the room.

Gurpreet, however, went up to Guruji and touched his feet. Guruji gave him his blessings, then turned back to his audience. 'I think that's enough for today.' He folded his hands and said, 'Hare Krishna.' Immediately there was a buzz as everybody got up, muttered 'Hare Krishna' and began to leave the room. Jatin came forward and stood next to Gurpreet.

Guruji smiled and nodded at him, then patted Gurpreet's shoulder.

'Bhai Gurpreet,' Guruji said, shoving a paan in his mouth as he spoke.

'Yes, Guruji?' asked Gurpreet.

'How's work in the college?'

'It's going well. I think I've won the support of most of the new students.'

'Good. I knew you'd do it. And don't forget . . .' he paused to spit out some of the betel juice, 'next time you speak to them, don't forget to mention how our boys have been beaten and put behind bars without any trial, for carrying out a peaceful procession.'

'I definitely will, Guruji. My blood boils when I think of the injustice of it all.'

'After all, what are we asking these Angrez for?' said Guruji. 'To give up the administration of our country. That's all. After all, this country belongs to us, it is our birthright. We are the citizens of this country, we live in this country, hence we want to govern it ourselves. That's all we want.'

'You're right, Guruji,' replied Gurpreet.

Some men walked into the room carrying bags and wooden boxes. They looked at Guruji and then at Gurpreet and Jatin.

'It's all right,' Guruji said. 'They're one of us.'

The men nodded and pushed aside the rug on which Guruji's disciples had been sitting a few minutes ago. They lifted a few logs off the wooden floor. Then they began emptying the bags and boxes. Jatin's mouth fell open as he watched them hiding guns, rifles, dynamite, bombs and other explosives into the cavity between the wooden floor and solid ground.

Gurpreet's eyes glittered as he picked up a rifle and ran his hand over its cool barrel.

'Guruji, these bombs?' Jatin uttered. 'Gandhiji would not approve . . .'

'Son, let Gandhiji do his work and let us do ours.'

'But Gandhiji says non-violence—'

'Non-violence means not hurting anyone. Rest assured these weapons are merely for cutting off the firangi lines of communication.'

But Jatin did not look convinced by Guruji's explanation. Gurpreet patted his friend's back and smiled reassuringly at him. Jatin did not smile back. Gurpreet looked at him thoughtfully. He knew the sight of all those arms and ammunition had shaken him. He watched him as he took out his handkerchief and wiped his brow with it. He always carried a white, starched, ironed hanky with him in his pocket. He was a shy, reticent fellow, his Jatin. So quiet that Gurpreet would have never known of his existence had it not been for the scuffle they had after their history exam last year.

Guruji drew Gurpreet and Jatin aside. 'You know, Jatin,' he said, 'a lot rests on your shoulders. You, the youth of today, are going to achieve India's independence. Do you know why?'

'Why?'

'Because you have nerves of steel. You have the zeal and courage that none of these leaders like Gandhi and Nehru have.'

Gurpreet gave Jatin an amused smile as he watched him look at the weapons and swallow. Jatin and nerves of steel! He wouldn't exactly call them that . . . He slapped his friend across the back.

Jatin groaned. 'My back's broken. Why can't you keep your hands off me?'

'You're as frail as a girl. Come home and have some lassi. It'll make you stronger.'

They left Guruji's house and walked in silence for a while.

Jatin finally spoke. 'I'm not sure I want to be a part of all this,' he said.

'Look, Guruji did say the weapons will never be used to hurt any living being,' said Gurpreet.

'How is that possible?' said Jatin. 'Where there is ammunition, someone is going to get hurt, sooner or later. It's like saying, "This is a pet tiger. Put your hand inside his mouth, he won't hurt you."'

'Come, yaara, you're overreacting,' said Gurpreet, putting his arm around his friend.

Jatin shrugged his arm off. 'No, Preeto. I think I should quit this movement. My parents don't know that I'm involved in this struggle for freedom. We're a simple middle-class family. They'll be shocked if they come to know.'

'Don't quit right now. Give it some time.'

'If you say so,' replied Jatin. He shook his head. 'But I feel very apprehensive about the future. As though something not quite right is going to happen. I can already feel the knots in my stomach.'

They fell silent again. Gurpreet let out a deep sigh. He

did not know how to convince his friend. Who knows? He might turn out to be right after all. Only time would tell.

Mili loved the smell of libraries – of musty old books and printing ink. Raven Sir was right. The school library seemed to have a copy of every single book ever written. *Lucy Poems . . . Lucy Poems . . .* William Wordsworth . . . where was it? Ah, there it was, hiding behind all the other books. Mili pulled it out and went and sat next to Vicky in the reading room. Vicky nudged her with her elbow and pointed to the far end of the table. Mili looked at her and then at the chair that Vicky was pointing at. Apart from some books, an open register and a black coat flung across the back of the chair, Mili could see nothing.

'Guess who's sitting there?' whispered Vicky conspiratorially.

'Who?'

'Angel. I saw her in that coat. Two days back. She was making fun of your name in class? I'll teach her a lesson.'

'What are you planning to do?'

'You sit here. Warn me if you see her coming.'

Mili watched Vicky tiptoe to Angel's chair. Angel had made herself very much at home, for she had not only taken off her coat, but her shoes as well. Mili giggled as Vicky put a couple of pieces of orange, that she had sneaked out of the refectory that morning, in each of Angel's shoes. Then with a demure face, barely able to conceal her giggle, Vicky came back to her chair. Mili hid her face behind *Lucy Poems* and waited.

She sat up straight as she saw Prof. Raven approach the reading room. He was reading something as he walked towards their table. Without looking up, he pulled out the chair with the black coat and sat down.

With a look of horror, Mili pulled at Vicky's sleeve. 'Vicky, those weren't Angel's shoes,' she whispered. 'Don't you know the difference between a man's shoes and a woman's?'

'Oh no! But I wear them sometimes. Men's shoes. They're more comfortable . . .'

'We've had it now. Hey Lord Kishan, hey Kanha – what's going to happen?' groaned Mili, biting her thumbnail.

A few minutes elapsed. Mili watched over the top of her book as Prof. Raven looked at the watch, then put his feet in his shoes. She heard a soft squelching sound and saw a look of surprise on Prof. Raven's face. He pulled out his feet and looked at his shoes, his eyes widening with bewilderment.

'Orange? I don't remember putting them in my shoes,' he muttered, scratching his head. He looked towards Mili and Vicky.

Mili quickly ducked behind her book.

Prof. Raven was looking at his shoes again. Then with a loud, 'What the hell . . . ?' he chucked the squashed orange bits in the bin. He then put on his shoes which were now squeaking like a toddler's rubber toy. Mili covered her mouth with her hand to suppress her laugh. She watched him as he put on his coat, gathered his books and papers and threw a suspicious look at her and Vicky, before shaking his head and leaving, his shoes squeaking with every step he took. As soon as he was out of hearing, Mili and Vicky threw down their books and burst out laughing.

Two months had elapsed. Mili was gradually settling down in school and getting used to not having servants to pick up after her. She looked around at the spacious school hall. They had been asked to assemble in the hall this morning instead of the classroom. All the students got up as Prof. Raven walked in. He was engrossed in conversation with an English lady.

'What?' asked Mili as Vicky nudged her with her elbow.

'Who do you think she is?' Vicky whispered.

Mili looked at the woman in question. 'She must be his fiancée,' she replied.

'Poor girl. She doesn't know what she's marrying,' giggled Vicky.

'Shh,' hissed Mili as she saw Prof. Raven looking sternly in their direction.

Raven clapped his hands to quieten the students. 'Today we have with us Miss Gonzales, who runs a theatre group in London. She's on a tour of India and has kindly agreed to put up a performance for us.' There was a sudden buzz in the hall as everyone started talking to each other. Raven raised his hand and there was silence again.

'But before that, one quick question. Does anyone know anything about Vidushi? It was brought to my notice this morning that she hasn't come to school for almost a month. Anyone?'

'Sir, her husband died,' answered Urmila. 'She's in the ashram.'

'What?' said Raven. 'I didn't know. Can you give me the details after class?'

'Yes, sir, I will,' replied Urmila.

'All right, class,' said Raven. 'Please welcome Miss Gonzales and her troupe with a round of applause.' So saying he moved to the back of the hall and the curtain on the stage began to rise.

Mili watched the adaptation of Shakespeare's *Romeo and Juliet* with fascination.

'Do you think he's going to kiss her?' Vicky whispered as Juliet sighed and Romeo took her hands in his.

'I hope so,' Mili tittered.

'What the devil!' Vicky exclaimed as Romeo brought his lips close to Juliet's.

'Keep it down, Vicky,' said Mili. 'Sir is getting cross. He's staring at us.'

'Let him. He can't eat us up. Can he?' replied Vicky.

After the performance, Prof. Raven walked up to the front of the hall and called out to Mili and Vicky, 'Stand up both of you.'

Mili gulped as she stood up and bit her thumbnail.

'Why were you two talking and giggling during the show?' His eyes were flashing like smouldering pieces of coal. 'For Christ's sake, you are in Junior Cambridge. You're not little children.'

Hanging her head, Mili looked sideways at Vicky.

Raven thrust his hands in his pockets and carried on his tirade. 'When are you two going to grow up?' He now looked at the other students. 'Remember, class,' he said, 'I will not tolerate this sort of behaviour. You are in Junior Cambridge, the second most senior class in school; behave like seniors.' With that he left the hall.

Vicky pulled a face. 'He didn't have to scold us in front of the whole class,' she sulked.

'Actually, it *was* our fault,' said Mili quietly.

'Now, don't you start . . .' replied Vicky. 'He should have been named Rav*an*, not Rav*en*,' she added as she stomped out of the hall.

Mili followed her.

'Why are you coming after me? Go to your Raven Sir,' said Vicky, pulling a face and mimicking – 'Raven Sir, Raven Sir . . .'

'Vicky, I've got an idea,' Mili sniggered. 'Come with me.' Snatching Vicky's hand, she ran towards their classroom. She peered into the room from the window. It was empty. 'Tell me if you see somebody coming, all right?'

'All right,' Vicky replied.

Picking up a piece of chalk, Mili started drawing on the blackboard. 'A nice oval face,' she said as she drew an oval shape on the board. 'A broad forehead . . . with three lines creasing it . . .' She drew three curly lines across the forehead. 'Thin, long nose . . .'

'That looks like Raven Sir,' said Vicky excitedly. 'Make the nose longer,' she added and laughed loudly as Mili drew an exceptionally long nose. She then drew another face. This one had a very small button nose. Then another. This one had a tiny moustache. Then another face. And another. Until there were ten faces attached to one another, staring down at them.

Mili finished her handiwork by writing the words 'RAVAN Sir' underneath the drawing. Then she stood back to admire her work.

'That's for scolding us in front of the whole class,' Vicky announced with satisfaction.

'We'd better run before someone sees us,' said Mili. Giggling hysterically, the two girls left the room, almost bumping into Prof. Raven in the corridor.

'Sir, you're still in school?' exclaimed Vicky.

'I know,' he replied. 'I've come to collect the assignments that all of you submitted yesterday. But more importantly, what are *you* two doing here?'

'Nothing. Nothing at all, sir,' said Mili, putting on her most innocent look and chewing her thumbnail.

'Aren't you late for tea?'

'Yes, sir, we're going, sir,' replied Mili taking hold of Vicky's hand and running towards the refectory. Oh, Lord Kishan, what was going to happen now?

'Sweetheart,' whispered Vicky, as soon as they were out of hearing, 'we're dead. Now he knows we made that drawing. Be prepared to be guillotined.'

Chapter Six

Uncleji's Tuck Shop. Strategically placed between STH and MP College, and hence the favourite haunt of most of the students studying there. Right next to the door stood an old piano, with its lid ripped off. Every now and then a student passing by would run his hands over the keys, adding to the cacophony. A quarter of the canteen was cordoned off by a low wall. Over the wall you could see Uncleji in his greasy vest frying pakoras in a giant wok and shouting at Bahadur to chop the vegetables faster.

Gurpreet lolled at his favourite corner table, watching the students as they walked in and out of the tuck shop in dribs and drabs.

'Preeto . . .' said Jatin.

'Have some shame,' said Gurpreet with mock horror. 'Calling me "beloved" in public.' He sighed theatrically. 'Now, if only a girl could call me that – Preet . . . Preeto

– I'd be on top of the world,' he said, as he slurped his tea noisily.

Jatin gave him a disgusted look. 'No girl's going to call you Preet unless you stop making those awful sounds.' He yawned. 'If the teachers had informed us there'd be no classes today, we wouldn't have had to come to college on a lovely day like this,' he grumbled.

'What's your problem?' Gurpreet asked, gulping down the remnants of his cup. 'Uncleji's set up this lovely canteen for us. Just stay put. Be—' He stopped speaking when he found a couple of eyes staring at him over the rim of a pair of glasses. She had a head full of short, curly hair and her glasses were bigger than Gandhi's. But her eyes – they were hypnotic and he could not look away.

'That blasted Angel has taken the last copy of the critical analysis of Keats' odes. Now how will we study for the test?' he heard her saying to her friend.

He walked over to their table. 'Hello, I'm Gurpreet. I study in MP College and couldn't help overhearing that you need a certain book on Keats. If you wish, I can get it from our college library.'

'Oh, can you?' Vicky asked, her eyes lighting up.

'Come hither this evening and it shall be thine,' replied Gurpreet, holding Vicky's gaze.

Vicky laughed, and pushing back her glasses with the tip of her finger, replied, 'Thank you, sir.'

'You can call me Gurpreet,' he said with a smile and extended his hand. 'Or if you prefer – Preet,' he added with a wink.

'Gurpreet,' Vicky said, giving him a crooked smile.

70

'I'm Vicky and this here is my friend Mili. We study at STH – Junior Cambridge.'

'Oye, Jatin, come here.' Gurpreet waved to his friend. Jatin walked over self–consciously.

'And this is Jatin,' said Gurpreet, thumping his friend across his back.

Jatin scowled, then nodded and smiled shyly at Vicky and Mili.

'They study at STH,' said Gurpreet again.

'STH?' said Jatin, raising a brow. 'Do you know a girl called Vidushi?'

'Yes,' Mili replied.

'Is she all right?' asked Jatin. 'I haven't seen her in a long time.'

'Her husband died,' said Vicky. 'She dropped out of school.'

'Where's she now?' Jatin asked anxiously.

Gurpreet looked at him. The news seemed to have perturbed him.

'Some ashram for widows. That's all we know,' replied Vicky.

'I'd better find her,' Jatin mumbled.

Gurpreet looked at him with narrowed eyes. Who was this Vidushi? And why was Jatin so worried about her? He'd have to find out. But first the book.

A few hours later Gurpreet swaggered into the college library, followed by Jatin. He rummaged through the bookshelves, looking for the book he had promised Vicky. 'This is the one,' he said, pulling out a book with one hand and holding a cigarette in the other.

'Excuse me, sir, smoking is not allowed here,' said the librarian, as he coughed and spluttered and waved the air before him with both his hands.

'Says who?' queried Gurpreet.

'It's the college rule.'

'All right, then,' Gurpreet replied, stubbing out his cigarette reluctantly. He then handed the book to the librarian.

'This book is only for reference, sir. You cannot take it out of the library,' said the librarian.

'Preeto, what now?' whispered Jatin to Gurpreet. 'You promised that girl. What'll she think of you now?'

'Don't worry,' replied Gurpreet in a low voice. 'I'm not going to give up so easily. I've finally found the girl of my dreams – how can I let go of a golden opportunity like this to impress her?'

Jatin chuckled. 'Girl of your dreams, indeed! That's what you call every girl you meet.'

Gurpreet turned to the librarian. 'What did you say?' he asked.

'This book is only for reading in the confines of the library,' the librarian patiently reiterated.

'Do you think I'm going to eat it if I take it outside the library? Believe me, I'm going to read it, that's all.'

'Sir,' the librarian tried again. 'Books in the reference section are to be rea—'

But Gurpreet had already snatched the book from his hand. 'I'm taking it with me,' he said. 'Put it on my account. I'll bring it back as soon as I'm done with it.' He tucked the book under his arm and strode out of the library, chin up in the air.

'I'll lose my job,' the librarian muttered, but Gurpreet pretended not to hear.

'Why are you always so aggressive?' Jatin asked as they entered the tuck shop for the second time that day. 'You think you can get anything by force. But that's not how things work.'

'That's the only way it works,' replied Gurpreet, pulling out a chair and sitting down. 'Didn't you see? You think the librarian would have given me the book, had I begged for it?'

Jatin did not reply.

Gurpreet continued speaking. 'If you want to acquire something, you've got to snatch it, yaara. That's what the British did. And that's what we need to do to get our freedom back.'

'I still think you can gain much more by peaceful means – like Gandhiji is doing.'

'Exactly. He has been negotiating with the British government for the last I don't know how many years. Anything happened? Nothing.'

He stopped speaking and waved to Vicky as he saw her and her friend Mili enter the tuck shop. Vicky waved back and the two of them moved towards the table where they were seated. Bahadur approached their table and grinned. He was still wearing his holey cap. He wiped the table clean with the gamcha he wore around his neck as a scarf. Then he fetched four glasses of water to the table, a finger dipping into each glass. Gurpreet suppressed a smile as he saw the look of disgust on Mili's face. She'd get used to it before the year was done, he told himself.

'What are my pretty damsels doing this weekend?' he asked.

'I'm visiting some relatives,' replied Jatin.

'Who's asking you?' said Gurpreet.

'I have to give my attendance at my local guardian's. Else news will be sent to Mummum . . .' replied Vicky pulling a face.

'Mummum?' Gurpreet asked.

'My mother,' replied Vicky.

'Oh,' said Gurpreet. He turned to Mili hopefully and asked, 'And you, ma'am?'

Mili blushed and replied shyly, 'I'm going with her.'

Throwing up his hands in exasperation, Gurpreet exclaimed, 'What luck. Two lovely ladies afore me, and neither wish to go on a date with me.' Everybody laughed as Gurpreet dramatically put his hand to his heart and let out a long sigh.

'You ought to join a drama troupe,' Jatin said, rolling his eyes.

Gurpreet looked at Vicky. She was engrossed in dipping her pakora in tamarind chutney. 'I almost forgot,' he said. 'Is this the book you wanted?'

Vicky looked up from her plate, licked her fingers and almost snatched the book from Gurpreet's hand. 'Why, yes. So you managed to get it from your library? I'd almost given up.'

Gurpreet crossed his heart theatrically and said, 'This is a mere book. For you, ma'am, I can even lay down my life.'

'Really?' asked Vicky. 'Prove it. Go to the summit of this mountain and jump off from there.'

'Haiyo Rabba,' Gurpreet exclaimed, smacking his forehead. 'That was such a romantic dialogue and look what you did to it.' He smiled as Vicky began to laugh. Her laughter made her eyes twinkle. He put his hands behind his head and watched the girls babble. Ah. Life was good, the tuck shop its quintessence. He would be haunting this place from now onwards, he thought with a grin.

Vicky drummed the windowpane impatiently as she looked out. There was no place like Kishangarh in May. The entire hillside was bursting with life and colour. Every single minute of this bright Sunday morning spent indoors was a waste. It was the kind of morning that was meant for riding. She looked longingly at the chestnut-brown horse tethered to a tree down in the valley below. She could visualise herself riding it bareback, the summer breeze on her face, the clippity–clop of the hooves, the horse sweating and foaming at the mouth as the two of them challenged the wind to a race. She could even smell it. Why had Mummum insisted she visit Uncle George when she spoke to her two days back?

'George and Ethel are your only relatives in Kishangarh, poppet,' she had said. 'There should be someone – a guardian you can turn to if something should happen.' What the devil. Mummum could be such a pain sometimes. But how she missed her. Even though she had never been able to see much of her. Mummum usually left for work before she woke up and got home after she'd gone to bed.

Vicky turned away from the window. Pushing back

her glasses which had reached the tip of her nose, she peered into Mili's bag. 'What *are* you packing? And all these heavy books? We'll be gone just one day.'

'Have you forgotten we have a test tomorrow?' Mili replied as she tried to put the bag over her shoulders.

Vicky shook her head with exasperation as her friend tottered under the weight of her bag. 'Here, let me carry it. You carry mine.'

'Where are you two off to?'

Vicky pulled a face as she recognised the voice. Angel. Such a busybody she was. Always poking her nose into other people's affairs. 'Here comes our guardian angel,' she muttered.

Mili giggled. 'We're going to spend the day with our local guardians,' she said.

'I hope you've signed the register?' asked Angel.

Looking at her over the rim of her glasses, Vicky asked, 'What register?'

'Haven't you read the rules the warden gave you? Each time you stay overnight at your local guardians', you must enter your name, place of stay and phone number in the register. Otherwise you can get into serious trouble.'

'Thanks for telling us,' Vicky replied. 'Now where's this register?'

'In the common room, of course,' replied Angel as she twirled a lock of her hair and strutted out of the room.

'The common room, of course,' Vicky mimicked. She smiled at Mili who was giggling hysterically, dumped her bag on the floor, then they hurried towards the common room.

'Have you noticed how long her nose is?' Vicky asked as they walked back to their room. 'Maybe that's why she's so nosy. Perhaps if we could grate it with a cheese grater, she'd become less inquisitive.'

The two friends looked at each other and sniggered, then picked up their bags and left the hostel.

Fifteen minutes later, they were walking hand in hand along the Mall, happily singing '*Kookaburra sits in the old gum tree . . .*' It was a beautiful day. There was so much to see – the flowers dotting the slopes, the soft mossy grass, the velvety butterflies, the nests with their speckled eggs, the crafty spiders, the clumsy daddy-long-legs.

Uncle George's house soon came into view as they reached the end of the Mall. It was a small cottage with a red-tiled sloping roof and walls the colour of buttercups. It stood on the hill, just a couple of paces above the last shop on the Mall. The black iron gate leading up to the house did not look welcoming, but rather like a giant Alsatian's teeth, snarling and ready to bite.

'Don't mention that I missed mass this morning,' Vicky whispered to Mili as she opened the gate.

Aunt Ethel was at the door. As soon as she saw Vicky, she exclaimed, 'Oh my God, Vicky, how you have grown! Come inside, my child.' Vicky and Mili followed her. Vicky smiled to herself. Aunty resembled Papa so much, she found herself warming to her almost instantly. Aunt Ethel wore a mauve cotton dress, her hair tucked neatly into a bun. Vicky could see why Uncle George hated Mummum so. While his own wife was the epitome of elegance, Mummum was as rough and clumsy as the bears that danced on the streets of Mohanagar on their hind legs. Vicky lifted her chin in the air. Bah! So what if Mummum wasn't prim and proper? She was the cuddliest and most huggable mother in all the land. She smiled as Aunt Ethel embraced her and nodded her head to acknowledge Mili's namaste.

'Come, come,' she said. 'I'm so glad you decided to visit us today. Your uncle has gone to Nainital and I was beginning to feel a little lonely.'

She led them through a dark, narrow corridor, with a number of doors on the right. It looked like a first-class compartment in a train rather than the interior of a house. Vicky looked around the living room – at the heavy teak furniture, the velvet curtains, the beautiful mosaics and tapestry on the floor and the walls. It definitely looked like the house of the Collector.

'You know, the last time I saw Vicky, she was only three,' Aunt Ethel was saying to Mili. 'She had lined up all her dolls and was saying to them, "I'm your princess and it's your duty to obey me."'

Mili grinned at Vicky. 'I didn't know you wanted to be a princess like me,' she chuckled.

'But we never got a chance to go to Mohanagar again,' Aunt Ethel whispered, as she rearranged the flowers on the table.

Vicky stared at her for a minute, then looked away. Grown-ups were terrible liars. It wasn't because they had never gone to Mohanagar again. It was because Uncle George wanted to have nothing to do with his native relatives after Papa's death.

Aunt Ethel chatted with them for a long time. She asked them about the hostel, the teachers, the food, Mummum, the clinic, her sisters, how long Mili and she had been friends . . .

'Can you two run to the shops and get me some fresh strawberries while I fix lunch?' Aunt Ethel was now asking.

Nodding, Vicky and Mili headed off towards the Mall. As they passed one of the shops, Vicky noticed some packets of cigarettes. She winked at Mili. Then turning to the shopkeeper, she pointed to the cigarettes. 'One of those for my uncle. And a box of matches please.'

As soon as they left the shop, Mili pounced on her. 'What do you need cigarettes for?'

'Mili, I'm sixteen. And you're seventeen. About time we tried it. Claudia and Michelle had it when they were twelve.'

'I don't think—' Mili began to protest.

'Shh,' hissed Vicky as she put a finger to her lip and pulled Mili to the back of Uncle George's cottage. She took out two cigarettes, gave one to Mili and held the other one to her nose. Ah, the ethereal smell of tobacco. She then put it between her lips. Her hands shook as she lit hers first and then Mili's. She lifted her chin in the air, feeling all grown-up and glamorous. She winked at Mili and together they drew their first puff.

And then she coughed and coughed. 'What the devil!' she spluttered and coughed some more. Tears were now rolling down her cheeks and she did not feel that glamorous any more.

'I feel giddy,' Mili said as she began to retch.

Vicky looked up with a start as a shadow fell across her. A burly middle-aged man had appeared out of nowhere and stood towering over them. He had to be Uncle George.

'Get inside the house, you two,' he barked.

The two girls scuttled indoors.

'So which one of you is Victoria?' he asked, his lips curling in disgust.

'I am,' Vicky answered quietly.

'I should have known,' he said. 'How could I have expected anything better from that heathen's daughter?'

Vicky shot him a venomous look. How dare he speak of Mummum like that? If Mili hadn't put a restraining hand on her arm and implored, 'Don't say anything, Vicky, please,' she might have hit him.

Chapter Seven

Raven thrust his hands in his pockets as he walked across the fields. The fields in Kishangarh were not flat like in the plains. They were terraced – in the form of giant steps cut into the hillside. He could see the hill women, singing as they tended their fields, in their blue gypsy skirts and heavy gold jewellery around their necks, arms and ankles. They were hard-working – hardy, stoic but always smiling. Some of them even had their little ones tied to their backs – fair-skinned, chubby babies with runny noses and red cheeks. And grime on their hands and mouth.

He looked down and espied two girls walking down the Mall. They looked familiar. He turned to Jatin who was walking beside him. 'Aren't they Malvika and Victoria?' he asked.

Jatin followed his gaze. 'Oh yes, they are,' he said. 'They must be on their way back from Vicky's local guardian's place.'

Raven looked at the two girls again. He hoped they were not up to any mischief today. He remembered the drawing they had made of him on the board. They had written 'Prof. RAVAN' under the picture. Whatever did they mean? Who was Ravan? He knew a little of Indian mythology. He had read the Upanishads and the Mahabharata. But he simply couldn't recall Ravan. Maybe it was a spelling mistake.

'We're almost there.' Jatin's voice broke into his thoughts.

'Are you sure she's in this ashram?'

'I'm certain, sir. Her own mother told me.'

'How long did you say you've known Vidushi?'

'Ever since we were little. We were neighbours. But I lost touch with her after she got engaged. Her parents and her in-laws are orthodox.'

'I can see that. Who would put a mere child in an ashram otherwise? I'm glad you overheard me when I was making enquiries about her.'

'Yes, sir,' Jatin replied.

As they neared the ashram, Raven became aware of a deep silence. The only sound that could be heard was the murmuring of the Bhoori river. An uneasy chill seemed to grip him. He saw a woman with short grey hair, clad in a white sari . . . 'Where can I find the head priest?' he asked. The woman pointed towards a small door. Raven lowered his head as he walked in through the door. The smell of incense and sandalwood greeted him. It was dark in there. And oh so cold. As though summer had abandoned the ashram. Just like the widows left there by their families – neglected and forgotten.

A thin, bald man in a saffron robe entered the room. 'Can I help you?' he asked.

'Yes,' replied Raven. 'I believe a student of mine called Vidushi is here and I would like to see her.'

'That's not possible. Widows are forbidden from interacting with men.'

'In that case I will have to take the help of the authorities,' Raven said.

The priest stared at him. Raven stared back. Was he really the head priest? Or was he Jack Frost?

'I see,' the priest finally replied. 'I will send her in. But please keep it short. Ten minutes.'

'I will. Thank you,' Raven replied.

He looked around. It suddenly struck him that the room had no windows. He suspected the rest of the rooms in the ashram were the same. He turned as a slight figure approached the door. His mouth fell open when he saw Vidushi. Her head had been shaved and she was clad in a flimsy white cotton sari. She stood before him, her head lowered, bare toes curling on the cold stone floor. This was not the Vidushi he used to teach. The girl with two thick plaits, who knew all the answers. Whose hand was up even before he had finished asking the question.

'Vidushi? What happened?' Raven asked.

She looked at him, then at Jatin, her lips quivering. 'My husband is no more. Soon after the wedding ceremonies he got a telegram and left for the war.' She swallowed. 'Two weeks later he was shot.' Vidushi paused and covered her mouth with the edge of her sari. 'I didn't get the chance to be alone with him even for a minute.' She looked down again and rubbed the floor with her big toe.

'And yet they have confined you to this?' said Raven, barely able to control his temper. 'I'm not leaving you here. You're coming with me.'

Vidushi gave him a startled look.

'I'm going to speak to Miss Perkins,' said Raven.

'Who will pay the fees, sir?' said Vidushi quietly. 'My parents have already forsaken me.'

'Hmm. We have an orphanage in Jeolikot. I'll arrange for them to take you. Anything will be better than this.'

'I agree,' said Jatin, who had been too shaken until now to speak.

'Sir, leave me to my plight,' said Vidushi.

Raven came closer to her. Vidushi sprang back in fright.

'Is this the same Vidushi who had come crying to me a couple of months back?' he asked. 'Begging me to plead with her in-laws to let her continue her education after marriage? Do you think I prostrated before them only to let you rot in this place for the rest of your life?'

Vidushi did not say anything.

Lowering his voice, Raven said, 'Vidushi, I'm going to get you out of here. You're too intelligent to waste your time in this hellhole. All right?'

Vidushi nodded. Her eyes were brimming with tears. She bent down, touched his feet, stole a sideways look at Jatin and fled from the room.

Kicking the door shut, Jatin muttered, 'Damn,' through clenched teeth.

Raven looked at him. He had spoken just once since

he had seen Vidushi and had kept his gaze averted while she was there. Yes, it must have been a big shock for him. Raven put a gentle hand on his shoulder. 'I'll get your childhood friend out of here, whatever it takes, I promise,' he whispered.

Jatin looked at him and nodded gratefully.

Later that night, Raven sat at his desk at home, before a pile of essays written by his students, but he could not concentrate. He could hear some noises outside, in the kitchen garden. Must be that fox rummaging through the rubbish again. He pulled the cord to ring the bell.

'You called for me, sir?' Digachand asked, as he came and stood behind him, head lowered.

'Yes, Digachand. Go and see what that noise is outside, and if all is well, you can go home now.'

'Yes, sir, good night to you, sir,' replied Digachand as he performed an awkward salaam and left the room.

Raven smiled as he heard Digachand cursing the fox. Then a yelp. He must have hit it with a stick . . . And now it was quiet again. Raven stared absent-mindedly at the framed photograph of his father that hung on the wall. But his thoughts were in the ashram. He was enraged by what they had done to that girl. He hated these Indian customs and practices. They held the Indian woman in its grip and crushed the life out of her; like a python tightening its coils round its victim until its bones get crushed. He knew he would not be able to rest in peace until he succeeded in getting her out of that hellhole.

So engrossed was he in his thoughts that he did not hear Mother walk into the room.

'Raven,' she said.

Raven turned around with a start. But he did not get up. His leg still hurt on days when he walked a lot, especially at the end of the day.

'You're still awake?' She straightened Father's picture, then averting her gaze asked, 'Do you miss your father?'

Raven was taken aback. It was an unwritten rule in their house – they never spoke about Father.

'No, Mother, never.'

Mother stood behind his chair and ruffled his hair lovingly. 'Are you just saying that? Not to hurt me?'

'No, Mother, really. I did miss him earlier, when I was little. But not any more. You've been for me all that he could never have been.'

'But surely you must wonder sometimes . . . where he is . . .'

Raven did not say anything. Yes, he used to wonder. And hear rumours. Some said his father had left for England for good. Some said he had settled down with an Indian girl and even had a secret family. How much truth there was in those stories, he could not tell.

He looked at Mother. 'But why this question? Suddenly?'

'I was sorting all the things in the storeroom today. I came across some old pictures. Of our wedding. It suddenly dawned on me that it would have been exactly thirty years this year, if we were still together.'

Raven got up and winced. He shouldn't have walked so much today. He couldn't have driven to the ashram as there were no roads, but he could have hired a palanquin or a rickshaw.

'Are you all right? Is it hurting?' Mother asked, lines creasing her brow as she spoke.

'A little,' Raven replied, accepting the support of her arm as he limped to his bed. He smiled fondly as she tucked the blankets around him.

'It's a miracle you can walk again, though,' said Mother. 'Most of the doctors had given up hope.'

'Yes, Mother, we have much to be grateful for,' replied Raven. He held her hand and kissed it gently. 'We don't need anyone else, Mother. Let's forget what happened so many years ago, shall we?'

'If only it were that easy,' she sighed. 'Goodnight, son,' she whispered, kissing him on the forehead.

Raven fluffed his soft, cold pillow and lay down. He watched mother as she switched off the light and slowly made her way to her room. She must get lonely sometimes. If only she would listen to him and marry again. But she was right. It was not easy to forget the past. And even if you did, it caught up with you when you least expected it.

Monday morning. Mili sat in the refectory and took a sip of the disgusting tea. There was so much din in the room at this time of the day. The sound of cutlery on china, the scraping of chairs on the floor, footsteps going in and out of the room, tea being poured noisily out of kettles and the incessant chatter. She looked at Vicky, who was busy wiping the crumbs on her mouth with a serviette. The mountain air had done her good. She had not been ill even once since they had left Mohanagar.

'Hurry up, Mili,' Vicky said. 'We can't be late today.

Ravan must be furious about the drawing of his cartoon on the board.'

Mili took a huge bite of the dry toast and got up.

'It's not good to gobble your food like a wolf, you know,' said Angel.

'Not her again,' she heard Vicky mutter as she grabbed her hand and dragged her out of the refectory.

'Oh Lord Kishan, my Krishna, please save us from Raven Sir's wrath,' Mili mumbled as the two of them quietly slipped into the classroom with the rest of the girls and took their seats right at the back.

'What is it?' asked Mili as Vicky nudged her with her elbow. Vicky pointed to the blackboard. Oh dear, her cartoon was still there. Nobody had rubbed it off. The whole class's eyes were glued on it and they were sniggering and whispering.

Raven clapped his hands and a hush fell in the classroom. 'Okay, class, I'm sure all of you have had a good look by now. I'm happy to announce that we have a talented artist in our midst. Would she do us the honour of standing up please?'

Mili stood up. Her head was bowed, her cheeks and ears flamed, and she was chewing her thumbnail mercilessly.

Vicky stood up as well. 'Sir, it was I who instigated her to do it,' she said.

'Never mind that,' Raven said, brushing her aside with a wave of his hand. 'Girls, we now know who we need to turn to when we have to make posters for the annual play and school fete.' Then picking up the duster he looked at Mili. 'Now, if you can kindly clean the blackboard, we can commence our work. Today we shall be looking at the Renaissance poets . . .'

Taking the duster from Raven's hand, Mili stole a glance at him. He wasn't smiling but his eyes seemed to mock her. She started rubbing the board vigorously, coughing slightly, choked by the chalk swirling in the air. Having rubbed off the last of the ten heads, she heaved a sigh of relief and slunk to her seat.

'Malvika?' said Raven, as he finished the lesson for the day.

Oh no. She looked up from her book, at Raven. Lord Kishan, what did he want now? And to think she had been congratulating herself for getting away so lightly. But no. He was a sadist. He was going to mete out his punishment bit by bit.

'Who is Ravan?' he asked.

Licking her lips, Mili stood up.

Raven picked up a piece of chalk from the chalk box, broke it into two and looked at her again. 'Malvika,' he said staring at her. 'I'm waiting for an answer.'

'Sir, he was the ten-headed demon king of Lanka,' said Mili. 'He abducted Sita and her husband Lord Ram had to wage a war to win her back.'

'So I'm a demon?' Raven asked, raising an eyebrow and smiling at her sardonically.

'No, sir,' Mili protested. She looked at Vicky, her eyes imploring her to help her out.

Vicky sprang to her feet. 'No, sir, it was a spelling mistake. She meant Raven, not Ravan.'

Raven smiled his cruel smile again. 'All right, if you say so. Why don't you two write a ten-page essay on this Ravan for homework? And I want it on my desk by tomorrow morning.'

'But sir,' Vicky wailed. 'We also have to submit our history project tomorrow . . .'

'I think Miss Agatha gave you that project two weeks back. You ought to have finished it by now,' Raven replied as he left the classroom.

The other girls began filing out of the room but Mili continued to sit at her desk. Pouting. Ten pages on Ravan. What was she going to write?

Vicky exploded as soon as Raven was out of earshot. 'What the devil! He *is* a demon. Ravan.'

Mili looked around to see if anyone had heard, then giggled. 'Yes,' she whispered and giggled again.

Mili leant against the pine tree as she watched the birds flying back to their nests. It was two and a half months since she and Vicky had left theirs. By now she had got used to life in a hostel. She had even got used to getting dressed and making her bed all by herself, without the help of Bhoomi. But she hadn't yet got used to queuing up outside toilets every morning, drinking tea that smelt of kerosene oil – just like the tea sold on railway stations – taking showers in tiny bathrooms without any bathtubs and gulping down the inedible food. The only things that were the same as Mohanagar were the classes; they were boring.

And the test tomorrow? She hadn't even started studying for it. But she had better. Unless she wanted to be admonished again by that Raven Sir. She grinned as she remembered the image she had made of him on the blackboard some days back.

'Doesn't Raven Sir look too young to be a professor?' she said aloud.

'He *is* young,' Vicky replied. 'He's only twenty-eight. I've heard he's one of the youngest professors in the country.'

'Only twenty-eight? Why, he's just eleven years older than me. But the way he scolds us, he sounds older than Bauji's grandfather.'

Vicky chuckled. 'Even the boys in MP College are scared of him. And he's just five or six years older than most of them . . .'

'Oh no,' Mili exclaimed as she realised she had got pine gum all over her fingers.

'You'll need turpentine to get that off,' Vicky said.

Mili tried to rub it off with her thumb, but the harder she rubbed, the harder it stuck and turned brownish–black.

'Vicky and Mili baba. You've got a visitor,' Bahadur crowed from the veranda.

'I wonder who it is,' said Mili as they made their way to the parlour, still trying to get rid of the gum.

'I hope it's not Uncle George,' said Vicky.

It wasn't. It was someone she had known all her life. She stopped at the door of the parlour as soon as she saw him – sitting under the oil painting of the three angels playing on a harp. Then with a yelp of 'Uday, what a surprise,' she sprinted across the room and hugged her brother. 'I didn't know you were coming.'

'I was missing you, so came to give you a surprise,' he said, tweaking her plait. He then turned to Vicky. 'What happened? How come you're so quiet? Has this place changed you?'

Vicky laughed. 'No, Uday. I was enjoying the reunion.'

'You mean Bharat milap?' Mili chuckled.

'What's that?' asked Vicky.

'You're as bad as Raven Sir. Don't you know – in the Ramayana, when Lord Ram has been exiled and his brother Bharat comes to see him? And the two hug each other and shed many a tear?'

'The only person I remember from the Ramayana is Suparnaka,' said Vicky. 'She too had a peculiar nose like Angel.'

Mili started giggling. Then growing a little sober, she asked, 'Uday, how are Ma and Bauji?'

'They're fine,' Uday replied. 'Bauji has sent his army to Burma to aid the British in the war. And Ma is busy with her saris and jewellery as usual.'

'I miss my saris. I hate this uniform,' Mili said, fiddling with the buttons on her cardigan.

'Now listen,' said Uday. 'I want to take you two out for dinner.'

'In that case, we'd better be off right away, before Angel appears and starts asking us whether we have signed the register or not,' chortled Vicky.

'So where should we dine?' asked Uday.

'Nataraj!' piped Mili and Vicky in unison.

Chatting excitedly, the three of them made their way down the hill. 'Uday, it's the best restaurant in Kishangarh. Wait till we tell Gurpreet and Jatin about it. They'll be so jealous.'

When Mili entered their room that night, she found Vicky looking out of the window. 'What's the matter, Vicky?' she asked.

Without turning around, Vicky whispered, 'You're lucky, Mili. You've got a brother.'

Mili put an arm around her friend. 'Uday is also your brother.'

'Yes, I know. But it's not the same,' Vicky replied. 'I've often wondered, what would it be like? To have an older brother? Or a dad? Would they be possessive? Or pamper and spoil me? And then . . .' She stopped talking and turned around.

Mili noticed her eyes were glistening.

'And then when I got married, my dad would lead me to the altar. I would have the first dance with him.'

'Aren't you supposed to have the first dance with the bridegroom?' asked Mili.

'Never mind the groom. He'd have to wait.'

'But I thought you didn't want to marry? I thought you wanted to work like Mrs Nunes?'

'Yes, that's true. Let's go to bed. We can't be late for class tomorrow.'

Mili nodded and slipped into bed. But she couldn't sleep. She kept thinking of what Vicky had just said. She had never seen her so solemn before.

Mili shot out of bed and looked at her watch. She was late again. She glanced at Vicky who had just finished brushing her teeth. Then she sat back on the bed and let out a sigh. 'I don't feel like going to class today. I feel exhausted, and the day has only just begun. And I haven't even studied for the test.'

Vicky came and sat down on the bed beside her. She

clicked her fingers and said, 'Let's do one thing. Let's play truant. Go shopping instead.'

'How can we do that? We'll get caught.'

'We'll have breakfast at Uncleji's. And sneak off from there.'

'And what'll we say when Prof. Raven asks us tomorrow why we missed the test?'

'We'll say – we weren't well.'

'Both of us?'

Vicky pushed back her glasses and thought hard. 'I know. We'll say we got an upset stomach. From something we ate. At the restaurant last night.'

The mere mention of the restaurant reminded Mili of the scrumptious meal they had eaten with Uday. The potatoes cooked in cumin seeds and garnished with coriander leaves were so delicious. As were the fried brinjal, the cauliflowers cooked in tomato sauce enriched with cashew nuts and raisins. And the smell of mint chutney was so strong, it remained on her fingers for a long time after she had eaten.

'But . . . do you think Raven Sir will believe us?' she asked Vicky.

'You think too much. Get dressed fast. And let's go.'

Mili grinned as she finished her breakfast and stepped out of the tuck shop. The thought of missing class and going shopping instead was exhilarating. She had never done anything like that before. But . . . who was that coming towards them? 'Raven Sir,' she wailed.

'Why are you spoiling your mood? Talking about him?' said Vicky.

'It's sir! He's coming this way. What do we do?'

'Oh, what the devil. We're dead now!'

'What are you two doing here?' Raven asked. He looked at his watch. 'School is going to start in fifteen minutes.'

'S-sir, we were just heading that way,' Vicky stammered.

'Good,' said Raven. He handed them a pile of papers. 'In that case, take these papers to your classroom and put them on my desk. I'll be there in ten minutes.'

'There goes shopping,' Vicky grumbled, as the two of them dragged themselves towards the classroom.

'What about the test? I haven't studied a word,' said a very worried Mili.

'We've got ten minutes. Let's make the most of it,' replied Vicky.

Nose buried in her poetry book, Mili paced the corridors in front of the classroom. Which Romantic poet should she study? Shelley or Keats or Byron? Wasn't Byron a pre-Raphaelite? *Oh Lord Kishan, please help.* She was so confused. She felt like the grasshopper that had wasted its entire summer singing and enjoying itself and now had to face the consequences. And why was that group of girls near the door chatting and laughing so loudly? How was she expected to focus?

There was a sudden hush followed by a murmur. Mili looked up. Raven was walking towards the classroom. Mili ran towards him, followed by Vicky.

'Sir, please postpone the test. Please, sir. My brother was here yesterday and took us out for dinner. By the time we got back, we were too tired to study.' She had said it in a single breath and now stood panting.

'Yes, sir, please don't give us a test today,' clamoured the other students.

'I don't care how busy you've been,' replied Prof. Raven. 'If you can't cope now, how are you going to cope in later life? When you will be working or married and taking care of a family?'

Looking down glumly, Mili grimaced.

Clapping his hands, Raven said, 'Get inside the classroom, everyone. The bell is about to ring.'

'Ravan, the demon,' muttered Vicky as they took their seats at the back of the class, as usual.

'Lord Kishan, where are you today?' Mili mumbled as she read the questions on the question paper. She only knew two answers. She watched Vicky as she slyly opened a copy of their notes and wedged it between the two of them. Mili smiled as Vicky looked at her and winked. Now every few minutes she would glance at the notes and scribble the answer on her answer sheet.

'What?' she whispered as Vicky nudged her with her elbow. She looked up, straight into Raven's eyes. Her brows knit together; she looked at Vicky, perplexed. Then not knowing what to do, she lowered her eyes and continued scribbling on her answer sheet.

Raven barked, 'Malvika Singh and Victoria Nunes, OUT!'

Mili winced as she heard their names. Everyone else had stopped writing and was looking in their direction. Her ears had turned red and felt hot. She wished the earth would open up and consume her, like it had swallowed

Sita when Lord Ram had denounced her. With eyes downcast she quietly gathered her books and slunk out of the classroom, preceded by Vicky.

'Wait for me in my office,' she heard Raven thunder after them. She closed her eyes and winced again.

Chapter Eight

Vicky and Mili stopped whispering when they heard footsteps in the corridor and braced themselves. The door of the office swung open and Raven strode into the room. He flung his jacket over the back of a chair, loosened his tie and unbuttoned the topmost button on his shirt, before turning his gaze on the two of them.

'Why were you two cheating?' he asked.

As always, straight to the point. Ravan didn't believe in mincing words, did he? Silence. Vicky pushed back her glasses and stole a sideways look at Mili. She was busy biting her thumbnail.

'Sir, we weren't the only ones cheating. Angel and—' said Vicky.

Walking around the desk to where she sat, Raven now stood glaring down at her. Vicky squirmed in her seat and wished she hadn't spoken.

'I don't care who else was cheating.' His voice had

dropped to a whisper but his tone was laced with ice. 'I saw you two. Were you or were you not cheating?'

Vicky and Mili did not say anything but hung their heads.

Raven went and sat down at his desk. 'Malvika Singh and Victoria Nunes, were you or were you not cheating?' he grated through clenched teeth.

'Yes, sir,' Vicky and Mili answered together, their voices barely audible.

Vicky gulped as he picked up their answer sheets, tore them into two and threw them in the waste bin.

'You two have brains. Why are you frittering your lives away?' Raven said, his eyes flashing angrily. He got up from his seat and paced the room, running his fingers through his hair. Then he veered around to face them. 'Do you know the plight of your classmate, Vidushi? I met her a few days back. Poor girl is rotting in an ashram. She would love to be in your place.'

He walked back to his desk. Speaking slowly, he thumped the desk with each word he spoke. 'You two are occupying seats that someone else might have occupied more fruitfully.' He paused for breath, then spoke again. 'Don't waste your time. Or mine. I don't want you getting into any kind of trouble again. Have I made myself clear?'

'Yes, sir,' Vicky murmured.

Then with a wave of his hand and a 'Go now, you're going to be late for your next class,' he dismissed them.

That night, after dinner, Vicky and Mili took their customary stroll in the hostel garden. After a while, they sat down on a little mound at the edge of the garden which was hidden from view by a thicket. Leading downhill from it was an unused dirt track that Mili fondly called the Hide-and-Seek Road. Vicky pulled gently at something on the ground and gave it to Mili.

Mili looked at it, smiled and said, 'Thanks.'

'Thanks?' Vicky exclaimed. 'What the devil. What happened? No whoop of delight? It's a four-leaf clover. You yourself told me it's lucky to find one.'

Mili smiled again.

The wind was howling tonight; Vicky wrapped her dressing gown tightly about her, then looked at her friend. 'You're quiet tonight,' she said.

'I was thinking about what Raven Sir said. You know, he's right.'

'I know. That was quite a scolding,' replied Vicky. She felt sorry for Mili. She was fragile. No one ever raised their voice at her at the palace. And if she did get into mischief on her instigation, the servants covered up for her. Couldn't that Ravan be less of a beast towards Mili at least? As for her – it didn't really matter. She was used to scoldings. Not a day had gone by in Mohanagar when she didn't get into some scrape or another.

'Be serious, Vicky,' Mili was saying. 'We can't keep getting into trouble. If Raven Sir complains to Principal Perkins, we can be thrown out of the school, you know.'

'I guess you're right. We can't go back to Mohanagar. In disgrace. Mummum would die. She'd disown me.'

'And what he said about wasting time . . .'

Vicky did not reply immediately but thought about what Raven had said that morning. 'Why are you

100

frittering your lives away?' he had said. It was true. She had never taken life seriously, never thought of achieving anything. She simply lived, or as he would have said, wasted each day as it came.

'Yes, Mili,' she said quietly. 'We need to get serious. I want to work all my life. Like Mummum. You know, Mummum's always been strong. She met with much opposition when she married Papa. Even after his death, nobody helped her.'

'Yes, I know. Even Ma thinks she's extraordinary.'

'She calls me her bravest child. Sometimes I wonder. What if I'm really not that courageous?'

'Vicky, you know very well you're the bravest girl I've ever come across. You were climbing trees even before you could walk. You rode your pony bareback when you were just four. It wa—'

'And you were a crybaby. Remember? When I forced you? To climb a tree? You were afraid to come down. You sat there and cried.' Vicky rubbed her eyes and pretended to cry. 'And cried . . .'

'You . . .' Mili lunged at Vicky. Vicky ducked and ran away laughing, with Mili after her.

The following week found Vicky and Mili traipsing towards the Mall. Vicky looked at Mili impatiently as she tripped over her sari for the third time. Whoever wears a sari when walking down a hill? A bicycle bell tinkled and she stepped aside to let it pass. But it halted right next to them. It was Gurpreet.

He looked at Mili and said, 'Oh, lucky day, seeing your lovely face, first thing in the morning! What good fortune! It seems as though the moon has come down to earth!'

The two girls laughed.

'Where's Jatin?' Vicky asked.

'In his beloved Jeolikot,' replied Gurpreet.

'He goes there a lot,' said Vicky.

'So where are you off to today?' Gurpreet asked.

Blushing, Mili answered, 'We've been invited for lunch by Vicky's aunt.'

'In that case I shall also pay her my respects,' said Gurpreet. 'I've heard she's very beautiful.' So saying, he grabbed Mili's bag from her hand and flung it over his shoulder.

'You better not come,' said Vicky. 'My uncle will also be there.'

But Gurpreet had already forgotten Vicky and was busy serenading Mili. 'What silky tresses you have,' he sang.

'My friend is not interested in you,' said Vicky. 'Leave her alone.' Why was he flirting with Mili? Was he trying to make her jealous? The rascal!

Gurpreet crossed his hands over his heart and sighed theatrically, 'Don't break my heart, my lovely . . .'

He could not continue as Uncle George's cottage came into view and Vicky and Mili hastily waved him goodbye.

Vicky sniffed the air appreciatively as she entered the house. Aunt Ethel was waiting for them with a smile and freshly baked bread. She ushered them into the living room. Uncle George looked up as they entered.

'Oh, you two,' he said and went back to his book.

Aunt Ethel cleared her throat as she fiddled with the cuffs of her dress.

'George, it has taken me a lot of persuasion to get Vicky to come and have lunch with us. She wa—'

'Why? Is she the Queen that she has to be invited with so much fanfare?' said Uncle George.

'Now, George,' said Aunt Ethel. 'We have agreed to be her local guardian. Let's be nice to our ward.'

'I didn't say anything wrong, did I? I caught her smoking that day, didn't I? I don't have the right to scold her? After all, as you said, we are her guardians and are responsible for her.'

'Come, girls,' said Aunt Ethel with an exasperated sigh. She put a hand on Vicky's shoulder. 'Let's go and see if the meal is ready.'

The dining room was small. Vicky looked at the food greedily while they waited for Uncle George to start grace. He was taking his time, tucking the serviette into his shirt, rolling up his sleeves.

Vicky looked at the food laid out before them. The food at the hostel was wholesome, healthy and tasteless. It lacked that something that set it apart from home food – the touch of the lady of the house. Like when Mummum would come to the kitchen and, taking the ladle from the cook, taste the stew. She would then look towards the ceiling while still chewing the meat and say, 'I think it needs to simmer for five more minutes. And a dash of pepper.' She would then sprinkle some pepper powder and *voilà*! The dish would be lifted from the ordinary to the divine. Like the dishes set before her right now – touched by Aunt Ethel's magic.

After grace, Uncle George read his book while eating and ignored them for the rest of the meal. Vicky and Mili chatted quietly with Aunt Ethel and left the house as soon as the meal was over.

As they made their way back to the hostel, Vicky said, 'You know, Mili . . . Aunt Ethel insisted I bring you along. Else I would have never let you meet Uncle George again.'

'Forget about him, Vicky,' Mili replied. 'The food was good. Just remember that.'

'How can you be so sweet? So forgiving? All the time?'

Mili smiled. 'Catch me if you can,' she challenged, running up the Hide-and-Seek Road. She tripped over her sari and fell.

Vicky smacked her forehead twice, as she ran after her friend to see if she was all right.

Chapter Nine

Uncleji's Tuck Shop was extremely busy that morning. Apparently, toast and boiled eggs that smelt like rotten eggs had been served in the school refectory. One look at the eggs and the girls had made a beeline for Uncleji's. In contrast, the tuck shop smelt of a strange mixture of omelettes, sausages, bacon, coffee, freshly baked cakes and scones, parathas and pickle. Strange mixture, yes, but appetising enough.

Gurpreet clicked his fingers at Bahadur and thumped his table. 'What happened to my tea? Are you getting it from Assam?'

'Two seconds, sahib, just give me a minute,' Bahadur replied.

Yawning, Gurpreet looked at Mili and Vicky sitting across the table. How did that Vicky always manage to look so alive? Especially in the morning – she looked as refreshing and bubbly as a freshly churned glass of lassi.

'What are you reading?' he asked as she laughed again.

'Shakespeare. *A Midsummer Night's Dream*,' she replied. 'This Bottom is so silly,' she giggled.

'I think Shakespeare as a playwright is highly overrated,' said Gurpreet. 'If you wish to study plays, read Ibsen or Shaw. Their work is much more relevant to today's society. If you look at the character of Ibsen's Nora in *A Doll's House*, or Eliza Doolittle in *Pygmalion*—'

'I'm impressed,' drawled a familiar voice, clapping his hands.

It was Raven. Standing there with his arms folded, looking down at the three of them. Gurpreet cringed. Damn, he should have known. What was he doing here? Trust him to interrupt just when he was trying to impress Vicky.

'I agree, sir,' said Vicky. 'Gurpreet, I had no idea you knew so much.'

A pleased smile hovered over Gurpreet's face as he shrugged his shoulders, pretending to be unaffected by the compliment.

'Why don't you come to school tomorrow and give a lecture to my girls on plays and playwrights? I'm sure they're bored of my teaching and would welcome a change,' said Raven.

'Yes, sir, that's a brilliant idea,' chirped Vicky.

Gurpreet looked at her and wiped his brow. His smile had vanished. He had to get out of this. 'But the principal?' he asked lamely.

'I'll get permission from her,' replied Raven. 'Don't worry about that.'

'Oh, what the devil. This sounds like fun,' said Vicky.

Raven touched Gurpreet's shoulder lightly. 'That's settled. Tomorrow, ten o'clock sharp. See you then.' So saying, he walked off, leaving Gurpreet staring after him, fuming and squirming. How he hated that Angrez. Especially after what Mother had told him about Raven's father.

Gurpreet looked at his watch and hastened his steps. He had spent all night preparing for the lecture and now he was going to spoil it by being late. As he reached the school building, he looked up and found Raven pacing the corridors. He glanced at his watch again. Damn, he was ten minutes late. 'Morning, sir,' he grinned at Raven as he followed him into the classroom.

He stumbled as he got up on to the rostrum.

'Have you been drinking?' Raven asked under his breath.

'Oh no, sir,' replied Gurpreet.

Raven proceeded to introduce him to the class. Then, with an 'All yours now', he went and stood at the back of the classroom.

Gurpreet nodded at him, then smiled at the class. He pulled out a handkerchief from his pocket and wiped his brow. *Pull yourself together, Gurpreet. You can't teach a bunch of girls and you want to fight for India's freedom? Stop being a chicken.*

He picked up a piece of chalk from the chalk box and broke it as he spoke. 'Hello, everyone. As Prof. Raven just said, I have come to speak to you about . . .' He picked up another chalk as he lectured and broke it.

Then another. And another. But soon he had got over his initial nervousness and was speaking confidently. Why, all the girls were listening to him with rapt attention. Even Vicky. Success.

At the end of the lecture Raven began to clap his hands. The whole class joined in. Gurpreet gave him a triumphant smile and winked at Vicky.

'Like I said yesterday, I'm impressed,' said Raven. 'I knew you could do it.' Then he addressed his students before leaving. 'Class is dismissed now. Don't be late tomorrow.'

'Yes, sir,' the students drawled as he left the classroom. They began to crowd around the desk, plying Gurpreet with endless questions. The room was filled with a buzz of voices.

After most of the students had left, Gurpreet looked around the classroom. Vicky and Mili were still there. He walked up to Vicky and said, 'Ma'am, aren't you going to say something? Everybody was full of praise . . .'

'It was—' Mili started to speak but Vicky interrupted.

'Umm . . .' she said, as she deliberately looked him over – from his turban to the two white streaks on his waistcoat where he had wiped his chalky fingers, the patch on the kurta, the dirty pyjamas and the old slippers.

Gurpreet grimaced and rubbed a hand consciously over his stubble.

'I might have said something if you weren't dressed as a vagabond,' replied Vicky haughtily. She looked him over again and said, 'Your appearance spoilt the whole show,' and walked off, followed by Mili.

*　*　*

108

The next morning, Gurpreet was slouched over his desk at home, when Jatin entered his room.

'Gurpreet? You're drinking? That too in the morning?' he said, alarmed.

'Shh, shut the door, you moron. Maji will hear.'

'But why are you drinking? Is something the matter?'

Gurpreet did not answer but looked at the plate of green chillies. He picked up one, twirled it around before putting it in his mouth, then took a sip of whisky. Then he bit into another chilli. He felt it explode in his mouth. Eating green chillies like this with whisky gave him a kick. Like a bomb exploding in the face of an Angrez.

'Bloody Angrez,' he muttered, twirling a green chilli.

'Who? Raven Sir? Why do you hate him so? He has always been good to us.'

'Jatin, you don't know what I know. All these firangis are brutes. Animals. Bloody palefaces.'

'That's not true, Preeto,' replied Jatin. 'You have no idea how much he has helped Vidushi.'

'He wasn't helping Vidushi, Jatin,' said Gurpreet. 'He just wanted to convert her. That's what they want to do with all of us – either destroy our religion or convert us. That's why he sent her to that orphanage run by Catholic nuns. Now, how is the orphanage different from the ashram?'

'I'll tell you how it's different,' replied Jatin. 'She doesn't have to live like a starving, shivering beggar any more. She has proper clothes to wear and food to eat. She doesn't have to shave her head. Do you know how humiliating it is for a woman to have to shave her head? And most important – she can study again.'

'How do *you* know all these things?' asked Gurpreet.

'I just do,' Jatin answered softly.

Gurpreet gulped down another mouthful of whisky.

'Look, if you don't stop drinking, I'm going,' said Jatin.

Gurpreet grabbed his hands. 'Jatin, my yaara, I need your help. Will you come with me to the shops?'

'What? You? You want to go shopping? You're drunk, Gurpreet, I'm leaving.'

'No. I'm serious. I need better clothes. That chit of a girl . . . that Vicky. How dare she taunt me?'

Jatin smiled as he fiddled with the gramophone that stood on a table near Gurpreet's bed. 'Are you in love?'

Gurpreet finished the remaining drink in his glass. He sniffed. Even his clothes smelt of whisky. He needed a bath.

'I don't know. But I've never felt this way for a girl before.'

Jatin chuckled. 'First of all, you need a good shave. And since how many days have you not washed these pyjamas?'

'Hey, stop playing mother. I've already got one to nag me.'

'You want me to help you or not?' said Jatin pulling Gurpreet to his feet. 'First stop – Kallu Barber.'

Gurpreet was seated on a bench outside Uncleji's Tuck Shop the following afternoon. He was rolling up the sleeves of his new shirt. It had been starched and felt uncomfortable. He cursed under his breath as he saw Jatin strolling towards him. Scoundrel. Couldn't he leave

110

him alone for a few minutes? He hoped Vicky hadn't eaten in the school refectory and would come to the tuck shop.

'Waiting for someone, Preeto?' Jatin asked with a sheepish smile.

'Not at all. Just enjoying the good weather. Kishangarh is beautiful in summer.'

'You got all dressed up to admire nature?' Jatin asked with a grin.

'Look, I'll give you my turban if you keep quiet for a few minutes,' begged Gurpreet, touching his turban.

'You didn't shave your moustache?'

'I shaved my beard,' said Gurpreet, glaring at him. 'That's good enough.'

'Relax, I was just curious. Keep cool, Preeto,' he said as Gurpreet shook his fist at him.

'Oh, she's finally here,' exclaimed Gurpreet.

'And we weren't waiting for anyone, right, Preeto?'

Gurpreet didn't answer. He was too busy shining his shoes with the back of his trousers. Then he got up and walked over to the two girls.

'So how are you two?' he asked self-consciously, feeling Vicky's eyes on him. 'Shall we go into the tuck shop and have something?'

The girls nodded and walked into the canteen. He followed them. Vicky turned to look at him and their eyes met. She was smiling. He knew Mili and Jatin were all ears, so he refrained from saying anything and gestured with his hands instead – how do I look? Vicky pretended to push a lock of hair behind her ear and gesticulated with her fingers – perfect.

Gurpreet grinned. 'Two minutes, I'll just be back,' he mumbled as he rushed out of the canteen. He jumped gleefully over the bench outside. Then he looked over his shoulder to catch a glimpse of Vicky and crashed into a group of students.

Chapter Ten

A few days later, Vicky stood near the fence pretending to look for something. It was the common fence between the STH playing field and MP College football field. She watched warily as Gurpreet kicked the ball hard. It bounced off the fence and Gurpreet ran towards it. As his feet shuffled the ball around, he slipped a note into Vicky's hand before kicking the ball back to his team. Vicky looked around the field furtively. No one had noticed. Miss Agatha was busy giving instructions to the other students. She opened the crumpled piece of paper in her hand and began to read it. *Everything to proceed according to plan. Will be waiting for you at the end of Hide-and-Seek Road at 4 o'clock. Don't be late.*

Vicky looked at Mili who was busy playing badminton. She pursed her lips. Coaxing Mili wasn't going to be easy today. She gestured to Mili to stop playing and pulled her to the edge of the field, behind a deodar tree. She showed her the note. 'I met Gurpreet and Jatin yesterday,' she whispered. 'We're going for a picnic. This evening. It's all planned out.'

'No, Vicky, we're not going.'

'Come on, Mili. Don't be a stick-in-the-mud.'

'If you want to go, you go, but I'm not coming.'

'Mili, this is our last chance. To go for a picnic. The monsoons will soon be here. And after monsoons it'll be too cold.'

'But how can I forget Prof. Raven has given us a final warning? And if this time we get caught, he's not going to forgive us.'

"We won't get caught. The plan is foolproof. We've worked out the details. At four o'clock we leave. After the last class.'

'I don't know . . .' Mili answered dubiously. 'But we have to be back in the hostel before eight,' she added.

'We won't be coming back to the hostel.'

'What?'

'The boys have booked some rooms,' said Vicky, pushing back her glasses. 'In a nearby rest house.'

'You're crazy, Vicky. You think the warden is going to give us permission?'

'We don't need her permission. We just sign the register. That we're off to our local guardians.'

'I see. But what if she finds out?'

'She won't, Mili. Half the boarders are going out this evening. She's not going to call up each one to find out if they're really there.'

Mili did not answer. She seemed engrossed in looking

at a bulbul that was trilling at the top of its voice from the upper branches of the tree. 'All right, then,' she finally said.

Vicky could see she still wasn't convinced. She put her arms around her neck. Mili did not turn around to face her friend but busied herself in plucking the needle-like leaves of the tree.

'Come on, Mili. Be a sport. Learn to live for the moment.' Vicky stopped speaking and dribbled the ball that had rolled over and stopped at her feet. She threw it back to its owner. She continued, 'That was one lesson Mummum learnt after Papa's death – to live for the moment. When Papa died, she had many regrets. There were holidays they'd planned but never went to. Promises made but never kept . . . She keeps telling us – do everything. Never have regrets . . .'

'But if we get caught, I'll never ever listen to you again.'

'You two, what are you up to?' called out Miss Agatha, who had spotted them behind the tree.

'Coming, miss,' Mili replied and picked up her badminton racquet.

Later that day, Vicky and Mili rushed to their room as soon as the last class was over. Throwing their books on the bed, they began to get dressed. Vicky pulled on a pair of jodhpurs while Mili hurriedly pulled out a pink silk kurta from the wardrobe.

Vicky watched Mili brush her hair as she ran a quick comb through her own. 'You've inherited your mother's smooth skin and silky hair,' she said. 'While I have Mummum's horrible hair and Papa's weak eyes,' she sulked. She tried to uncurl a lock of hair. But as soon as she let go, it curled right back – ping. 'I wish I had long, straight hair like you,' she sighed.

Mili laughed. 'If you had long hair, it would always be matted like that of the three witches in *Macbeth*. Birds would build nests and lay eggs in them and you wouldn't even come to know.'

Vicky scowled and stuck out her tongue at Mili.

'I used to love watching Ma get dressed for dinner every evening,' said Mili, looking at herself in the mirror and fiddling with her earrings. 'It was such an elaborate affair. Five or six maids would hold out her outfits one by one and Ma would take her time deciding which one to wear. Then once the sari had been selected, the same procedure would be carried out for the jewellery.'

'I remember,' replied Vicky. 'I was there on a couple of occasions. But hurry now. The boys must be waiting.'

Just as they were about to step out of the room, footsteps were heard in the corridor.

Mili looked at her and raised a brow.

'Quick. Hide,' Vicky whispered.

They hid behind the curtain. It was Angel. She came into the room and started packing a bag. Vicky remembered – she had mentioned that morning that she was going to pay her aunt a visit that weekend. She was humming a song completely out of tune. Mili began to giggle. Angel looked around. Vicky quickly covered Mili's mouth with her hand and held her breath.

Vicky let go of Mili and let out a long sigh of relief as Angel left the room. Clutching their bags, the two friends quickly signed the register, then made their way to the Hide-and-Seek Road. The boys were waiting in a jeep at the end of the dirt track. Gurpreet was behind the wheel and grinned happily at Vicky as she got into the jeep and sat down beside him. He looked back to make sure Mili and Jatin were seated, then with a shout of 'Sat Sri Akal' started the engine.

The four of them chattered and joked for a while. But soon the hum of the jeep's engine and the weariness that comes with attending boring lectures for an entire week lulled Vicky into a deep sleep. She was awakened when the jeep crunched to an abrupt halt. Opening her eyes, she saw before her a vast expanse of undulating land. Little smooth hillocks, unmarred by stones and rocks and covered with grass as soft as moss, rolled into one another.

Jumping off the jeep, Vicky took off her shoes and padded over the grass barefoot. She looked at Mili and winked, her eyes flashing underneath her broad-rimmed glasses. "Shall we?' she asked.

'Yes, let's,' Mili replied with a grin.

The two of them darted off to the top of a smooth hillock. Climbing right to the top, they lay down on their sides. Then closing their eyes, they went rolling down the hill like Jack and Jill, right down to the bottom. They sat up laughing and spluttering. Vicky dusted the mud and grass from her clothes and looked at Mili who was holding her head to get over the dizziness. She smiled as the boys came towards them, carrying the picnic hamper, rugs and blankets.

Spreading a rug, she sat down and looked around.

She noticed a couple of horses tethered to a nearby tree. Their faces were buried in the chaff bags tied around their necks. Eventually they'd come up with a mouthful, which they chewed lazily. Vicky's eyes lit up and she pushed back her glasses. 'Anyone coming riding and exploring these hills with me, before it gets too dark?' she asked.

"Me, me, me,' shouted Gurpreet, putting up his hand.

'Put your hand down, Preeto, we're not in class,' said Jatin.

Vicky laughed as Gurpreet pulled a face at Jatin, put his forefinger over his lips and mimicked, 'We're not in class.'

'Anyone else?' she asked, her eyes roving over the other two.

They shook their heads.

'No, you two go ahead,' said Jatin.

'Both of you are so lazy,' said Vicky as Gurpreet pulled her to her feet.

'What if the owners of the horses come back before you do?' asked Mili, a frown creasing her forehead.

'Just make up an excuse,' replied Vicky. Patting the horse confidently, she swung her leg across its back. She loved horses. She had been riding them ever since she was five. Riding came to her as easily as eating, sleeping or playing truant from class.

She pointed to a hill in the distance. 'Let's go there,' she said as she kicked the horse. Soon they were galloping towards it. They got off the horses when they reached the top. With a look of awe on their faces, they sauntered towards a jutting piece of rock on the edge of

118

the hill. Gurpreet whistled. From that vantage point, they could see for miles and miles around. A river meandered down the hill surrounded by lush vegetation on either side. Cottages and fields could be discerned in the valley below. Cars no bigger than toys in a doll's house could be seen on the road. And beyond the valley were a chain of mountains – purple and formidable.

As she sat down on the rock, Vicky took off her glasses. 'What the devil!' she exclaimed. 'This place is amazing.' As she wiped her glasses, a mist slowly began to descend on them. Within minutes the entire place was engulfed in a fog so thick that all Vicky could see was Gurpreet and the rock they were sitting on. It was as though they were sitting at the end of the world. Nothing existed beyond that rock, which seemed to be hanging in mid-air. Like when she was little and used to think the earth was flat and if she kept walking on and on and on she would reach the very end.

Just then a vulture flew over their heads and they ducked. And in a split second, the atmosphere had turned eerie. The vulture was circling their heads as though portending some evil and Vicky got a sinking feeling at the pit of her stomach. She shook her head. Since when had she become superstitious like Mili?

She was about to put on her glasses, when Gurpreet pulled them out of her hands.

'You have such beautiful eyes,' he said. 'Why do you hide them behind these hideous Gandhi spectacles?'

'My eyes are very weak. Inherited it from Papa. I was born with the sight of a seventy-year-old. I've worn glasses since the age of two.'

'Really?'

Vicky nodded, her mind far away. One of her earliest memories was of waking up at night in her room, frightened. She must have been three or maybe four. It was summer and Mummum had left the window open. Her bed was right next to the window. She could hear the leaves of the trees rustling in the breeze outside, but couldn't see a thing. She groped for her glasses, but couldn't find them. Ayah had told her a ghost story that night and the trees were now assuming the shape of ghosts and witches. And then she heard another sound – the crickets. And then a flapping sound. A bat. It made her sit up and scream. Papa was beside her in a trice. 'Relax, princess, it was just a dream,' he whispered, as he carried her to his room. Clinging to him, she gradually drifted off to sleep. She didn't know then that it was the last time she would be sleeping with him. The next day Mummum moved her bed to Claudia's room, much to her big sister's annoyance.

Vicky sighed and plucked at the moss growing on the rock. 'You know, Gurpreet . . . I still remember what Papa smelt like when I slept with him the last time,' she said, with a shaky laugh. 'He died a few months after.' She swallowed and her voice changed, but she carried on speaking. 'I used to feel very secure. Sleeping in his powerful arms. They felt like a protective shield around me.' Her voice had dropped to a whisper. 'I've never felt secure. After he died.'

Gurpreet covered her hand with his and gently caressed it. 'What did he die of?' he asked softly.

'He died in an accident. Where he worked.' She got

120

up abruptly. Suddenly she felt very self-conscious. She had revealed more about herself than was necessary. 'I think we'd better go back and join the rest,' she said.

'Yes, I think we should. Else they might start getting worried.'

They did not speak much after that. Vicky was grateful for the silence. And their friendship had been permanently sealed by the intimacy they had just shared. They tethered the horses to the tree where they had found them, then walked hand in hand down the hill to where the others were. By the time they reached Jatin and Mili, they were talking again and laughing quietly.

Jatin winked at Gurpreet and said, 'Someone's looking cosy.'

'Aren't they?' Mili enthused. 'Won't it be great if they fall in love?'

'Stop your nonsense, Mili. We were just riding and chatting,' said Vicky.

Gurpreet gave a loud sigh. Holding his hand theatrically over his heart he leant close to Mili. 'But when art thou going to give me thy heart?'

'Behave yourself, Preet,' Mili said, blushing and giggling. 'Everybody's looking at us.'

'Preet!' cried Gurpreet. 'Did everyone hear? She called me Preet. Say it again. It sounds so romantic coming from your lips.'

Mili shook her head in exasperation as everybody guffawed.

'Stop flirting with both the girls,' said Jatin, as he pulled Gurpreet to his feet. 'At least leave one for me.'

'Shut up, you two,' said Vicky, rubbing her hands

together. It was getting a little nippy. She watched the boys trundle towards the trees in search of firewood. A syce appeared from the opposite direction and made his way towards the horses. He untethered them and led them away.

'One thing I really like about Kishangarh . . .' Mili was saying.

'What?' Vicky asked, as she watched the horses disappear behind a cluster of chinar trees.

'There aren't any mosquitoes here. I could never dream of sitting outside like this in Mohanagar and not be plagued by them.'

Vicky laughed. 'Yeah, your hands and face used to get covered with those little reddish bumps.'

'You remember the smoking incense that used to be lit every evening in the palace in silver urns? That the servants would carry from room to room? It was to keep the mosquitoes out.'

'Really? I thought they were for the evening prayer—' Vicky stopped speaking as the boys were back with some branches, brambles, twigs and dry leaves. She got busy helping them light a bonfire. As the fumes began to rise, the strong smell of smoke filled their nostrils and began to choke them. They wheezed and coughed and blinked back the tears. After a while the leaves began to crackle, the smoke died down and was replaced by a roaring fire.

Edging towards the hamper, Gurpreet said, 'C'mon, let's have some food, I'm starving. Girls, get busy.'

'Excuse me?' Vicky stood up with hands on her hips and glared down at Gurpreet. 'You expect us girls to serve you?' She shook her right hand. 'You've got hands and feet. Get your own food.'

'That's not fair, Vicky,' said Gurpreet. 'We've been chivalrous for our part. We carried the hamper, rugs, everything, all the way from the jeep. We even went and gathered firewood. It's only fair that you two serve the food.'

'Yes, how is it you girls never helped us carry all this? Or collect the wood and light the fire?' added Jatin.

'Stop arguing. Let's eat,' said Mili, opening the lids of all the boxes in the hamper.

The smell of home-made food distracted everyone. There were parathas with fried potatoes, black lentils, chickpeas cooked in khada masala and loads of pickled onions. But what made Vicky's mouth water was the sight of chargrilled chicken.

'A meal without a non-vegetarian dish is not a proper meal,' Vicky stated, taking a second helping of the chicken.

'Try the dhal. It's out of this world,' said Mili.

'How can you like dhal? They are all the same and so bland,' said Vicky.

'No they're not,' Mili retorted. Pointing to her plate she said, 'This here is ma ki dhal – dark, mysterious and spicy. Then you have the yellow toor dhal which is bright and sunny, and not to forget the shy pink masoor dhal. How can you say they are all the same?'

'You've lost it, Mils,' Vicky said as she looked at Mili and shook her head. 'You really have. Hostel food is affecting your brains.'

With a 'huh', Mili turned her back to Vicky and carried on eating.

'Did anyone read the newspaper this morning?' Gurpreet asked, looking up from his plate for a moment. 'I don't understand Gandhi's stance on the war. He says he doesn't want to raise an independent India from the ashes of Britain. Now, whoever thinks of being considerate to the enemy, other than Gandhi?'

'But surely you don't support that fascist Hitler?' said Jatin.

'No, I don't,' replied Gurpreet. 'But that doesn't mean that to fight one evil, we support another evil.'

'Hmm. I too am beginning to lose my faith in Congress,' said Jatin.

'Stop talking politics,' Mili whined. 'It's boring.'

'Jatin, we need to identify the students who are serious about supporting us in our struggle and take them to meet Guruji. He wants to train some of them to make bombs.'

'What are you two talking about?' asked Vicky, who had been hitherto engrossed in watching a handful of ants. They had appeared out of nowhere and were laboriously moving the crumbs on her plate onto their backs. She wanted to kill them but Mili would kill her before she could do that.

Looking questioningly at Jatin, Gurpreet asked, 'Shall we tell them?'

Jatin nodded his assent.

Gurpreet looked around and lowered his voice. 'We are part of an organisation called KFF – Kishangarh Freedom Fighters. We support the Congress in its bid to gain our country's freedom.'

'Oh,' said Vicky.

'You don't approve?' Gurpreet asked, his face ashen.

'I don't really care.'

'You don't *care*?' Gurpreet looked at her incredulously. 'How can you be indifferent when the whole country is grip—'

'Look,' Vicky said. 'All my relatives – both English and Indian – deserted us when we needed them the most. Why should I care?'

A hush fell over the group.

'Anyone for some cake?' chirped Mili. She had just discovered an unopened box at the bottom of the picnic basket.

Gandhi, the Congress and the freedom struggle were forgotten as everyone bit into the freshly baked fruit cake. Soon every single crumb in the hamper had been eaten. The rubbish had been collected and a quiet lull descended over the satiated group. Gurpreet lit up his cigarette. Mili and Jatin sat around the fire, speaking in murmurs.

It was quite dark now. Vicky had found a smooth, round rock. Using it as a pillow, she lay on the grass looking up at the stars above. It was a clear night and not a single cloud could be seen in the sky. She smiled to herself as she remembered her conversation with Gurpreet. Funny thing, though – she had never spoken to anyone, other than Mili, about herself before. What was it about him? Last night she had even dreamt of him. They were attending some kind of a fancy dress party. And Gurpreet kept thanking her and saying how much he was enjoying himself. Vicky sat up abruptly. Was she in love? No. She wasn't the sissy type to fall in love.

They were just great friends. Like Mili and she were. She enjoyed his company. He made her laugh. But he could also be sensitive and serious as she had just discovered. And yes, she did feel flattered when he complimented her. But that was all.

But then – what about the dream? A sound coming from the road made her look over her shoulder. She saw a palanquin. A girl with blonde hair was peering through the curtains. Was that Angel? But before Vicky could ascertain if it was indeed Angel, the curtains had been closed and the palanquin-bearers were huffing up the road.

Chapter Eleven

Mili and Vicky walked quietly up the Hide-and-Seek Road. The flowers and blades of grass were drooping sleepily under the weight of the dewdrops. The wind, however, was fresh and wide awake. They entered the hostel building through the back door of a toilet, left ajar for the purpose. It was about seven in the morning and the other hostel inmates had just started to stir. Mili turned white as she heard the sound of footsteps in the corridor. 'Who can that be, so early in the morning?'

Vicky clutched her hand. 'Listen, if it's the warden, we tell her we just got back. From our guardian's house. We forgot to take a change of clothes, that's why we had to come back early. All right?'

'Yes. But my clothes have a smoky smell,' whispered Mili.

'The warden's not going to come and sniff you,' Vicky answered.

It wasn't the warden, but Angel. Mili heaved a sigh of relief as she watched Angel wipe her face on a towel and put away her toothbrush.

'Thank goodness it's you, not the warden,' Vicky blurted.

'Don't worry, she'll be here soon,' said Angel, looking at them with a mocking smile on her face.

Vicky darted a quick look at Mili before asking warily, 'What d'you mean?'

'Where were you two last night?' Angel asked.

'At our guardian's, of course,' replied Vicky.

'Really?' Angel twirled a lock of her hair with her forefinger. 'Save your lies for the warden, sweetheart.' Perching herself on the edge of the bed, Angel folded her arms, then looked at both Mili and Vicky. 'Look, you two are in big trouble. I thought I'd better warn you.'

'Why? W-what happened?' Mili stuttered.

'I told the warden,' said Angel, smiling maliciously. 'I had to come back to the hostel last night as Aunt had taken ill. And I saw you on my way here. I thought it my duty to inform her.'

'So it *was* you in the palanquin last night.'

'Yes, I saw everything. The bonfire, the boys. And you two behaving like hussies—'

'Mind your language,' Vicky retorted.

'Well, I thought it might help if you knew what was in store for you beforehand. But since you don't seem to appreciate my good intentions, I shall be off.'

'Good intentions indeed,' muttered Vicky through clenched teeth.

Mili pursed her lips. If there was one person Mili hated more than Uncle George at the moment, it was Angel.

Mili and Vicky knocked timidly on Raven's door. Without looking up, he gestured to them to come in and sit down. Mili bit her thumbnail as she looked towards his desk. He was hidden behind a pile of books and reports, and reams of paper. She hastily lowered her gaze as he looked up.

'You two seem rather fond of my office,' he said.

Silence. Without looking up, Mili stole a sideways look at Vicky. She was staring straight ahead at the cross on an otherwise bare wall.

'I believe you two were absconding from the hostel last night?' Raven asked.

The two of them did not answer but hung their heads.

'I will take your silence as a yes,' said Raven. 'Do you realise the gravity of your crime?' His voice rose as he said this. He got up and walked over to the window. Folding his arms across his chest, he looked out, his back towards them.

The two girls sat up straight and waited with bated breath for him to speak again.

'You're not little children any more. You are young girls. How old are you?'

'I'm sixteen and Mili is seventeen,' Vicky replied.

'Do you know what a young girl staying out all night with two boys implies?' asked Raven.

Mili and Vicky averted their gaze.

'Do you or do you not?' Raven asked again. 'Answer me.'

'Yes, sir,' Mili and Vicky answered meekly.

'But sir,' added Vicky, 'we didn't do anything of the sort.'

'I know,' said Raven, his voice softening. 'But the fact remains – you broke the hostel rules and you could get suspended or even expelled for that. Don't you girls ever think about the future? Tomorrow you'll be engaged to be married. What'll happen if your in-laws hear of this incident?'

Sitting down, Raven put his elbows on the table and clasped his hands. He spoke again. 'I gave you two a warning last time. I thought you'd improve.'

Mili shifted uncomfortably. He was staring down at them.

'Sorry, sir,' they said in unison, their voices barely audible.

'This time you've gone too far. I'm afraid the matter is no longer in my hands. It has reached the vice chancellor,' he said.

Mili's heart began to pound and she chewed her thumbnail furiously.

'Believe me, you two are in very serious trouble,' he said quietly.

Vicky finally spoke. 'We weren't the only ones. Gurpreet and Jatin were also there.'

'Don't worry,' replied Raven. 'I'll speak to them. But remember, they're boys. They don't have a Cinderella time at their hostel. But you girls . . .'

'Sir, but that's not fair,' Vicky grumbled. 'We're going to be expelled while the boys go scot-free – for the same crime?'

'Who said life was fair?' Raven said. 'Is it fair that you two, who have absolutely no interest in studies, should be sitting here comfortably while an intelligent girl like Vidushi has to rot in an ashram? Tell me, is that fair?'

Mili grimaced and looked down again.

'Well, unfortunately, that's how it is,' said Raven.

'Yes, poor unfortunate us,' grumbled Vicky.

'You two? Unfortunate?' Raven raked his fingers through his hair and looked at them incredulously. 'I find it hard to believe what you just said.' He got up, thrust his hands in his pockets, took a few angry steps towards the door, then turned back abruptly and gave them a hard stare. 'Do you know how fortunate you are to have parents who are willing to send you to a school like STH? How many girls would die for a chance like this – girls like Vidushi? They'd love to change places with you . . .'

Mili looked out of the window. Once Raven Sir started scolding, he went on and on and on. A lot like Bauji. Beads of perspiration broke out on her forehead. Gosh, how was she going to face Bauji if they were expelled from school and sent back home in shame?

There was a knock on the door. It was Bahadur. He handed a note to Raven who read it, nodded briefly at Bahadur, then turned to Mili and Vicky. 'Prof. Keating would like to see you in his room at 3 p.m.'

'Prof. Keating? The vice chancellor?' Mili swallowed hard.

'Yes, the very same,' replied Raven. 'You may go to your class now. And make sure you're on time. Prof. Keating hates to be kept waiting.'

Mili looked at the clock in dismay. It was only eleven o'clock. The next four hours dragged painfully. Mili felt as though they were being subjected to the Chinese water torture. Each tick of the clock felt like a cold drop of water dripping on her forehead. At ten minutes to three, she looked at her friend. Vicky got up and made the sign of a throat being slit with her forefinger. Quietly they left the classroom.

School was over. Mili and Vicky dragged themselves to Uncleji's Tuck Shop and sat in silence for a while. Even the smell of freshly fried onion and cauliflower pakoras could not whet their appetite today.

'That Angel!' Vicky finally spat out. 'If it hadn't been for her we wouldn't have got caught. The warden wouldn't have checked the register. Nobody could have seen us. No one knows there's a dirt track behind that thicket. The warden has often seen us sitting on the mound. She wouldn't have suspected a thing.'

'If it wasn't for Raven Sir . . .' said Mili, her voice breaking, still shaken from all that had transpired that day.

Vicky put her arms around Mili's shoulders as she pushed back her glasses. 'At the picnic, when I was talking to Gurpreet . . .'

'Yes?' Mili's eyes lit up. 'What were you two talking about?'

Just then, as though on cue, Jatin and Gurpreet walked into the tuck shop. Vicky winked at Mili, and they both looked down, their faces grim, as the lads came towards them.

Jatin asked, 'What happened?'

'What we had feared,' replied Vicky.

'What?' asked Gurpreet.

'Yes,' replied Mili. 'We've been expelled.'

'No!' Jatin and Gurpreet spoke together.

'We were first grilled by Ravan,' said Vicky. 'Then four hours later by the vice chancellor.'

Mili cleared her throat and said in a gruff voice, '"I had a meeting with your principal, your warden and the dean of your hostel this morning and this is what we decided . . ."' Mili paused and looked at Gurpreet and Jatin. They had turned white.

'Damn,' ground out Gurpreet, banging his fist on the table. 'This is all my fault. I shouldn't have coaxed you to come for the picnic.'

'Does this mean you're going back to Mohanagar?' asked Jatin.

Mili began to giggle.

Vicky gave a broad grin as she pushed back her glasses. 'We were let off. With a warning.'

While Jatin slouched with relief, Gurpreet got up and shouted, 'Balle balle,' and slapped Vicky across her back.

Vicky turned white and glared at him. 'I feel as though I've been hit by a hammer. So is this what Jatin has to endure everyday? Poor thing.'

'Yes, poor me,' said Jatin.

Gurpreet tried to change the subject. 'So tell us, what exactly happened?'

Mili mimicked Prof. Keating again: '"Since this is the first time you have committed a crime of this magnitude, we've decided not to expel you and give you one last chance."'

'What if we had been?' said Vicky. 'Mummum would've been shattered. She was so proud of me when I got admission. She even threw a party.'

'If we'd been expelled, Bauji would have married me off straight away, to the first prince he came across,' said Mili, shuddering involuntarily at the thought.

'And can you imagine?' said Vicky. 'It was Ravan who put in a good word and saved us . . .'

'See? I keep saying that professor is a good man,' said Jatin.

'So?' retorted Gurpreet, his eyes flashing. 'I don't care if he's good or bad. He's an Angrez. And I'm wary of *all* firangis.'

Mili sat on her bed finishing her home assignment. She looked out of the window and absent-mindedly put her pen in her mouth. It was raining again. It had been raining incessantly for the last three weeks. Ever since they'd got back from the picnic. The raindrops were not big, heavy drops like the ones in Mohanagar during the monsoons, but millions of little drops racing each other to hit the ground. They were ricocheting off the road, the rooftops, the street lamp, at breakneck speed. She could almost hear them shout 'wheee' as they slid down the roof into the gutter. And the raindrops bouncing off the street lamp looked beautiful – like sparklers on Diwali night.

The monsoon rains had also brought with them the leeches, Mili realised with horror, as she noticed a red stain on her leg. She sprang out of bed and began dabbing the spot with a wet cloth.

Vicky rushed into the room, panting and wet, leaving a muddy trail on the floor. She threw her arms around Mili's neck and exclaimed, 'Guess what, Mili. I'm in love. I'm so much in love.'

'You, in love? I don't believe it,' Mili chuckled. 'I think I know who he is,' she added, with a mischievous glint in her eyes.

'You know Gurpreet . . .' Vicky said as she dried her hair with a towel.

'Yes!'

'Well, I went with him to his aunt's place . . .' Vicky said as she sat down on the chair and began taking off her shoes.

Sitting down on the floor, at her feet, Mili clasped Vicky's hands and said, 'Yes, go on.'

'You won't believe what I saw there. Their dog has given birth to six adorable puppies. I fell for them.'

'So you're in love with a puppy?' said Mili as she smacked her forehead and shook her head.

'The youngest one is so tiny,' said Vicky, as she cupped her hands together to show how small he was. 'He looks like a snowball. He sleeps all day. Doesn't even wake up to feed himself. And when he does, he gets bullied and shoved aside. But my favourite is this fat—'

Mili sighed. Alas, her tomboy friend was never going to fall in love. She was certain of that now. 'Don't run off to see them on Sunday,' she said. 'Remember, you promised to go shopping with me?'

'Yes. We'll leave early. I forgot to tell you the best

part. Gurpreet's aunt has promised to let me take my favourite one to Mohanagar. During the holidays.'

Mili wasn't listening any more. She pointed to the floor. 'You'd better clean that up before our guardian Angel arrives and starts rattling off the hostel rules.'

'Yes, I'd better,' said Vicky with a grin, stepping out of her wet skirt.

Chapter Twelve

Raven leant back on the bench in the park, by the side of the lake, his eyes half closed. It was the first week of July. He could not decide whether Kishangarh was more lovely in summer or during the monsoons. Especially on rare days like this, when it chose not to rain. The hills were lush, green, throbbing with life and energy. He could hear the shrieks of the children playing cricket in the distance. Some little children were throwing breadcrumbs into the lake, which had brought a dozen ducks quacking excitedly to the edge. The little ones stamped their feet in delight as the ducks dived into the water after the crumbs. Raven smiled to himself. He folded his arms across his chest as he leant back some more, his hat shading his eyes. A light breeze rustled through the grass and carried with it the smell of roses and fruit sorbet. A toddler clapped his hands, as he watched two ducks fight over a single piece of bread, before getting distracted by a yellow butterfly.

Loud shouts of 'Sir, sir' woke him from half-slumber. He sat up and looked in the direction of the sound. It looked like . . . Malvika and Victoria. They were running towards him.

'Sir, come with us,' panted Vicky. 'They're beating up this boy. They'll kill him.'

Raven sprang to his feet and followed the two girls. Sure enough, a couple of English lads were beating up an Indian boy who did not look a day older than twelve. They had now pushed him into the lake. Raven charged towards them. As he neared them, he saw one of the lads was applying pressure on the child's head so as to prevent him from bobbing up to the surface.

'What the hell do you think you're doing?' Raven growled.

The lads were taken by surprise and let go of the Indian boy. The Indian boy came up to the surface, gasping for breath, his arms flailing. Raven rushed towards him and pulled him out of the lake. He put him on the ground and turned his head to the side. Water began draining from his mouth and nose. Then he turned his head around and began giving him mouth-to-mouth resuscitation. He breathed heavily into his mouth and pinched his nose. Then he put his ear near his mouth and watched him breathing. Finally, he checked his pulse and heaved a sigh of relief. The boy was out of danger.

'Sir, you're helping a thief!' said one of the lads who had been pushing the Indian boy into the water.

Raven stared at him. 'What could have been so

precious that he should pay for it with his life?' he asked as he patted the Indian boy's back. He was now sitting on his haunches, bent double, coughing and spluttering.

'It's the principle, sir. Stealing, however petty the object, is a crime and must be punished.'

'And that gives you the right to kill a fellow human?' said Raven, catching hold of the English lad's collar. 'Leave this park right now if you do not wish to be handed over to the police.' With that he abruptly let go of him.

The lad's cheeks were inflamed. He gritted his teeth as he adjusted his collar, then turned on his heel and walked away.

Someone started clapping his hands from behind. It was Gurpreet, with his friend Jatin close on his heels.

'That was a brilliant act, sir,' said Gurpreet, continuing to clap his hands.

Raven looked at him quizzically, a frown creasing his brows.

'You're one to talk, sir,' Gurpreet taunted. 'The son of a murderer.'

Colour drained from Raven's face as he stared at Gurpreet, too shocked to move or speak.

'How do you know?' he asked after a long moment.

'My grandparents were two of the innocent victims,' said Gurpreet, his eyes full of hate, before he strode off.

Raven stared at Gurpreet's receding back for a long time. How long does a son have to bear the burden of his father's sins, he wondered?

* * *

'What's the score?' Raven asked as he took his seat beside Prof. Keating in the front row.

'Kishangarh University made 264 runs while our boys are struggling at 101 for four.'

Raven looked around the main playing field of MP College. It was an important day for them – the annual cricket tournament with their arch-rivals, – Kishangarh University, for the Lions Trophy. He looked at the thirteen players on the field – all sparkling in white, except for a couple of fielders at the boundary whose trousers were speckled with mud. The bowlers too had brown marks on the front of their trousers, where the ball had been rubbed mercilessly.

He watched the bowler take his run-up. He was trying to throw a yorker, mistimed and threw a full toss instead. 'Ah, what a miss,' exclaimed Raven, as the batsman ran for a single. If he could still play, he would have definitely hit that ball for a six. After all, if there was one passion he had in life other than books, it was cricket. 'He plays with a straight bat'; 'He plays every shot according to the book,' people used to say. Yes, he used to be a good batsman.

But the accident had changed all that. 'I'm afraid you will never be able to ride or play cricket or football ever again,' the doctor had stated matter-of-factly. He had stared at the doctor's hands as he wiped them with a towel and thought of the two prisoners who had been sentenced to Kaala Paani, the cellular jail in Port Blair, the previous day. He now understood how they felt and why one of the prisoners had wept when he heard the sentence.

Raven looked around the field. The girls of STH were also there, including Malvika and Victoria. Malvika caught his eye, smiled timidly and mouthed, 'Good morning, sir.' He smiled back and nodded, then turned his attention back to the game. The bowler took his run-up. Right arm over the wicket . . . and . . . clean bowled. A stunned silence fell over the MP College supporters, which consisted of three-quarters of the audience, as they lost their fifth wicket.

'Have you heard? About the German attack on Russia?' Prof. Keating asked Raven during the drinks interval.

'I think Hitler has dug his grave by dragging the Soviets into the war,' replied Raven.

'That's true. I hear there are talks of an Anglo-Soviet agreement.'

'I'm not entirely sure if that is a good—' Raven stopped speaking as the new batsman took his position at the crease.

It was Gurpreet. Colour drained from his face as he remembered his words – 'son of a murderer'. Sitting on the edge of his seat, he tried to concentrate on the game. The fielders were jumping and shouting 'Out!', but all he could hear was 'Fire!'

Twenty-two years. Yes, it had been over twenty-two years and yet he could visualise that scene clearly, as though it had happened yesterday. The sound of firing, the look of shock on Kartar and Ayah's faces, mirrored in Mother's eyes. And the shrieks that followed, he could hear them even now. When would they stop haunting him?

Raven wiped his clammy hands on his trousers and gratefully accepted the sherbet from the waiter. The cool drink made from fresh strawberries eased his nerves. He sat back, a little more relaxed.

. . . Nineteen more runs to win the match. The crowd was now cheering each and every run that the batsman took, as though they were hitting a four or a six. MP College was cruising along. Ten more to go. The crowd was on its feet as Gurpreet thrashed the ball for a six and with that he got his century. A jubilant Gurpreet pointed his bat at the crowd in acknowledgement. Raven stared at him. No, it was not a gesture of thanks to his supporters. He was pointing the bat at him, accusingly – *son of a murderer*, his eyes were saying. Raven wiped the perspiration that had formed on his forehead and was now running down the side of his cheeks.

. . . He watched Gurpreet as he came forward to hit the ball. The crowd was on its feet and went berserk as he hit the winning shot. MP College had finally snatched the Lions Trophy from Kishangarh University after nine long years. The students of MP College were euphoric, they were hugging each other, shaking hands and jumping with joy, but all Raven could see and hear were dead bodies and the sound of firing.

Mili and Vicky made their way to the Mall for the second time that week. Some money had arrived from home that morning and Mili couldn't wait to spend it.

'You know, Mili,' said Vicky, 'I just remembered. When we went for the picnic and I took off with Gurpreet . . .' Vicky paused.

'Yes, I'm listening,' said Mili, looking at her from the corner of her eye.

'We were sitting and chatting on the edge of the cliff. It had gone a bit foggy—'

'How romantic.'

Vicky gave Mili an exasperated look before continuing, 'Suddenly a vulture appeared. Out of nowhere. Circled over our heads a couple of times. Then disappeared just as suddenly.'

'That's not a good sign, Vicky.'

'Yes. It was weird. And eerie.'

'It's a bad omen. You better come with me to the temple tomorrow.'

'Come on, Mili. Don't talk like an illiterate.'

The two of them fell silent after that. Seeing a sari shop, Mili said, 'I want to buy a sari for Ma.'

'Come, come.' The shopkeeper ushered them inside. 'What would you like to see – saris, lahengas, suits . . . ?'

'Saris,' said Mili.

'In that case, go straight upstairs,' said the shopkeeper. He peered up the stairs and shouted, 'Tandon, show these customers the new lot that arrived this morning.'

The two girls went up the creaking, narrow wooden stairs, and entered a room covered with thin mattresses, which in turn were covered with white sheets. They took off their shoes and sat down.

'Would like cup of tea or coffee?' Tandonji asked.

'No, thank you,' said Mili.

Tandonji pulled out a sari from the shelf and began unravelling it. 'These coming here today morning,' he said. 'I can guarantee – each sari unique. You not find a similar sari in all of Hindustan.' He started spreading out various saris one by one.

'These are too expensive,' said Mili running her hand over the smooth silk sari.

'No matter,' replied Tandonji. 'What you like to see? Cotton, georgette . . . ?'

'Silk is fine,' replied Mili. 'But not so expensive.'

'I understanding,' said Tandonji. 'What about these?' he asked, pulling out another sari.

'Can I have a look at that one?' Mili said, pointing to a red Banarasi sari with gold embroidery all over.

'Madam. That a wedding sari. Too expensive.'

'Let her see it,' said Vicky.

'All right, madam,' replied Tandonji.

Mili's eyes shone as he spread the sari before her. Instinctively, she pulled the edge over her head and peered at herself in the mirror. Seeing her distracted, Tandonji turned to another customer.

'You will be a beautiful bride,' Vicky whispered softly. Mili blushed.

Vicky chuckled. 'You're blushing. As though I'm the groom.' She smiled. 'I'll dress you up. On your wedding day.'

'Oh heavens, no,' protested Mili. 'I don't want to look like a clown on the most important day of my life.'

'I'm not that bad,' sulked Vicky. 'I do know a thing or two . . .'

Mili did not reply.

Vicky clicked her fingers in front of her face. 'What's up, dreamer?'

'Nothing,' said Mili in a subdued voice. 'I just realised

– when I get married, I'll have to live without you. How will I survive?'

'Don't worry about that. Leave it to me. I'll come with you. As your trousseau.'

'I'm sure my husband would love that,' Mili grinned as she selected one of the thin silk saris for Ma and gave it to Tandonji to pack.

'You know what my fondest dream is, Vicky?' she said, turning her attention back to her friend.

'No, tell me, I've heard it only about fifty times till now,' Vicky said.

Mili grinned. 'Seriously, Vicky, I'm waiting for the day when I will fall in love with a prince who in turn will love me immensely, serenade me, praise me. We shall marry and live in a palace filled with lovely children and I shall have the most exquisite saris and jewellery in the world.'

'Your sari, madam,' said Tandonji.

'Thank you,' Mili replied, as she took the package and paid him.

As they left the shop, she could smell pickled onions and chicken being roasted on a tandor. Vicky sniffed appreciatively and said, 'We have some time. Let's have supper. At Nataraj.'

'But after that we won't have any money left,' replied Mili as they left the shop.

'Oh, come on. I'm in no mood to have that broth-like stew at the hostel tonight.'

'Isn't it too early?'

But Vicky wasn't listening. She snatched her hand and pulled her towards Nataraj.

* * *

Mili reluctantly entered the restaurant. She smiled to herself as she remembered the last time they had come to eat there. It was with Uday. She missed him.

The food was delicious and the two devoured it greedily.

'I'm still hungry,' said Vicky. 'Let's order some more.'

'But we won't be able to pay the bill,' whispered Mili.

'Don't worry. I'll take care of it,' said Vicky as she pulled out a cockroach from her pocket.

Mili opened her mouth to scream, but before she could do that, Vicky had clamped her hand over her mouth.

'You want us to be kicked out?' Vicky chided, as she let go of Mili.

Slyly, she put the cockroach in the bowl which had a little bit of pahari murg still left in it.

Then she started screaming, 'Cockroach! What the devil! Cockroach in the food. I'm going to sue . . .'

The manager of the restaurant was at her side in a trice. 'Madam, please cool down,' he placated. 'This has never happened before. We are very particular about hygiene.'

'Really?' said Vicky, raising her voice. 'Then how did a cock—'

'Please don't make a fuss, madam. I'll fire the cook right away,' he said as he wiped the sweat from his forehead.

Vicky winked at Mili.

'Banthia,' the manager was saying. 'Bring another pahari murg and a couple of chapattis to this table.' He then turned to Mili and Vicky. 'I assure you, madam, this'll never happen again. And eat as much as you please. I will not charge you a single paisa.'

Vicky nodded. The manager bowed and left them to enjoy the rest of their meal. She giggled as soon as he was out of earshot. 'Now I can eat in peace. And not worry about the bill.'

'What was a dead cockroach doing in your pocket?' asked Mili.

'It looked so real, didn't it?' whispered Vicky. 'But it's not. I bought it from one of the Tibetan shops. When you were busy looking at the jewellery.' She stopped speaking as she concentrated on cutting a piece of the chicken. 'I was thinking of putting it in Ravan's drawer. But, well . . .' She shrugged her shoulders as she put the fork into her mouth.

The two friends quietly trekked back to the hostel, after enjoying a sumptuous meal at Nataraj. It was late evening and getting dark. Vicky burped loudly, then grinned as Mili looked at her in horror.

'Be glad one of the teachers didn't hear you,' said Mili. 'She would have jumped into her grave.'

'These teachers don't know anything. Nothing can beat the taste of a fraudulent chicken curry,' Vicky said as she winked at Mili.

'The poor chicken must be turning in its gravy,' grinned Mili.

'Very funny,' said Vicky as she stuck out her tongue. She looked at Mili thoughtfully. 'Mili?'

'Yes?'

'What would you have done if Bauji hadn't given permission?'

'But he did, Vicky. Lord Kishan meant us to be together, for ever. So the question doesn't arise, you see.'

Vicky smiled. This is what she loved about her friend. She saw life so simply. 'Your Lord Kishan has an answer for everything?'

'Of course. He's omniscient, omnipotent—'

Vicky covered Mili's mouth with her hand. 'And omnivorous,' she finished for Mili.

Mili laughed. 'That's not Lord Kishan. That's you.'

The two girls hastened their pace. The opposite hill was shrouded in indigo-grey rain clouds. The rain would soon be upon them. They ran into their room, still chatting and laughing, and found Angel waiting for them.

'Your Uncle George was here,' she said.

'Whatever for?' Vicky asked.

'Your mother had called him up.'

'Mummum?'

'She was worried about you. Apparently, you haven't spoken to her in ages?'

'I'd better go. If I don't call Mummum tonight she won't be able to sleep,' Vicky mumbled as she hurriedly put a set of nightclothes in her bag.

'I'll come with you,' said Mili.

'No no, Mili,' said Vicky. 'I'll go myself. I'll be back in the morning. Before school starts.'

'It's drizzling,' Mili said, looking out of the window.

Vicky pulled out her mackintosh from under the bed and put it on. There was a clap of thunder.

'Looks like a storm,' said Mili.

'Stop worrying,' said Vicky, putting an arm around

Mili's shoulder as they left the room. 'I'm not made of sugar. I won't melt.'

'Don't forget to sign the register,' Angel called out after them.

Vicky shook her head and looked at Mili. They both laughed. 'What would we do without our guardian angel?' she said. Just as she was about to cross the road, a grey cat ran across.

'Come back, Vicky,' Mili yelled from the hostel door. 'A cat just crossed your path. It's bad luck.'

Vicky chuckled. 'Mili, stop being superstitious.' She waved to her, blew her a kiss and was off, her bag bobbing up and down as she marched down the hill.

She thought of Mummum. She felt guilty she hadn't written or called her in a month. Her sweet, huggable Mummum. How helpless and lonely she must have felt after Papa's death. All her relatives had cut off ties with her after she affronted them by marrying a cow-eating Englishman. And then the person for whom she had given up everything had left her – alone, with three children.

It was then that Mili's mother, the ever-practical Queen of Mohanagar, had come to her rescue.

'How can I work now? How will I cope with the house, the children, the loss of Francis?' Mummum had protested.

'If you don't work now, you never will,' Her Highness had said quietly.

Mummum had her doubts. Even though she had done some training in nursing, the only practice she had was on the cuts and bruises of her three brats. Yes,

Mummum had worked hard to bring the three of them up. Sometimes, by the time she got home, it would be very late. And even though tired and hungry, she'd sit beside them and ask them how their day had been. And if they were already asleep, she'd let Vicky sleep, but wake Michelle and Claudia up to enquire about her.

Vicky smiled sadly to herself. Children can be so cruel sometimes. The next day she would tell Mummum she was a terrible mother, coming home late at night, leaving her kids all alone. Mummum would laugh then, her loud boisterous laugh, and pulling her cheeks, say, 'Sorry, Grandma, it won't happen again.' Vicky would then feel very pleased and grown-up for telling off her own mother. She'd push back her spectacles, then with nose in the air, she'd say, 'It's all right. Next time be home before dark.' Mummum would give her a salute and say, 'Aye aye, captain.'

The drizzle had now turned into a heavy downpour. Vicky hastened her pace. Kishangarh was depressing during the monsoons. Not like Mohanagar, where she could make paper boats and splish-splosh in the puddles all day. But the smell of rain was the same. Oh, how she loved the earthy, heavenly smell of rain. It was just seven in the evening but it was already dark. A solitary frog croaked noisily from a nearby puddle. Vicky pulled up the collar of her mackintosh to stop the raindrops from seeping in. A strong, gusty wind brought with it the stench of an overflowing bin. Vicky stepped aside to let a mother and her little boy pass. The boy tripped and let out a long, annoying wail.

But the rains were a little different tonight, she

thought, as she heard the thunder rumble, followed by a streak of lightning. She ducked instinctively. There was more variety today. As though the rain of the last few days had been a rehearsal and today was the final performance, with all the sound and light effects.

Aunt Ethel's marigold-coloured house soon came into view. Vicky looked at it through a veil of rain. It did not look pretty and sunny any more – rather, like a stain on a rain-shrouded Kishangarh. The gate creaked as she opened it. It was wet and slimy and smelt of rust.

'So you decided to grace us with your presence,' said Uncle George as the servant led Vicky into the living room.

Vicky looked at him as he lay sprawled on the sofa, smoking a hookah. When Mummum had told her she had an uncle in Kishangarh and he was a collector, she had visualised him as a lean, athletic, suave man, not a slothful hippo. She looked around as she unbuttoned her mackintosh. 'Where's Aunt Ethel?' she asked.

'Her father was very ill. She rushed to Calcutta a couple of days back. He died this morning.'

'Oh, I'm sorry,' Vicky mumbled. This was great. The day just kept getting better. Now she had to sit and make small talk with Uncle George. She looked down at her feet. Drops of water were dripping from her raincoat and forming a puddle where she stood. Absent-mindedly, she began tracing a pattern on the water with her shoe.

'I think you'd better speak to your mother,' said Uncle George, pointing to the telephone. 'She sounded rather worried.'

'Yes,' replied Vicky as she took off her mackintosh and

handed it to the servant. She picked up the mouthpiece and waited for the operator to connect the line.

'Hello, Mummum?'

'Victoria, my poppet,' Mummum gushed. 'How are you? Why haven't you written to me or called me up for so long?'

'I'm fine, Mummum. Don't you worry,' replied Vicky.

'The telephone in your hostel is always engaged,' said Mummum. 'And I heard about your aunt. Please give her my condolences.'

'I will, Mummum.' She paused to look at the servant who was standing at the door. He had come to announce that dinner had been served. 'I've to go now,' she said into the mouthpiece. 'I'll call you again. Soon.'

Dinner was a dismal affair. Well, not quite, since Uncle George had decided to have his meal in silence, which suited Vicky just fine. She had already eaten, so she just nibbled at some salad. After the servants had left and she sat on the sofa in the living room, sipping her coffee, Uncle George finally broke his silence.

'I heard you were almost expelled from school,' he said. 'Have you come here to study or to run riot with boys all night?'

Ah, so that was the reason for the silence. Wouldn't do a collector good to admonish his niece for playing truant in front of the servants, would it now? Vicky smiled disdainfully at his choice of words. *Run riot* indeed.

'They're my friends.'

'But why? Why do you spend so much time with those bloody natives? Your father was English, have you forgotten?'

'So? My mother is an Indian. I live in India. I look like an Indian. I *am* an Indian. And what I do is none of your business,' she replied. She realised her voice had gone shrill and she was shouting.

'Oh yes it is. I'm your local guardian, remember? And while you're in my charge, there's no way I'm going to let you become a hussy like that mother of yours.'

Vicky walked slowly towards Uncle George, anger written all over her face. 'How could you speak about my mother in that manner?' she said through clenched teeth. 'How dare you? Just because she's an Ind—'

'Ha! Don't I know? She was pregnant even before she tied the knot with Francis.'

Vicky was livid. Before she knew what she was doing, she had slapped Uncle George right across his face. He looked stunned for a moment. And then he slapped her right back, so hard that Vicky staggered and almost lost her balance. 'How dare you?' he spat out. 'You hit *me*? The Collector of Kishangarh? Whom everyone respects?' he barked as he pushed her down on the floor. He pinned her hands above her head with one hand and hit her again with the other. This time the blow landed on her nose and it began to bleed.

Vicky's eyes widened with fear as he fumbled with his trouser buttons. She tried to pull her hands free but his grip was much too strong. He was now on top of her. She felt suffocated. His heavy frame was smothering her. She wriggled as he yanked up her frock and tried to push him off with her feet, but he was much too heavy. Vicky began to shake and broke out in a sweat.

Her heart was beating rapidly. She felt numb. And cold. So cold. She wanted to scream, but all that escaped her lips was a defeated sob. She heard a clap of thunder. She had always been afraid of thunderstorms. 'Papa,' she sobbed.

Chapter Thirteen

Raven massaged his knee with his hand. It had been a long day. He switched off his lamp and was about to get into bed when there was a frantic knock on the door. It was still raining heavily. He frowned. Who could be out in this kind of weather? Pulling on his robe over his pyjamas, he answered the door. Gurpreet, Jatin and two other boys rushed inside even before he could ask them to come in. Gurpreet shut and bolted the door, then leant against it with a sigh.

Raven raised a brow as he looked at him and then at the other three lads. 'What is it?' he asked. 'Have you lost your notes again?'

'No, sir – the police,' replied Jatin, panting.

'What?' asked Raven.

Just then there was a knock on the door. Raven pursed his lips and looked at the boys. They looked at him pleadingly, with folded hands. Pointing to a door, he said, 'Go into the living room.' Once the boys had done his bidding, he opened the main door. There were two policemen.

'Yes?' he said.

'Some natives have been creating trouble at the theatre. They made their escape before we could catch them,' said one of the policemen.

'What kind of trouble?' asked Raven.

'They were enticing the Indians to protest against the management for not being allowed in the balcony,' said the same policeman. 'They might have come this way. Have you seen them?'

'I have no idea what you're talking about,' Raven replied brusquely. He looked at his watch and then pointedly at the two men at the door.

'We're sorry to have bothered you at this hour, sir,' said the other policeman. 'We shall take our leave.'

Nodding, Raven shut the door. He strode into the living room. 'You lads have some cheek. Coming to your teacher's house in the dead of the night to hide from the police? What were you thinking?'

He glared at Gurpreet and Jatin as they looked at each other.

'But sir . . .' said Gurpreet. 'You yourself said we could come to you for help any time, day or night . . .'

'As students. For your studies,' barked Raven.

'You helped Vidushi, sir, so I though—' muttered Jatin.

'That was a different matter,' said Raven walking out of the room. He came back after five minutes with a couple of blankets that smelt of mothballs. Throwing them on the sofa, he said, 'You can stay the night in this room. But I want you out of here at daybreak. Have I made myself clear?'

'Yes, sir,' the boys answered softly in unison.

Raven left the room.

'I told you so,' he heard Gurpreet speak and stopped at the door to listen.

'After all, he's an Angrez. Son of a murderer. These firangis are no good, Jatin. You can never trust them. Never ever.'

Raven strode back into the room and walked up to Gurpreet. 'I'm sorry for what happened to your grandparents, but I had nothing to do with it. I was only six. It wasn't in my hands, was it?' He retied the belt of his gown which had come undone and looked Gurpreet in the eye. 'It was my father who did it. And who knows? Maybe it wasn't in his hands either? Maybe he had no choice but to obey the orders.'

Gurpreet smiled scornfully. 'If you say so, sir.'

'Look, I'm not here to defend my father,' said Raven. 'Hell, I don't even know whether he still lives or is no more. All I'm saying is that I'm not him.' He waved a finger at the four of them. 'If I was, you'd all be in prison right now.'

With that he left the room and made his way slowly to his bedroom. Taking off his slippers and robe, he lay down, but sleep eluded him. He lay on his bed, his head resting on his arm, staring up at the ceiling. He wondered why he was so upset. Was he upset because his own students were plotting against his fellow brethren? Was he really angry with them or with

157

himself? Because he did not know where he belonged? Because he himself could not decide whether he was English or Indian?

The next morning dawned bright and sunny. As though the storm that had raged all night had never happened. Raven squinted as he traversed the short gravel path leading up to the church. He winced as the church bells began to ring. He had slept badly and his head hurt. He was about to enter the church when he heard a voice from behind.

'I say, Raven . . .'

He stopped in his tracks and turned around. It was the vice chancellor.

'Yes, Prof. Keating?' he said, stepping back and away from the door to let the others enter.

Prof. Keating led him to the back of the church. 'It has come to my notice that you gave shelter to some Indian boys in your house last night,' he said, lowering his voice. 'You hid them from the police. Are you insane, Raven?'

Raven raised a brow. News travelled fast in Kishangarh.

'I did no such thing, Professor,' Raven lied. 'They were my students and had come to me for help with Shakespeare.'

'This is most irregular,' said Professor Keating, shaking his head.

'What is, Professor? I'm afraid I don't understand.'

'Oh yes you do,' said Professor Keating giving him a long hard look.

Raven looked askance.

Prof. Keating spoke again. 'You're getting too involved with your students, Raven. Protocol requires a certain distance be maintained.'

'Yes, Professor, I shall keep that in mind.'

'You had better. Otherwise the consequences can be worse than you could ever imagine.'

'Yes, Professor. Good day to you,' said Raven, lifting the edge of his cap slightly, and he walked into the church without waiting for Prof. Keating to reply. He sat on the empty pew right at the back and closed his eyes as the smell of roses and lilies enveloped him. It was peaceful in there. He wished he could say the same for himself.

Mili was still in bed. She could hear the other inmates stirring – washing, cleaning, getting dressed. She knew she ought to get out of bed, but she didn't feel like attending classes today. Not today, not the rest of the week, not ever. She wished Bhoomi was there with her. To tidy her bed, help her dress, braid her hair and to bring her breakfast in bed. Mili rolled over on her stomach. Then propping her chin on a hand, she lifted the curtain with the other and looked out of the window. She blinked as she looked at the calm sun. Not a trace of the storm last night. There wasn't a single cloud in the sky. Not even those soft, fluffy clouds that looked like cotton balls. It promised to be a beautiful day. And yet she felt that lurking fear, the kind of dread she had felt seeing the look on Ma's face – just a minute before she had told her that Nani was no more.

The door creaked open and Vicky walked into the

room quietly. Mili looked at her, surprised. It was not like Vicky to enter a room softly. She burst into rooms. 'What's wrong?' Mili asked as Vicky slumped down on her bed. Mili let out a gasp of horror as Vicky lifted up her eyes and looked at her. Her eyes – they were not twinkling. They were dull, vacant and lifeless and were staring at the wall beyond.

Mili looked at her friend carefully. Her lips were puffy, as were her cheeks. There were scratches and bruises on her cheeks and neck. Her frock was torn at one shoulder and crumpled. Mili clutched Vicky's hands. 'What happened, Vicky? Didn't you go to Uncle—?'

'He raped me, Mili,' Vicky sobbed, tears flowing down her cheeks. 'First he hit me . . . my nose and lips were bleeding.'

Mili wrapped her arms around her friend.

'It . . . hurt . . . so much,' said Vicky. She was crying hysterically now.

Mili held her best friend to her bosom, her tears falling onto Vicky's face and mingling with her own. They clung to each other, holding tight, cradling each other and crying softly – for a long time.

'I want Papa. I need him. He'll clobber him . . .' Vicky sobbed, as she put her head on Mili's lap, her knees drawn up.

'Shh,' whispered Mili, caressing her hair and face. 'I know, Vicky, I know. Relax. Don't speak any more.'

'Mummum will die. She was so happy. That I got admission here. How proud she was. Announced it to the whole world. This will kill her. She can't show her face to anyone. No more.'

'No, Vicky, she loves you,' said Mili, wiping her tears with the back of her hands.

'But I've let her down. She always called me her bravest child. She'll never forgive me. For being such a coward.' Vicky started shivering uncontrollably. 'I'm cold – very, very cold,' she whispered.

Mili wrapped a shawl around her, then covered her legs with a blanket. She then started rubbing her hands with hers. Vicky slowly drifted off into a deep sleep.

Getting up, Mili hastily got dressed. She had to get some help. Should she get a doctor? But she didn't know any doctors in Kishangarh. Who should she go to? She'd go to the warden. Yes. She'd know what to do. She went to the warden's room and was about to knock on the door when Angel appeared out of nowhere.

'She's away. The dean is in charge now,' said Angel.

'Dean? Raven Sir?'

'Yes, now if you'll excuse me, I'm getting late for class. And you'd better hurry as well.'

Mili hesitated outside the hostel building. She wasn't sure what she ought to do. It was Vicky who always decided what was to be done in moments of crisis. Should she speak to Raven Sir? But he hated the two of them. But then, he was also in charge. Yes, he would know what to do. Mili headed for the faculty residences. She banged frantically on Raven Sir's door. No answer. She banged again. And again. Then tired, emotionally and physically, she sat down on the parapet at the edge of the front garden. She gazed absently at the dirty gutter flowing behind the parapet. She thought of Vicky, her bruised appearance and what she had told her. She wasn't sure she fully understood the meaning of rape, but it must be something horrific to have affected Vicky in that manner.

Now, where was Raven Sir? It must be around ten o'clock in the morning. Mili knew he didn't have any class that morning. Then where? Could he be taking a class in MP College? Mili scratched her head. Or maybe he was in the library? Yes, it was his favourite haunt. Why hadn't she thought of it before?

He was indeed in the library. Mili rushed over to his table. 'Sir, sir . . .' she said.

Raven put his forefinger on his lips. 'This is the library,' he said in a low voice. 'We can't talk here, as you know. Wait for me outside. I'll be there in fifteen minutes.'

'It can't wait,' Mili said, on the verge of tears.

'What is it?' Raven folded his arms and looked at her.

Mili averted her gaze. 'Sir, Vicky has been raped.'

'What?' said Raven, shocked.

Mili nodded her head.

'Where is she?' he asked.

'In the hostel.'

Raven sprang to his feet and followed Mili to the hostel. It was eerily quiet. All the inmates were attending class. Mili tried to open the door of her room but couldn't. It was bolted from the inside. Raven banged on the door and called out Vicky's name several times. Mili did the same. She then looked at Raven and wondered what they ought to do now. He did not reply, but taking a short run, threw himself at the door. Nothing happened. He did it again. And again. The fourth time the bolt gave way and the door opened. Raven fell into the room.

'Oh Christ,' she heard him mutter as she entered the room. She stared. And stared. Beads of perspiration broke out on her forehead. She wanted to scream but not a sound left her throat. She turned white and clutched onto Raven's sleeve.

Vicky's body swung from the ceiling fan, Mili's red dupatta wrapped tightly around her neck.

Chapter Fourteen

'Hurry up, Mili. We're going to be late,' Vicky said as she picked up her bag.

'I can't wait to get there,' Mili squealed excitedly as she put her arm through Vicky's.

The two girls alighted at the Mall and made their way to the theatre, which was situated at the heart of Kishangarh. They were going to watch the English adaptation of Kalidas' *Shakuntala*. As they pushed through the crowd, Mili noticed people sniggering and pointing their fingers at her. Some stared at her unashamedly while others began clicking their tongues – tut tut tut!

Mili tugged Vicky's sleeve frantically. 'What's the matter with these people, Vicky? Why are they staring at me like this?'

'Don't be ridiculous,' Vicky replied. 'Let's walk a little faster. Or we'll miss the first scene.'

As the two of them took their seats in the front row of the theatre, Mili felt uneasy again. She looked around and then over her shoulders at the rest of the audience. She found a hundred pairs of eyes gaping at her instead of the stage. Beads of perspiration appeared on her forehead. She clutched Vicky's elbow as the audience began to chant, 'Murderer, murderer, murderer.'

Mili sat up with a start. She was drenched in perspiration. Two weeks had elapsed since the fateful day on which Vicky killed herself. Or was it three weeks? Or four? She couldn't remember. It was as though she had been living in a haze. If only she had not left Vicky alone that day. She would have been still alive.

She lay back in her bed, gazing at the ceiling fan – the monster that had devoured her friend. The hostel was quiet. It must be almost empty. All the girls were in class. A tap was dripping somewhere. Then the sound of footsteps which gradually faded away. The windows of her room were open but there was no breeze. The air was still. Mili began to feel claustrophobic and switched on the fan. The droning of the ceiling fan did nothing to stifle the heat but added to her feeling of desolation. As she continued to gaze up at the ceiling, the walls of the room seemed to close in on her. She felt a desperate need to escape.

She ran down the Hide-and-Seek Road and did not stop till she had reached the edge of the lake. She sat there motionless, gazing at the still waters. *Why did Vicky have to die?* she asked herself for the hundredth time. She had always been so brave, always taking chances, always in charge, never afraid. Why did she have to die such a horrible death?

They had been friends ever since they were babies. When they were about five, they would sneak out a couple of Ma's saris, wrap them around themselves and pretend to be Ma and Mummum. Then, when they were about a year older, mothers were replaced by the princes and princesses from the fairy stories that Nani used to tell them at bedtime. Vicky would always play the prince and come to rescue Mili from the clutches of the wicked witch. One of Mili's dolls would be the witch, or on the rare occasion, Uday. Mili was content to play the sad forlorn princess, singing mournful songs. She had the voice of a cuckoo, Nani used to say.

She also used to say the two of them were Kishan and Sudama in their previous birth. But then Kishan didn't leave Sudama and disappear into oblivion like Vicky had. Or did he? According to the Hindu scriptures, the two were inseparable in school. And even when they met each other again after years, Krishna knew exactly what ailed Sudama and showered his friend with wealth and prosperity. Maybe Vicky was up there with Nani, waiting for her to join them? And then they would be reborn again . . . together . . .

'There you are.'

On hearing the familiar voice, Mili turned around. She started to get up. 'Good evening, sir . . .'

'No, no, keep sitting,' Raven said, sitting down on the grass, beside her. 'You mustn't go wandering off on your own like this. It's not safe.'

Mili did not answer. She picked up a long stick lying

next to her and began to stir the still waters of the lake with it, making little ripples.

'I was speaking to Miss Perkins and Mrs Nunes a few minutes back.'

Mili shot him a questioning look.

'Yes, Victoria's mother had come to my office. She's leaving in a couple of days.' He collected some pebbles in his hand and threw them one after another into the water, making little whirlpools in the process. 'She told us she had decided to close the chapter on Victoria's rape and begged us to do likewise,' he finally said, as he threw one last pebble into the lake, as hard as he could.

'What? She's not going to take that man to court? Is she out of her mind?'

'I'm not surprised,' said Raven, averting his gaze. 'Don't forget, she's a widow. And she has two other daughters to think of. If she filed a case, everyone would know it was her own brother-in-law who had committed the heinous act. Who would marry her daughters after such a scandal?'

'*No!*' Mili shouted vehemently, shaking her head. 'Her reluctance to go to court is not because of her daughters. She doesn't want to lose face. After all, she's always been so pompous and a show-off.'

Raven spoke quietly. 'Malvika, hurling abuses at Mrs Nunes is not going to bring Victoria back.'

But Mili wasn't listening. 'What reason is she going to give everyone for the suicide?' she asked.

'Low grades in exams,' replied Raven.

Mili laughed. A hollow, mirthless laugh. 'Vicky committed suicide because she got poor marks? Do you think she ever cared about marks? That is so ludicrous. She'd never kill herself for that. Low grades indeed!'

She looked at Raven as he got up. He stood with his hands in his pockets, feet slightly apart, looking askance. Mili continued speaking. 'There we were, almost expelled from school for an innocent picnic at night, while this man rapes a girl half his age and is allowed to roam free? And she was supposed to be his ward? He was her local guardian!'

'True. But we are both helpless, Malvika. Unless you're able to cajole Mrs Nunes to go to court. Or force the police to lock him up. You are forgetting George is a powerful man. He's not only English, but also the Collector of Kishangarh.'

'You know, sir, if Vicky was English or her father still alive, and the man who raped her was an Indian, he would have been hanged for sure. Forget rape, he would have been killed like a dog even if he had just kissed her.'

Raven did not reply but merely stared at her. She saw something in his eyes that she could not fathom. He spoke after a long time, his voice barely audible.

'Let's go back,' he said. 'It's getting dark.'

'Sir, you don't understand what I'm going through right now. And even if you did, you don't care. After all, you never did like Vicky and me.'

Again, no reply. Mili's hands curled into fists as she watched him stride towards his car, get in and start the engine. He gave her a slight nod. Reluctantly, she walked to the car and slid into the passenger seat. He reversed into the main road before slanting a sideways glance at her. They drove back to her hostel in silence.

When they reached the hostel, Raven Sir switched off the engine and turned to face her. 'I'm sorry,' he said softly. 'I shouldn't have spoken so harshly. But what you said back there isn't true.' His Adam's apple moved and his voice dropped down to a whisper. 'I do care. Very much so. I guess that's why I got upset. It wasn't you I was angry with. I was angry with myself. For not being able to help my own student.'

'Don't worry, Raven, sir, we're used to your scolding by now,' said Mili.

Raven grimaced slightly. 'I think I've scolded you two more than all my students put together.' He looked down. 'But this time, I'm sorry,' he said softly.

'I'm sorry too,' replied Mili. 'It's just that . . . I feel awful. My dearest friend has died and I can't do anything about it. Not a thing. You have no idea what that feels like.'

'I do. Only too well,' Raven said quietly. 'I felt the same way when my father walked out of my life. And I couldn't do anything to ease my mother's pain . . . Sometimes, nothing is in our hands.' He sighed. 'Believe me, if it was up to me, I would move heaven and earth for you. I would never let my students down.'

Swallowing the lump rising in her throat, Mili stepped out of the car. 'Yes, sir,' she murmured. 'Thank you, sir; goodnight, sir.'

'Before you go, promise me something?'

Mili raised a brow.

'Promise me that you will start attending classes from tomorrow. I haven't seen you in class for the last two weeks.'

'Yes, sir, I will.'

'Promise?'

Smiling slightly, Mili replied, 'Yes, sir, I promise.'

'Good.' With that, he drove off.

Mili looked at the road for a long time after the car could be seen no more. Then with a sigh, she dragged her feet towards her room.

Raven had dinner on Mother's insistence, but ate very little and in silence. And as soon as he was able to, he excused himself from the table. He was grateful that, although Mother gave him a questioning look when he threw down the serviette and pushed back his chair, she chose not to say anything or follow him to his room.

He sat down at his desk and tried to check some of his students' assignments but he could not concentrate. He kept thinking of Malvika with a tenderness he had not known before. It had hurt him to see her hurting so.

He had been taken aback by all that she said. It seemed her friend's death had made her grow up suddenly. How solemnly she spoke. He sighed. He missed the old Malvika. Always up to mischief with that Victoria, always in trouble, fluttering around like a butterfly. Her words kept coming back to haunt him. 'If Vicky was English . . .' She was right. If George had been an Indian, he would have been hanged . . . that's for sure. Raven picked up the dome-shaped glass paperweight, twirled it like a top on his desk and stared at it.

He recalled what had happened earlier that day, when Mrs Nunes had come to his office.

'I've never liked George much. And for what he

did to my poppet, I'll never forgive him,' she said. 'He snuffed out my daughter's life, the most precious thing in the world for me, and for that may he rot in hell.' She paused and looked down at her hands. 'But I've decided not to take him to court. And I wish to hush this matter completely, once and for all.'

'Are you sure, Mrs Nunes?' Raven had asked.

'What purpose is dragging George to court going to serve? It's not going to bring my Victoria back to life, is it?' Her voice shook as she spoke. 'Everyone will spit at us when they come to know that Victoria's own uncle raped her. I have two other daughters. One has just got engaged. To an orthodox Catholic family from Kerala. They would break off the engagement in an instant should they come to know the details surrounding Victoria's death.'

'I understand,' Raven had said. 'What do you want me to do?'

'I have spoken to Prof. Keating as well as Principal Perkins and they have promised no one shall come to know about the rape. I want you to do the same.'

'Rest assured, Mrs Nunes, the circumstances surrounding Victoria's death shall go with me to my grave.'

'One more thing, Prof. Raven . . .' She hesitated.

'Yes?'

'I believe, in the absence of the warden, you are in charge?'

'You're right. The warden has gone to England for two months, possibly three. The political unrest in the country is making a lot of the English insecure.'

'Malvika is also like my daughter. I don't know how to break this news to her. Will you do it for me?'

'You have entrusted me with a very difficult job, Mrs Nunes, but yes, I'll speak to her.'

Raven took out a cigar and lit it. He drew in a long puff and sighed.

Speak to her he did. He knew she'd get upset but what he didn't realise was how affected he himself would be after speaking to her. He used to despise her and Victoria because of their juvenile behaviour and careless attitude towards studies. But today . . . the way Mili's eyes welled up with tears and yet the conviction with which she spoke – his heart went out to her. She looked so lost and lonely, so vulnerable. He felt like kicking himself; here was his student, his ward – miserable and in pain – and he was unable to do anything to ebb her sorrow.

It was Janamashtami, the birthday of Lord Krishna, after whom Kishangarh had been named. Raven stopped his car for a moment, as he passed Gopeshwar temple. It was beautifully decorated with flowers today. The statue of Krishna had been washed and adorned with new clothes and jewellery. Legend had it that when Krishna was a cowherd, one of the calves in his charge gambolled off towards the hills of Uttaranchal. Krishna ran after it, until he reached Kishangarh. Tired from the long chase, he sat down to catch his breath and began playing his flute. It was on that spot where he had rested that Gopeshwar temple had been built. And it is said that even today, when the north wind blows and rustles through the leaves of the trees in

Kishangarh, you can hear Lord Kishan playing on his flute.

Raven listened. Could he really hear the flute? He shook his head and grinned at his own foolishness. Since when had he started believing in all this nonsense? He started the engine and slowly made his way to Jeolikot.

He thanked Sister Therese as she pointed to the green in front of the school building where the children were playing. He smiled as he espied Vidushi, hopping about on one foot, trying to catch the children fleeing from her. Her hair had begun to grow. Though it was still short and looked like a boy's, she looked much healthier as well as happier. She turned around as a shadow fell across her.

'Sir,' she said, a smile instantly lighting her face.

'How are you, Vidushi?' Raven asked with a smile. He pointed to the children she was playing with and who were now staring at him curiously.

'Sir, they also live here. Older students like me help the sisters take care of them.'

'I see,' said Raven, shooing the children off with a wave of his hand. Then turning to Vidushi he said, 'Walk with me. I wish to speak to you.'

'Yes, sir,' Vidushi replied, walking alongside him.

'Are you happy, Vidushi?'

'Very,' Vidushi replied. 'And sir . . .' she gushed.

'Yes?'

Raven narrowed his eyes as he looked at her. She was blushing.

'Nothing, sir,' she giggled.

'Come now. You can tell me.'

'But what if you get angry, sir?' Vidushi replied, wringing her hands nervously.

'I don't believe an angel like Vidushi can ever do anything wrong,' Raven replied with an affectionate smile.

'Sir,' she replied, looking down. 'There's a boy in MP College. He is . . . a little . . . fond . . . He has proposed to me.'

'Jatin?'

Vidushi nodded, continuing to look down.

'That's wonderful news.'

'But I'm a widow,' Vidushi said, her smile vanishing. 'How can I marry?'

'I'll see what I can do.'

'But sir, I don't wish to convert . . .'

'Of course not.'

'But . . .'

'Vidushi,' said Raven with a frown. 'I recall you as being a bright student whose essays were always brilliant. Do you not know, starting each sentence with a "but" is not good English?'

'Sir, bu—'

Raven put a finger on his lips. 'Don't worry. Leave it to me. I'll take care of it.' He bent down and picked up a broken pine cone. It looked like a wooden rose but smelt of pine. Giving it to Vidushi, he said, 'Congratulations.' Then he smiled, winked at her and left.

'Someone here to see you, Mili baba,' announced Bahadur. Mili wondered who it was as she went into the parlour. It was Mrs Nunes.

174

'I'm going back to Mohanagar tomorrow,' she said. 'I wanted to see you before I left.'

Mili sat down quietly beside her. 'I can't believe she's no more,' she said softly.

Mrs Nunes looked down. 'Yes, I know,' she whispered. 'When I saw her body . . . I couldn't believe it was her. To see someone who was always full of life, still and lifeless . . .' She paused as she wiped the tears running down her cheeks with the back of her hand. 'Why, when she was just a month old, she rolled off the sofa—'

Mili looked straight ahead at the painting of the angels playing the harp. 'And yet you do not want to get her justice.'

Mrs Nunes looked sharply at her. 'Mili?'

Mili continued to look straight ahead. She shook her head slowly. 'You're not Vicky's real mother. You must be her stepmother.'

'What are you saying, Mili?'

Mili looked at her, her face contorted with anger. 'If you were really her mother, you would not rest in peace until you had avenged your daughter's death,' she said, her voice rising.

'What can I do, my child?' said Mrs Nunes, her eyes brimming with tears. 'What can I do?' she whispered in a defeated tone.

'You can drag that . . . that man to court,' said Mili. She could not bring herself to say his name any more.

Mrs Nunes looked down at her hands. 'I met George the other day. He said to me that he hasn't seen Victoria for almost two months. I reminded him that Victoria had called me up from his house that night. He said she must have called from elsewhere. It was most certainly not from his house.'

'But what about the entry in the register?' said Mili.

'That's not enough, my child. After all, didn't you and Victoria put in a similar entry, the night you went off for a picnic? Besides, you two didn't exactly endear yourselves to the warden or to any of the other teachers, did you?' She stroked Mili's head gently. 'There's no point going to court. None at all. We can't prove anything.' She walked over to a table that stood at the end of the room and poured herself a glass of water.

Keeping her face averted, she spoke again. 'Don't forget, Mili, I'm an Anglo-Indian. On the fringe of society. The English make fun of us, the Indians hate us. It has taken me a long time to earn some respect. And Michelle is engaged to be married. Into a very good family. Do you think they would want to marry into a family where the uncle is a rapist?'

'You never did love Vicky. It was always the other two. You were never there for her. Most of the time she was with me. In the palace. You were always too bus—'

Mrs Nunes put a finger on Mili's lips. Mili darted an angry look at her. Mrs Nunes cupped her face with her hands. Mili looked down. 'Look at me, Mili,' she said. Mili slowly looked up into Mrs Nunes' eyes. Tears pricked her eyelids.

'I know you didn't mean that, my child,' said Mrs Nunes quietly. 'I know how you hurt.' She pulled Mili to her bosom. Mili could not control her tears any more. The two of them clung to each other and sobbed uncontrollably.

She spoke after a while. 'As a mother, I shouldn't say this – but of the three, Victoria was my dearest. She was my baby. I felt guilty not being able to spend any time with her because of my work. The other two would bully her. I would tell her when she came crying to me – shame on you, crying like a little girl. You're the man of the house. Go and scold them, hit them back.'

Mrs Nunes got up and walked over to the window. Then turning back, she looked at Mili again, a faraway look in her eyes. 'You know, when I first saw you, you were . . .' she paused to put her left hand two inches below her right palm '. . . see? That's how small you were when I first saw you. I was the new nurse and couldn't find my way to your mother's room. There are so many rooms and corridors in your palace. And they all look the same. I was bewildered. I stood in the corridor, watching the khus mats beating against the walls in the breeze and wondering what to do, when I heard you. I followed the sound of your crying and what do I see? You alone in the cot, your face puckered and scarlet from all that crying.

'That was not all. Crouching over you were two of the ugliest black cats I have ever seen. They didn't look like cats at all. More like Cerberus, straight out of hell. They were sniffing you hungrily. By now my heart was going thump, thump, thump. And you were crying harder and harder. And the more you cried, the more Victoria kicked me in the tummy. And I'm thinking – oh my goodness, oh my goodness, what do I do? What do I do? Unable to think of anything better, I charged towards the cats shouting at the top of my voice and clapping my hands. Thanks be to Jesus, they ran away.

177

'With my heart still beating fast, I picked you up. The moment I did that, you stopped crying and Victoria stopped kicking. Just like that.

'Shortly after that your mother came. She snatched you from my arms. "Who are you?" she asked suspiciously. I think she thought I was going to steal her baby. I narrated the whole incident. Her eyes grew moist and she showered a hundred kisses on you. And then she thanked me profusely. "You saved my baby. The cats would have mauled her for sure." "Speak nothing of it," I replied. "I was only doing my job."

'Then she demanded where the midwife was, in whose charge she had left you. We searched and found the deaf midwife fast asleep on the other side of the crib. She was sacked and I became your mother's best friend and counsellor.'

'Oh, Mrs Nunes, I had no idea,' Mili said, her voice choked and moist.

'That's not all,' Mrs Nunes continued. 'A few months later, when Victoria was born, your mother brought you to our house to see her. You smiled and cooed at my little princess. And then you grabbed her little finger and closed your fist around it and—'

'And our friendship was sealed. Yes, Ma told me this part,' Mili said, with a soft, sad smile.

Mrs Nunes caressed her hair. 'You were more of a sister to her than either of the two brats,' she said lovingly. 'I can understand your loss, my child.'

'Oh, Mrs Nunes, I can't live without her,' Mili sobbed, hiding her face with her hands.

After some time, Mrs Nunes got up to leave. She

hugged Mili once again. 'Come and see me whenever you're in Mohanagar.' She looked heavenward. 'I'm sure Vicky would like that.' She covered her mouth with her hand to control her sobs from escaping and rushed outside.

Mili stood alone in the room, with only the angels in the painting that hung on the wall staring down at her. She felt lost. And alone. Yes, for the first time in her life she was alone. How was she going to live without Vicky? Who was going to tell her what to do? Vicky had always been there to take care of her, to protect her. But now . . . Mili swallowed. She was afraid. Very, very afraid. Oh Lord Kishan. Why did he do this to her? Why did he snatch her away from her? Mili sat down on the sofa and held her head between her hands as tears flowed down her cheeks yet again.

She did not know how long she sat there. Or when the evening gave way to twilight. It was the caretaker, who had come to lock up for the night, who found her there – curled up on the sofa like a foetus, two vertical lines running down her smooth cheeks, eyes swollen from too much crying.

Chapter Fifteen

Gurpreet swaggered into Uncleji's Tuck Shop and sat down at his favourite table, right at the back of the room. He was sipping a cup of coffee when Mili walked in. He waved to her with one hand and pulled out a chair for her with the other. Then he clicked his fingers at Bahadur. As Bahadur approached his table, he gulped down the remaining coffee and, banging the cup down, asked him to get him another one.

'How are you?' Mili asked.

'How do I look?' he answered in a clipped tone.

Mili fell silent. Gurpreet listened to the radio. Gandhiji was again waffling about how dishonourable it would be to launch a campaign against the Raj when it was engaged in a life and death struggle with the Fascists. He looked at Mili and said, 'I feel like defecting to the Forward Bloc. Gandhi and his idealisms!'

'What's Forward Bloc?' Mili asked.

'Netaji's army? Haven't you heard of Subhas Chandra Bose?' he asked irritably.

'Oh, yes yes,' replied Mili, biting her thumbnail. 'Where's Jatin?'

'He's gone for a meeting. With Guruji.'

'You didn't go?'

Gurpreet did not answer. He fumbled in his pocket for his cigarettes, found them, lit one, then blew out smoke. 'Mark my words, Mili,' he said, 'India is never going to become independent. This Congress and the Angrez are going to keep playing their cat-and-mouse game . . .' He drummed his fingers on the table before continuing, 'I want to get out of this country. I don't mind going anywhere, be it Australia, Canada, America – anywhere. I want to forget everything that happened here. I don't feel like talking to anyone any more. I want to be left alone.'

'I know, I understand,' replied Mili. 'I too am tired of hearing the same empty words over and over again. They say time heals all wounds, it's not at all true.' She bit her thumbnail, then continued, 'The pain, the loss will always be there. Yes, perhaps I'll learn to live with it. Some people say they understand my loss. How can they? It was a very personal loss which only I can understand.'

'Why did she do it, Mili? Why? I feel like burning down this whole world. Everything. Set this bloody canteen, school, college, everything ablaze. A world that did not have room for Vicky doesn't deserve to exist. All of us should be dead. You, me . . .' He got up abruptly and pushed the table over with all his strength. Their cups and saucers smashed to the floor.

'Get a hold on yourself, Gurpreet,' said Mili turning red.

He noticed everyone had gone quiet in the canteen and was staring at him. He didn't care.

Mili got up and, tugging at his sleeve, pulled him towards the door.

Uncleji walked up to them. 'Hello, son of Bhim, where are you sneaking off to?'

'We'll pay for all the damage, Uncleji. Just leave him alone at the moment and let us go,' Mili pleaded.

Uncleji looked at Gurpreet, then at Mili. 'All right, but I'm sending the bill to your hostel through Bahadur. You better pay up or . . .' he looked threateningly at Gurpreet.

'Yes, we will,' Mili muttered pulling Gurpreet out of the canteen.

'Do you know somewhere quiet?' asked Gurpreet.

'I know just the place.'

Just then, they bumped into Raven.

'Mili,' he said.

'Yes, sir?' Mili answered, walking over to him.

Gurpreet leant against the canteen wall and lit another cigarette as he watched Raven and Mili speaking to each other.

'So what was Raven saying? Was he scolding you again?' he asked, as they made their way up the Hide-and-Seek Road.

'No, no. He was just saying that if I have any problems, I can approach him anytime.'

'He can be nice sometimes. During the first trimester,

Jatin and I went to his house in the dead of the night. He was most understanding and said studies were more important than anything else in the world, even sleep . . . But he's an Angrez after all. You just can't trust them.'

Mili nodded.

'Isn't this where you and Vicky used to sit often?' he asked as Mili led him to a mound behind the hostel building.

Mili nodded again. She brushed aside the prickly pine needles before sitting down. They sat in silence for a while, Gurpreet pulling impatiently at the blades of grass and Mili tracing patterns with a little stick on the muddy ground.

'You can see the lake from here,' he observed.

'Yes, just a glimpse,' said Mili, smiling slightly. 'Vicky used to say—'

Gurpreet cleared his throat. 'I haven't mentioned this to anyone.' He felt Mili's eyes on him as he continued. 'A few days before Vicky died, she had come with me to my aunt's place.'

'Yes, she told me about it.'

'Then she must have also mentioned that she saw some puppies there . . .' Gurpreet plucked a grass and chewed its tip. 'It was then, as I watched her playing with those puppies, that I realised I was in love with her.'

He looked at Mili from the corner of his eye. She did not say anything for a while but continued making patterns on the ground with her stick. 'I had guessed,' she said finally.

'You know after the cricket match? Remember, we won the match and I made a century?'

Mili nodded.

'She came running onto the field, hugged me and said, "You play well." The whole of MP College was on its feet at the time, cheering and shouting my name, but all I could hear were Vicky's words – "You play well, you play well . . ." I did not know . . .' Gurpreet's voice broke and he could not continue. After a long time he spoke again. 'Siyappa . . . why did she do it, Mili?'

'I guess, because of low grades in class,' Mili answered carefully, avoiding eye contact.

'Rubbish,' he said through gritted teeth. 'Surely you don't believe that? A girl like Vicky is not going to commit suicide for something so trivial.'

Mili did not answer.

'You know, Mili, if I ever come to know the cause of her death, I will kill the person responsible. Whoever or whatever it is that caused her death, I will annihilate it from the face of this earth,' he said, as he yanked an entire tuft of grass.

He looked at the blades of grass he had just pulled up, clenched his teeth and crushed them with his fingers. He felt like setting fire to the whole universe. Reduce it to ashes. Just like his Vicky had been reduced to nothingness.

With October came Diwali, the festival of lights. Everywhere Mili looked, there were signs of celebration. Houses decked with diyas, which glittered like gold jewellery on a pretty maiden. And yet her heart was plunged in darkness. The hostel was almost bare – most of the inmates had gone home for Diwali. Mili had decided not to go. She did not know how to cope with Vicky's death in front of her family.

She thought of home. It must be beautifully lit today. All her favourite sweets – barfis and laddoos – and dahi vadas and puris must have been prepared. Their chef was famous for making the softest dahi vadas in all of Mohanagar. They would be soaked in curd and sweet-and-sour tamarind chutney and would melt the moment you put them in your mouth. And there would be a grand fireworks display in the palace gardens after dark. *Hey Lord Kishan, when will there be light in my life?*

There was a polite knock on the door. It was Bahadur. 'Phone for you, Mili baba,' he said. Mili sprinted to the common room. It must be from home. Sure enough, Ma was on the other end of the line.

'Happy Diwali, my child. We are all missing you so much. Why didn't you come home?'

'I have a lot of work to do, Ma,' Mili lied. She cleared her throat. 'Exams are around the corner.'

'And how is Vicky? Wish her happy Diwali as well.'

So Mrs Nunes had not told them yet. Mili took a deep breath. 'She's no more.'

'What?'

'She killed herself because she . . . . because of . . . she failed her exams.'

'Hey Ram. Mrs Nunes must be devastated.'

'Yes, Ma, do go and meet her.'

'But what about you? How are you?'

Mili pushed back the lump that had risen in her throat. 'Don't worry about me, Ma. I have lots of friends. Even the teachers are very supportive. They are all mollycoddling me.'

'Are you sure, Mili? I'm getting worried now. No wonder you didn't want to celebrate Diwali.'

'Ma, I'm fine. Really. Don't worry. There are a lot of people here to take care of me.'

'Listen, Mili, I'll come there.'

'No, Ma, no. Don't come here. You cannot leave home on Diwali. You're the Lakshmi of the house.'

'But . . .'

'Ma, I'm fine. Believe me, there are lots of people here. And then, in a couple of weeks, our exams will be over and I'll be home for the winter holidays.'

'All right, if you insist. But I'll call you again tomorrow.'

'Yes, Ma.'

Mili went back to her room to study for the forthcoming exams. Her mind began to wander. She thought of home and the long summer vacations when she was studying in Mohanagar. Much of her summer holidays were spent in Nani's home. There was a little temple dedicated to Lord Kishan in the house. And not only the temple, but the whole house smelt of sandalwood. It was a huge mansion built in the seventeenth century, sprawling across acres and acres of land. Central to the building was a large square courtyard with rooms all around it. The floors and steps were made of huge slabs of stone, which were always cold, no matter what time of the year it was. There were marble-topped tables and walls and floors covered with ornate tiles and mosaics.

At one end of the terrace was a single low-roofed

room. It had a large window covered with net from where the entire neighbourhood as well as the local bazaar could be seen. Once the room had been used for storing grain, but it had lain empty for the last few years and had become the favourite haunt of Mili and her younger cousins.

The children's makeshift bedroom used to be a long hall *without any* furniture. The floors were covered with row upon row of mattresses, and it was here that all the children gathered around Nani every evening after dinner.

Nani would take out a paan from her betel box, fold it from all sides, then tuck it into the right-hand corner of her mouth. She would then clear her throat and start. She would tell them stories from days long gone by, about brave kings and warriors, tales from Indian mythology and from the two great epics, the Ramayan and the Mahabharata.

The story Mili liked most of all was that of Prithviraj Chauhan, the valiant Rajput king of Mewar. Her eyes would light up each time Nani reached the part where Prithviraj came riding to Princess Sanjogta's swayamvar, and whisked her off on his horse, much to the amazement and chagrin of the assembled kings and princes. Every other day Mili would ask Nani to tell them the story of Prithviraj Chauhan, until Nani exclaimed in exasperation, 'Mili, I will tell you any other story but that!'

Mili then saved up her pocket money to buy the book. She would often read it before going to bed and fantasise that one day a prince, equally valiant and handsome, would come and sweep her off her feet. But even in her wildest dream, she had not thought that men could be animals like George. How she loathed men now, especially the Angrez. Maybe men like Prithviraj Chauhan were only found in fables? Maybe they never really did exist . . .

Autumn had given way to winter. Gurpreet rubbed his hands together in an effort to warm them as he looked around the examination hall. He had not studied for the exams. He might fail again. He didn't mind. He wasn't here to garner marks, but freedom fighters. He looked at the clock at the back of the classroom and yawned. Half an hour was still left.

He glanced at Jatin, who was sitting in front of him. He had been studying all night and was now scribbling furiously on his answer sheet. Leaning forward, he whispered, 'Why are you writing so much?'

'Shut up. I have two more questions to answer.'

'I've finished,' Gurpreet grumbled. 'I'm getting bored.'

'No talking in the class, please,' boomed Raven's voice, as he looked pointedly at Gurpreet.

'Sorry, sir,' he whispered and looked down at his answer sheet. Ever since he had called him the son of a murderer, he had been unable to look him in the eye. He shouldn't have called him that. After all, Raven was his teacher, his guru and had only ever been good to him. It wasn't fair to hold him responsible for what his father had done. But then, how could he forget what had happened to his grandparents?

He looked at Jatin again. He was calculating

something on his fingers; now he had gone back to writing. Gurpreet smiled. He remembered the first time he had noticed Jatin. It was last year, in the same hall, during their history exam.

Gurpreet had raised his hand.

'You want to drink some more water?' the invigilator asked, walking over to him.

'No, I need to go to the toilet,' replied Gurpreet.

The invigilator looked at him incredulously, over the rim of his glasses. 'I'm sorry, I can't give you permission for that,' he finally said.

Gurpreet turned his question paper over and pointed to the instructions. It was mentioned that students could be given permission to go to the toilet one at a time.

'I'm afraid I don't have any instructions to that effect,' said the invigilator.

'Sir, it's urgent,' replied Gurpreet.

'Why did you drink so much water?' the invigilator asked.

'I was thirsty,' replied Gurpreet. He grinned unashamedly as Jatin gave him a dirty look.

'I'll have to ask the principal,' replied the invigilator. 'Jatin, take my place and make sure no one cheats.'

'Yes, sir,' replied Jatin, standing up.

The invigilator soon returned. 'You can go now,' he said, looking at Gurpreet.

But Gurpreet was busy cutting and buffing his nails. Without looking up he said, 'I don't want to go now.'

He watched in amusement as the invigilator turned several interesting shades of red, blue and purple, before asking, 'Why?'

'I don't need to any more,' Gurpreet coolly replied. He hid his smile as the invigilator glared at him. He would have loved to strangle him, he was sure of that.

Jatin muttered under his breath, 'Bloody drama king, doesn't spare us even in the examination hall.'

Gurpreet had given him a lopsided grin and continued buffing his nails.

Whistling happily, now that the exams were over, Gurpreet had made his way to Uncleji's Tuck Shop. He was about to go in when a couple of his classmates called out to him.

'We have distributed all the leaflets,' said one of them.

'That's good,' replied Gurpreet, patting him on the shoulder. 'Now don't forget to come for the party meeting at Guruji's house tomorrow.'

'We won't,' replied the other. 'We'll be there.'

Just as the two lads left, someone caught hold of Gurpreet from behind, by his collar. Gurpreet turned around in surprise. It was Jatin.

'Why the hell did you have to ask for water every ten minutes?' he said through gritted teeth.

'Why do you think? I was thirsty,' said Gurpreet. 'Ahh,' he cried out in pain as Jatin punched his nose.

'Thirsty indeed! Because of you I couldn't finish my paper,' thundered Jatin. 'Sir, water . . . sir, toilet,' he mimicked.

Swiping at the blood running out of his nose with the back of his hand, Gurpreet was about to hit Jatin back when Uncleji arrived on the scene.

'Look, what had to happen, has happened,' Uncleji said, after listening to the sissy Jatin tattling about him.

'It can't be changed. So what's the point of fighting?'

'Uncleji, you don't know how many times he's failed,' said Jatin. 'And now because of him, I'm going to fail. He should be kicked out of college. Good for nothing.'

'Don't speak in that manner about your friend,' Uncleji admonished as he gave his handkerchief to Gurpreet.

'Friend indeed,' Gurpreet growled, grabbing the hanky from Uncleji and dabbing his nose with it.

They did become friends. Eventually. Not just friends but the thickest of friends. And he was glad he had him. Especially now, after Vicky's death. Even though they never spoke about it, he knew Jatin understood and was always there for him. And for that he was glad.

Chapter Sixteen

Uday had come to the station. He hugged Mili and held her tight. 'I've missed you so much,' he said, hugging her yet again. He had chattered all the way home and Mili had let him. It used to be the opposite. But this time she was relieved she didn't have to do all the talking. She snuggled up to Ma as soon as she reached the palace. It was comforting to feel the soft folds of her sari, to smell her familiar aroma of sandalwood, after such a long time. Bauji was equally pleased to see her, although, as always, he did his utmost to hide his emotions.

Mili was happy to be back home, to the warmth and security of familiar surroundings. Ma led her to her room excitedly. She had something new to show her. 'Look,' she said, pointing to the ceiling as soon as they entered her room. 'We've had one of these installed for you. They are much more efficient than the manual ones.'

Mili stared at the ceiling fan vacantly. She turned

pallid as the vision of Vicky's body swinging from her red dupatta flashed through her mind.

'What's the matter, Mili?' Ma was concerned.

'I think I'm a little tired,' she replied. She looked at the ceiling fan again and shook her head. And she had thought coming here would help her get away from it all.

'Yes, it was a long journey,' said Ma. 'You'd better go to bed. Bhoomi . . .'

Bhoomi, who had been hovering near the door, grinning at Mili from ear to ear, stepped forward and said, 'Yes, Your Highness?'

'Help her into bed,' she said, before turning to Mili. 'Goodnight, my child. Sleep well. We'll speak in the morning.'

Mili looked at Bhoomi who now stood by the bed with her nightdress, ready to help her undress. She took the nightdress from her and said, 'Thank you, I can manage.' She smiled slightly at the look of shock on Bhoomi's face. She had never thanked a servant before.

'You can go now. I can manage,' Mili repeated.

'As you wish, Princess; goodnight, Princess,' Bhoomi mumbled, and backed out of the room.

The next morning Mili was ravenous as she sat at the dining table. She thought of the babble that greeted her every morning in the refectory at STH. Even before entering the building, you could hear the din emanating from that huge hall. It was so wonderful to be able to dine in peace, with a golden sun throwing a quiet light on the cutlery and making it glitter. She sniffed appreciatively as the smell of pureed tomatoes and chopped onions roasting with cumin seeds wafted into the room and her stomach growled in anticipation. She had still not got used to the gunk dished out in the hostel.

Ma came in, followed by the servants bringing in the breakfast. 'Your favourite – aloo bhaji and poori,' she said as the waiter served her.

Mili took a sip of the sweet mango shake and poked a finger through her poori as was her habit. She took a spoonful of the rich badam ka halwa, made with almonds, ghee and sugar. She gobbled a couple of pooris and wanted more, but suddenly felt shy. It was silly but she felt embarrassed asking for more. She hadn't realised, but as the days away from the palace had turned into weeks and then into months, she had grown more and more distant from home, so much so that a strange formality had now crept in . . .

Days passed slowly in Mohanagar without Vicky. Mili could not wait for the holidays to be over. It was good to be home, to be with her family, to sleep on her own Dunlopillo mattress and yet . . . she longed to get back to Kishangarh. Maybe it was the freedom that she had grown accustomed to. Or the privacy of not having servants following her every move. She was glad to have Bhoomi at her beck and call again but her overenthusiasm to do everything for her irritated her now.

But what rankled the most was how everyone was cautious not to mention Vicky's name. Like the Harijan slums on the edge of the city that everyone avoided. Hey Kishan, please let someone say something about Vicky so that she could pour out her heart to that person. But sadly, that did not happen.

Ma wanted her to meet some of her old school friends, but she declined. All her friends had always been conscious of the fact that she was a princess. Hence, however friendly they were, however rowdy the game was, there was always that slight deference that they treated her with. It was only Vicky who never cared for such proprieties and had treated her as an equal. And Mili loved her for that.

'You don't need to go back, you know,' Bauji said for the nth time, as the holidays drew to a close. 'You can continue your studies at Mohanagar. You can go back to your old school or we can get you a tutor at home.'

But Kishangarh beckoned her. She had to go back. Even the basket of her favourite sitaphal, which had arrived from their orchards that morning, could not tempt her enough to stay back.

'You have been very quiet ever since you came home,' Ma said, as she lovingly tucked a stray hair behind her ear. 'Is the hostel all right?'

'Yes, Ma,' Mili replied. She found herself speaking in monosyllables more and more often these days.

'A distant cousin of mine lives in Kishangarh,' said Ma. 'She's a widow and lives by herself. You can stay with her if you wish.'

'I'll think about it,' Mili replied, turning her attention to Bhoomi who was packing her trunk. 'No, take out those two saris. I won't need so many of them in Kishangarh.'

'As you wish, Princess. I will miss you, Princess.'

Mili did not say anything. She realised she was not as

emotional now as she used to be. Something within her seemed to have hardened and she could not wait to get away from everyone.

February. 1942. Mili stood on the balcony of her hostel room. The holidays were over. School had reopened early. She couldn't believe she had been at STH for almost an entire year. Even Bauji had not expected her to last in Kishangarh for more than three months. She watched the other students coming to the hostel with their bags and trunks. They all seemed happy to be back. Mili envied them their happiness. She stood on the balcony for a long time, alone, filled with memories and nostalgia. She remembered the first time she had come to STH with Vicky. And how Angel had called their room 'freaky' because of the ceiling fan. Little did she know then that the 'freaky' would soon assume gruesome proportions.

The weather didn't help lift her spirits. The sky was overcast. Scudding, low, dark clouds spread a melancholy hue over the landscape. They were a dirty grey, the clouds. And the more she looked at them, the more they felt like a leaden blanket, smothering her. The birds were winging their way back home, back to their nests, back to their soulmates and their little ones, cawing and screeching. Mili gazed up at the menacing clouds. It was going to pour.

She shivered involuntarily and hugged herself. She felt alone and desolate and oh so cold. Just a year back she and Vicky had arrived at the same hostel, full of exciting dreams and a sense of adventure. So much had changed since then. Life had certainly not turned out the way she had imagined. She had such rosy dreams then and now she had nothing to look forward to.

Just then a single ray of the sinking sun broke through a cloud, illuminating it. The spectacle was magnificent. Mili looked at it mesmerised and felt her spirits rise. Maybe Lord Kishan was trying to tell her that all was not lost. As she watched the cloud, it dawned on her that the only way to get over her grief was to leave the hostel. She would go and stay with Mausi, just as Ma had suggested.

Mili made her way to Mausi's house after class. It was snowing. Thick and fast. Soon everything looked white and blank – like her heart. Blank, empty and drained of emotion. And the deathly stillness. As though she was the only person inhabiting Kishangarh.

The sound of a horn made her jump. It was Raven.

'Where are you off to?' he asked.

'To my Mausi's. That's where I live now.'

'Come, I'll drop you,' he said, opening the passenger door.

Mili hesitated.

'I know it's not a grand car like your Rolls-Royce,' he said, 'just a humble Morris, but . . .'

Mili smiled as she slid into the car. 'She's beautiful. I love the expression on her face . . . and the lazy smile.'

Raven chuckled. 'You make her sound like a very attractive woman.'

Mili grinned. She had felt numb with the cold out there and was glad of the warmth the car now afforded.

She looked sideways at Raven. He looked handsome in his long coat. He was driving very carefully and slowly. She suddenly realised they were going off the beaten track. Her lips went dry and she exclaimed, 'This is not the way to M—'

'The other way is far too dangerous in this weather,' Raven replied, concentrating on the road ahead.

Just then the car spluttered and came to a halt. Raven cursed under his breath and turned the key. The car spluttered again, lurched forward, then stopped. Raven got out of the car and lifted the bonnet.

Mili looked around uncomfortably. The place was deserted and it was beginning to get dark. No one could be seen for miles around. And there wasn't even a house nearby, not even a street lamp. Her heart began to race. So Raven Sir had purposely chosen this deserted route? It was all a ploy. No. It couldn't be. Not Raven Sir. He would never stoop so low. But then, weren't all men the same? she thought bitterly. Especially Englishmen. They were animals. All of them, with just one thing on their mind. Oh, Lord Kishan, what was she to do? What could she do? *Stay calm, Mili, stay calm.* Relax. *Breathe in. Okay, that's better.*

She put her hand on the door handle. Raven was still behind the bonnet, pretending to sort out the car. She pressed the handle. Yes, she'd run for it. Sprint across the road as fast as she could. *Run, Mili, run. Now's your chance, when he's not in the car. Just run.*

No, she couldn't get out of the car and run. Not in this snow. He would soon catch up with her.

Raven closed the bonnet and slipped back into his

seat. He turned to Mili. 'It's not a big problem. We've run out of petrol. We just have to wait till somebody comes along and helps us.'

Mili squirmed. Soon it would be pitch dark. And then she'd be alone in the dark with this Angrez. *Quick, think fast, Mili, think. What are you going to do?* Oh good, somebody was coming that way. She darted a look at Raven. He was looking the other way. This was her chance. She would run across to that man coming towards them. But what if he did not help her?

Drat. The man was drunk. He could not possibly be of any help. Some more minutes passed. Then finally, hope, in the shape of a car. Mili almost leapt out of Raven's car with relief. It was Jatin, with his uncle. She had never been so glad to see him before.

'Any problem, sir?' Jatin asked, leaning out of his window.

'We've run out of petrol,' Raven replied.

Jatin and his uncle got out of their car. Between them, they were able to find a tube and an empty jar and transfer petrol from one car to the other.

Soon they were on their way. Much to Mili's annoyance, Raven chatted amiably all the way to Mausi's house.

'It's so late,' he said. 'Your aunt must be getting worried. Imagine, forgetting to fill up my tank! I'm becoming more and more of an absent-minded professor. One day I might even forget to eat. Come to think of it, I did forget to have lunch this afternoon . . .'

Mili did not say anything but kept looking straight ahead. The car swerved around the corner and stopped in front of the little gate leading to Mausi's cottage.

'You've been awfully quiet today,' Raven observed as he turned his gaze on her.

Mili was covered in a cold sweat and shivered involuntarily.

Raven frowned. Then exclaimed, 'No, Malvika, no! You didn't think I contrived that, did you? Oh, what do you think I am? I'm your teacher and your dean, for Christ's sake. You're my responsibility. How could—' He broke off.

'George was Vicky's local guardian. She was also his responsibility,' Mili replied quietly. She continued to sit in the car, motionless, as Raven covered his eyes with a hand, then smacked the steering wheel. He again turned to look at her.

Touching her shoulder gently, he whispered, 'Look at me, Mili. Not all Englishmen are beasts, not all men . . .'

Nodding slightly, Mili bolted out of the car. She ran up the driveway and rang the doorbell.

Chapter Seventeen

Raven was in the school library, which was on the second floor. It was his favourite haunt after school hours, when it was practically empty. Just he and the books, spending an evening together, accompanied by the wondrous musty smell of manuscripts mingling with the aroma of hot coffee.

Books had been his best friends for a long time now. It was books that had enabled him to turn a deaf ear to his parents' quarrelling, that had given him solace when Father left them. And it was books that had entertained him when he'd been bedridden after the accident.

After a while Raven got up to get a breath of fresh air. As he stepped out into the corridor, he saw a girl stop at the school gate. Was it? He scrunched his eyes. Yes, it was Mili. He recalled the incident that had taken place a week back, when he had offered to give her a lift. He had been hurt that she had put him in the same category as

George. Of course, it was silly of him. After all, the poor girl had been traumatised by her friend's suicide. It was only natural for her to feel that way towards all men. He shouldn't take it personally and feel hurt. But he did. For some strange reason, it hurt him immensely.

He looked towards the gate again. Mili was turning back now and walking towards the building. Raven went down the stairs. She had seen him and was walking towards him timidly.

'Anything the matter?' Raven asked. 'I thought you were going home?'

'Yes, sir, I . . . ,' Mili licked her lips and started chewing her thumbnail.

'You look pale,' said Raven. 'Come into my office.'

Mili nodded and meekly followed him.

'Sit down,' he said, as he switched on the lights. Mili sank into a chair. He noticed she was trembling. He handed her a glass of water. 'Here, have a drink,' he said.

'Thank you, sir,' said Mili as she took a sip.

Raven gathered all the papers scattered on his desk and put them into a neat pile. Then he collected all the stationery and put it away in a drawer, while he waited for Mili to get a grip on herself.

He glanced at her. He had been shocked when he had seen her for the first time. Miss Perkins had told him she was a princess. But most days, with her hair worse than Medusa's, she had looked anything but that. Today, however, she had brushed her hair, which reached well below her waist, until it shone. Her face gleamed like that of a little boy's, scrubbed by his mother after playing in the mud, until he screamed. She had baby-like soft skin.

Why, she even smelt like a baby. Must be the soap or the powder she used. Her sallow complexion had turned an angry red right in the middle of her left cheek, where a solitary pimple was pushing its way through. She was pretty, he had to admit, and did look like a princess today. Albeit a frightened one.

'Now, would you like to tell me what's bothering you?' he asked.

'Sir, it's nothing important.'

'Anything that makes a student of mine look like she's just seen a ghost is important.'

'Sir . . .' Mili traced a line with the drops of water that were condensing on her glass. 'Sir, yesterday, when I was walking home from school, an English boy appeared out of nowhere. He said, "Hey, darkie, don't you know only the English can walk down this road?" I ignored him and continued walking.' Mili paused and began plucking at the bobbles on her cardigan. Then he grabbed my scarf. When I tried to snatch it away from him, he jeered and blocked my path. I tried to dodge him . . .' Mili faltered, took a sip of water, then with a bowed head continued speaking. 'And then he pinched me.'

'The swine,' spat Raven. 'Then . . . ?' he whispered, encouraging Mili to continue.

'Then I swung my bag with all my strength and hit him. And would you believe it, sir, that fellow turned on his heels and ran away.'

Raven threw back his head and laughed. Then he looked at Mili affectionately. She was looking at him with a mixture of bewilderment and annoyance. 'My little lamb turns out to be a wolf in lamb's clothing,' he said with a chuckle. Then added seriously, 'I'm proud of you. You know something? Underneath all that frailty of yours, there's a backbone made of tungsten!'

'Sir?'

'Well, you fought that lad and frightened him away, didn't you? Besides, I've seen . . . how you gathered yourself together after the . . .' Raven paused, stumbling for the right words. 'I know you and Vicky were inseparable, it was no ordinary tragedy that you went through. But I never saw you wallowing in self-pity. Rather, you have picked up the pieces of your life all by yourself. You're a brave girl, little one.'

'But sir, I *am* frightened. Very much so. I'm afraid to go alone. Can you . . . umm . . . give me a lift?'

Raven was taken aback by her request. 'Are you sure? I think your piano teacher, Mrs Kapoor, is still in the library. Let me ask her if she can drop you.' He turned on his heels and was about to walk towards the stairs leading to the library, when Mili put a hand on his arm.

He raised a brow questioningly. She lowered her gaze and said, 'There's no need for that, sir. I trust you.'

This time it was Raven's turn to look shocked.

'I'm ashamed of my behaviour the other day,' said Mili, continuing to look down.

'Think nothing of it, little one,' Raven replied softly as he strode towards his car.

'I trust you,' she had said. He felt like jumping over the gate and dancing a little jig right there – in the middle of the street. Or shouting from the roofs of STH: 'SHE TRUSTS ME. MALVIKA TRUSTS ME.' He switched on the engine of the car and stole a look at Mili, seated beside him. Thank goodness she could not read his thoughts. After all, they were just three simple words – and yet they had filled him with a profound happiness that he found hard to explain.

Gurpreet sat outside the college gates, smoking his cigarette. He watched the smoke curling out of the chimney of the caretaker's cottage. It reminded him of the smoke that came out of the funnels of train engines.

Trains used to fascinate him as a child. He remembered the first time he had travelled by one. It was alone with Maji. They were going to Amritsar to see his grandparents. That was the last time he would see them. They were late and had to rush to the platform. And Maji in her nervousness had boarded the first-class compartment, which was only for the English. She realised her mistake only after the guard had blown his whistle and the train had started moving.

Gurpreet had eagerly taken a window seat and looked around importantly. He had often looked at trains with longing and wondered what it must feel like to travel in one. And here he was. It felt grand, he had to admit. He felt delirious as the houses, trees, fields, shops, people on foot hurrying along, people on horseback, carriages, cars whizzed by. It was like watching a movie at the talkies or jogging really fast in a pair of running shoes.

He noticed nobody was taking the seat next to him. Now and then someone would glance at the empty seat, then at him, then hastily walk away. They looked at him as though he had just crawled out of a septic tank. He didn't mind. He was too young and having too much fun to be bothered by such things. This was the first time he was travelling by train and he was not going to let these firangis spoil it for him.

He did look out of place, though. With his brown skin, his unsmart clothes, greasy hair and muddy feet. He noticed the English mem sitting across the aisle screwing up her nose at him and Maji and smiling disdainfully.

Gurpreet took another puff of his cigarette. Yes, back then these racial discriminations didn't bother him. But now they did. And very much so. It filled him with such a loathing for the English and an anger that he sometimes found hard to control.

The train ride was all that he remembered of his last trip to Amritsar. Maji used to tell him how she would take him to the Golden Temple and how much he loved the langar food there. How he danced around the fire on Lohri with his grandmother. But they didn't go there again. Because three months later, in the April of 1919, his grandparents were shot down like animals along with hundreds of others, in Jalianwala Bagh. He did not understand what it meant when he was told that his grandparents were no more. He just remembered his mother crying. A lot. For days. And it frightened him to hear her wails.

He got up as he saw Jatin approach him with a mountain of books. Throwing down the cigarette stub and squashing it with his shoe, he took some of the books from his friend, then asked, 'Done? Shall we go home?'

Jatin nodded and the two of them made their way down the hill to Gurpreet's house. He kicked the door to his room open and dropped the books on his bed. Then he hung his waistcoat on the peg. He looked at Jatin. He had pulled out the chair in front of his desk. Sitting down, he was now fiddling with the wick of the oil lamp.

'Preeto, have you heard? There is talk about Gandhi planning another march across the country like the Dandi March in 1930,' said Jatin.

'I'm telling you, the Congress needs to change its leaders. Gandhi and Nehru will never get us freedom,' said Gurpreet, sitting down on the bed and taking off his shoes.

'Why do you keep saying that all the time?' said Jatin, lighting the lamp.

'Because he said the same thing in 1920. Did we become free? Been twenty long years since he said that. Besides, it was because of Bhagat Singh that the bloody Congress started demanding total swaraj. And Nehru and Gandhi got the credit for it.'

'So Gandhi hasn't been successful yet. But tell me, have violent means met with any success? You know what happened to Bhagat Singh, Sukhdev and Rajguru? All three of them were hanged. And have you forgotten what happened in 1857? The way the Uprising was crushed? The carnage, the killing, the destruction – all in the name of retribution.'

'1857 was different.'

'How was it different? They were also fighting for freedom. Besides, violence leads to so many innocents getting killed.'

'And non-violence leads to hundreds of innocents being beaten up and put behind bars.'

'Look, we can never match them in the field of battle. They're much too strong. Ahimsa is the only way we can defeat them. You've got to believe – there's a different kind of strength in non-violence.'

'I don't think I believe in anything now, not after Vicky's death.' Gurpreet walked over to the window and curled his fists tightly around its bars.

'Preeto,' whispered Jatin, putting a hand on his shoulder.

'Let it be, yaara, you'll never understand because you've never been in love.'

'That's where you're wrong. I'm not only in love, I have even proposed to her.'

As soon as he had said that, Gurpreet punched Jatin so hard, he toppled over and fell.

Just then Maji knocked on the door and entered. 'You're home, Preeto?' she asked with a smile. Then she noticed Jatin on the floor. 'Haiyo Rabba, what happened?'

'Nothing, Maji,' Jatin mumbled. 'I just fell off the chair.'

'Oh, do be careful,' Maji said, as she put two glasses of lassi on the table and left.

'What's wrong? Why did you hit me?' Jatin asked.

Gurpreet punched him again.

'Stop it. I believe in Ahimsa, otherwise I can also hit back.'

'When were you planning to tell me? After your secondborn started going to school?' said Gurpreet.

'Stop being so dramatic. I was going to tell you.'

'Who is she?'

'Vidushi.'

'That girl in the orphanage at Jeolikot?'

Jatin nodded.

'That explains . . . all those visits to your mysterious "relatives" in Jeolikot.'

Jatin grinned, caressing his cheek where Gurpreet had hit him.

Gurpreet walked over to the table, picked up the glass of lassi and emptied the tumbler in one gulp. Then he wiped his mouth with the back of his hand. He loved Maji's lassi. So cool and invigorating. He used to call it 'liquid yogurt' when he was little.

He turned back to Jatin. 'But have you gone insane? You want to marry a widow?'

'You talk of winning India's freedom?' Jatin's voice rose. 'First free yourself from these age-old prejudices, Preeto. Then talk about freedom.' He strode angrily to the window. Gurpreet walked up to him and handed him his glass of lassi. Jatin snatched it from his hand and took a sip. He spoke again. 'And for that matter, that Vicky, she wasn't a Hindu either. You were planning to marry her, weren't you?'

'What's the point of talking about her when she's no more?' said Gurpreet, averting his gaze. He busied himself in putting away the books he had carelessly thrown on the bed, onto the bookshelf. For some reason, the mere mention of Vicky's name made his eyes burn and throat go dry.

'I'm sorry. It's just that it upset me . . . the way you lashed out. I'd thought you'd be happy for me when I broke the news. Now I wish I hadn't told you.'

'Hey, hey, hey, this wishing business can be very dangerous. I mean, Jatin . . . just imagine that this girl you love . . . umm – what's her name?'

'Vidushi,' replied Jatin, glaring at him.

'Relax. It's a difficult name, I'll memorise it eventually. As I was saying, let's suppose Vidushi is . . .' He winked at Jatin.

Jatin kicked him hard.

'Ouch! Yaara, we're just supposing. So where was I? Yes, supposing she's sitting in her classroom and wishes you were there with her and her wish is granted. And precisely at that moment you're taking a bath and you're transported to her classroom. Wahe guru, can you imagine the scene?' he chuckled.

Jatin slapped his forehead, then burst out laughing.

Gurpreet put his arms around his friend. 'So when are you taking me to meet her?'

'Soon,' Jatin replied with a shy smile.

Mili yawned. When was the history class going to end? She was trying her hardest to listen to Dr Anne Miller's lecture. But she was droning on and on and on: '. . . As I was saying, this book here – *Down the Ages* – is your bible, especially if you want to pass your Senior Cambridge history exam with distinction. You've got to read it, chew it, digest it, then read it all over again until you know it back to front and can even see it in your dreams.'

Mili groaned. That was all she needed. Dream about books. Whatever next? She was pleased when the bell rang and class was over. As she left the classroom, Bahadur came running up to her.

'Raven saabji calling you to his office, Mili baba.'

As she knocked on the door, Mili wondered what she had done wrong now.

'Good afternoon, sir,' she said.

'Afternoon,' Raven replied and nodded to her to take a seat.

She sat down carefully and looked around.

'I've been thinking about what you told me the other day. About that English lad who was harassing you. Now, don't get me wrong, but I won't always be there to drop you home. So how do we solve this problem?'

'I don't know, sir,' Mili replied, shrugging her shoulders. 'Maybe I should leave early for home, before it gets dark?'

Raven shook his head. 'No, that's not a solution. During the last semester you might have some extra classes that may run late . . .'

'Sir, please don't ask me to come back to the hostel,' Mili begged, chewing her thumbnail.

'No, of course not . . . Although hitting that lad was the right thing to do.'

Mili shifted uncomfortably.

'And I'm proud of you, that you didn't get intimidated by him,' Raven continued.

Mili looked down at her hands and didn't say anything.

'Why don't you arrange for a palanquin to take you home everyday? Or perhaps a pony? I've heard the syce in Kishangarh are simple and loyal and they'll take good care of you.'

'Oh no, sir, not a pony, never.'

Raven raised a brow. 'Why? What happened?'

'Sir, the only time I rode one was on Vicky's insistence in Mohanagar. I sat on the horse, straight and tense, too scared of falling off. That night, when I lay in bed, my entire body was stiff and aching all over. It was then that I swore never to go riding again. Even the horse had not taken to me for some reason. It galloped off at top speed, as soon as I got off, with the horseman running and swearing after it.'

Raven laughed aloud. Mili smiled. She marvelled at how his eyes changed colour with his emotions. When he used to scold her and Vicky, they used to flash angrily and turn dark; they looked almost black then. But right now, as he laughed, they looked light brown. He had the softest, warmest eyes she had ever seen.

'Your horse must have seen a terror called Vicky approaching,' he was now saying.

She smiled sadly and said, 'No, sir; Vicky was brilliant with horses. And they in turn used to love her.' She again looked down at her hands and whispered, 'It was Vicky's dream to rid me of my fears and make me adept at horse riding one day.'

Leaning forward, Raven put his forefinger under her chin.

He had long, tapering fingers, Mili noticed. Slowly, she lifted up her eyes to his.

'Let go of old dreams, Malvika,' he said softly, 'and new ones will follow.'

Mili nodded, a lump in her throat and tears pricking her eyes.

'And I'll teach you to ride . . . but no . . .' he said as he remembered something.

Mili looked at him, puzzled.

'Not any more. I can't ride a horse any more, not after the accident.'

'What exactly happened, sir?'

'It happened a few months back, during one of the demonstrations against the English. Although it was a peaceful protest at the start, some of the revolutionaries got carried away and began pelting the English with hand grenades.' Raven stopped speaking, pulled out a handkerchief from his trouser pocket and wiped his brow.

'Someone threw a bomb at a building right next to where I sat on horseback. Prancer, my horse, panicked and reared up. I was thrown off his back. My knee hit a sharp rock as I fell. Prancer began to gallop. My left foot was still in the stirrups and I was dragged along for half a mile. My knee got totally smashed. When I came around, my foot was touching my knee as the bones and cartilages had got crushed. It's a miracle I can walk still . . .'

'It must have been so painful . . .' Mili said.

'Ah, yes.' He frowned. 'But why am I telling you all this? Go now,' he said with a wave of his hand. 'And remember to get a palanquin from tomorrow.'

'Yes, sir. I will.'

'Good, now off with you,' he said, and without waiting to see if she had left the room or not, he opened a file and began leafing through its contents.

Shaking her head Mili quietly left the room.

* * *

213

That night, Mili lay in bed, a book in one hand and absent-mindedly plucking the bobbles on the blanket with the other. She smiled to herself as she saw a face: Raven – his hazel eyes, his smile. She saw him throw back his head and laugh. He looked so handsome whenever he laughed – so young, boyish even. And he was laughing at her. He wasn't scolding her, he was laughing. And then she heard him say, in a voice so tender . . . 'Let go of your old dreams, Malvika, let go of your old dreams . . . and new ones will follow.' Mili smiled again. She hugged her pillow, rolled over and tried to sleep.

Chapter Eighteen

A couple of days later, Mili and Mausi were walking down the cobbled streets of the inner Mall. They passed Vikram Bhandar, the local grocery store; then the tiny candle shop which sold candles of every shape and form. Candles in the shape of Christmas trees; candles shaped as ducks – yellow ducks, black ducks, red ducks, ducks with golden beaks and wings. She had bought a candle shaped like a beautiful Kathak dancer once. Vicky had lit it after the warden had turned off the lights, when she had managed to smuggle a copy of *Lady Chatterley's Lover* to the hostel. They had giggled through the night, until the entire candle had burnt away. What a mess that candle had left behind and what a lot of trouble they were in the next day.

They had reached Mehta School Uniforms. Stepping inside the shop, Mausi and Mili sat down on the chairs provided, while the shopkeeper attended to another customer. Mili tapped the counter top with her fingers and looked around. She wrapped her coat tightly about her. It was extremely cold today and a fierce wind was blowing.

Hearing footsteps, Mili turned around, and who should be coming up the steps leading to the shop? George. He looked stouter and more slothful than the last time she had seen him. Her first impulse was to hide. But it was too late. He had seen her.

'Now, isn't that our dear Malvika?' he piped.

Mili squirmed inwardly and looked at him with disgust. He had never addressed her so lovingly before. What was he playing at now, the bastard?

'You seem to have forgotten the way to our house,' he was saying. 'Come over sometime. Ethel will be pleased to see you. She misses the two of you.'

The gall of that man. Mili glared at him, speechless. 'You murderer!' she shrieked. 'Have you no shame? Speaking to me as though nothing has happened?'

Uncle George looked around surreptitiously, nodded politely at Mausi who looked totally baffled, then said, 'Now now, child, calm down. I have no idea what nonsense you're talking about.'

Oh, how she hated that man. Clenching her hands into fists, Mili opened her mouth and spat on his face.

'Mili!' exclaimed Mausi, shocked.

Uncle George wiped his face with the ends of his muffler. 'You forget who I am. You shall pay for this. Uncivilised heathens!' he said, before turning on his heel and walking away.

On the way back to Mausi's house, sitting huddled

in a palanquin, Mili felt her anger rise again as she remembered her encounter with George. The injustice of it all. Her innocent friend had paid with her life for a crime that he had committed, while he himself roamed free, totally unaffected by what had happened. The more Mili thought about it, the angrier she became.

She did not sleep at all that night. By the time dawn was breaking, her mind was made up. Once she had completed her studies, she would do something to help other girls like Vicky and make sure people like George got what they deserved. She did not know how she was going to do it, but do it she would. 'I'll do it, Vicky,' she whispered hoarsely to Vicky's photograph, kept on her bedside table. Yes, she would make things happen. She'd show everyone how the British Raj was hollow and rotting from the inside. She'd make everyone sit up and listen. She would challenge the court. She would change the world in which innocents suffer and the criminals go scot-free. She would not let another Vicky commit suicide. You wait and see, George, you wait and see.

Mili was still fuming over her encounter with George the previous day when Raven called her into his office during the lunch break. There was a small bouquet of flowers on his desk.

'What type of flowers are these, sir?'

'Blue poppies.'

'They're beautiful. I've never seen them before.'

'That's because they only grow up here in the mountains where it's cooler. Vidushi sent them. She has been helping the nuns in the gardens. She is such an asset . . .'

Mili felt a twinge of jealousy. Always praising Vidushi. As though she was an angel or something. If he liked her so much, why didn't he marry her?

'You are aware that Jatin and Vidushi are getting married?' Raven asked.

'No,' replied Mili with a start. It was as though he had read her mind. 'Jatin never mentioned it.' She smiled. For some strange reason, she felt relieved that Vidushi was marrying Jatin and not Raven.

'The date has been set for May, I'm told. I'm not sure whether you are aware – Vidushi's family has disowned her ever since she left the ashram and started living at the orphanage. And the only other people she knows are the nuns and the little children who live there. So is it possible for you to be with her that day, help her get dressed and just be there for her?'

'I guess I could do that,' replied Mili with a shrug.

'I had thought you'd be ecstatic. Anything the matter?'

'No, sir, I'm fine.'

'I'm waiting.'

'I bumped into George yesterday.'

'I see. Forget him, Mili. Petty p—.'

'Yes, you'd think like that. After all, you too are English. It's a petty matter for you. Your life has always been so easy and rosy for you, Raven, sir.'

Raven stared at her open-mouthed. He got up slowly and strode towards her. Mili bit her lip, then chewed her thumbnail. Now why did she say that? Why was she turning the anger she felt towards George on Raven

Sir? But it was too late. The words had been uttered. She could not take them back.

'How dare you,' he said catching hold of her by her shoulders and shaking her. 'You have no right to speak to me in that fashion, especially when you don't know anything about me.' He let go of her and putting his hand on his forehead turned towards the window. 'Besides, I did not say it was a petty matter. I was going to say that petty people like him are best ignored.' He turned around to face her again. 'And what d'you mean by "rosy"? Do you know what it's like for someone to be taunted and call—' He stopped speaking abruptly.

'To be called the son of a murderer?'

Raven stared at her for a long moment.

Mili spoke softly. 'Sir, tell me what happened.'

'I think you already know.'

'I want to hear it from you.'

'You want to hear an Englishman's words as opposed to all that you've heard from the Indians?'

'Sir, I don't care what the others say. I believe you and that's all that matters to me.'

She lowered her eyes as she felt Raven's eyes on her.

He cleared his throat. 'We used to live in Amritsar then. I was six years old. I remember clearly because it happened just two days after my birthday. Kartar was my Ayah's son. She often brought him to our house. We played together while she worked. That morning she greeted me with a cheery "Happy Baisakhi, baba" and gave me a box of sweets. A little later that day, Mother wanted to go to the shops. She asked Ayah to come along as chaperone.'

Raven paused, loosened his tie and began rolling up his sleeves. 'On the way, as we passed the Jalianwalla Bagh, we heard some bullets being fired. I looked at Mother, not sure what those sounds meant. She looked shocked. The driver stopped the car and stared out of the window. Our car was at an elevated part of the road and we were able to look over the high walls of the bagh. There were a lot of people there, on account of Baisakhi. "Papa," I cried out as I noticed my father right in front – among the soldiers who had opened fire.'

Raven stopped speaking, picked up his glass of water and had a long drink. 'Mother covered my eyes. But it was too late. I had already seen what a six-year-old boy should never have to see. People running wildly, screaming, jumping into the well in a state of panic and the agonised shrieks as bullets pelted down on them. I can forget the dead bodies, the smell of blood, but the shrieks haunt me even today.' He paused and covered his ears with his hands. 'Parents, children, grandparents – all shot down within minutes.

'The next morning Ayah came to inform Mother that she wouldn't be working for us any more. Her husband had said to her that it was better to starve than work for murderers. I clung to her and wept. I was rather fond of her . . .' Raven's voice broke and he did not speak for a couple of minutes. 'Two days later I saw a huge bonfire in the park in front of our house. Ayah was there. She and her husband were throwing all the clothes that Mother had given her into the fire. And then I saw Kartar throw a toy I had gifted him into the flames.' Raven's Adam's apple moved. 'That broke my heart, it did. Lots of fires burnt in the city for days. The smell of burning flesh . . . Mother shut all the doors and windows, and yet that smell permeated the house.'

Raven wiped his forehead with the back of his hand. 'From that day on, wherever I went, whispers followed me – "son of a murderer".' He looked right into Mili's eyes. 'Was it my fault that my father obeyed an order and fired? I did not give that order . . .'

Mili did not know what to say and merely nodded.

'Mother is a very gentle woman and a stickler for what is right and wrong. She knew what the English had done that day in the Jalianwala Bagh was wrong. And the fact that one of the wrongdoers was her husband disturbed her immensely. She was not happy in her marriage anyway . . .

'He was fond of drinking, my father. And frequenting Lol biwi's kotha. But this incident was the last straw. That summer Mother and I came to Kishangarh like we did every year. But this time we never went back when the rains came. I never saw Father again.'

'I'm sorry, sir, I had no idea.'

Raven looked at his watch. 'Oh no, I hope I haven't kept you from your lunch. Run along, little one, before you get into trouble.'

'Yes, sir, I'll go and meet Vidushi on Sunday and work out all the details.'

'Thank you, Malvika,' he said in a voice that was barely audible, and smiled softly.

Mili smiled back and left the room. For the rest of the day, she kept thinking about Raven Sir's revelation about his childhood. What a terrible ordeal for a boy that age. What impression must those killings have made on his mind? And then to have to lose not only his friend and Ayah, but eventually his father as well. No wonder he was so reserved and often kept to himself.

She tried to remember what her life was like when she was six. At that age she must have romped around the palace all day, with a train of servants picking up after her and attending to her every tantrum. And she had accused him of having a rosy life. Mili winced. How her words must have hurt him. If only she could take them back. The way his voice had broken when he was speaking about his Ayah and Kartar, a lump had risen in her throat as well. He had looked so sad, so vulnerable.

Mili used to admire Raven as a teacher, but now she found herself in awe of the man himself.

It was Holi and school was closed for two days. It used to be a day of great excitement for her and Uday. Bhoomi would wake her early and massage oil all over her, including her hair. Donning a white salwar kameez she would wait impatiently for Vicky. And then they would spend the whole morning running after Uday and all her friends with water pistols, squirting each other with colour and gorging on gujjias. The afternoon would be spent scrubbing the colour off. And in the evening there'd be a sea of visitors – friends and relatives with whom they would exchange sweetmeats, hugs and the latest gossip.

But now, ever since Vicky's death, she preferred spending her holidays either alone or studying. It helped her cope and kept disturbing thoughts at bay. She had come to Raven's house to borrow a book. Through the open window of his study she could see groups of children and grown-ups going up and down the hill, singing phaags and shouting 'Holi hai'. They were covered in pink, red, green and yellow gulal. Pink seemed to be the dominant colour and their faces were smeared with that colour as well.

Unlike in Mohanagar, Holi in Kishangarh was dry. Perhaps it was owing to the cold winds that still blew in from the Himalayas and kept the temperatures very low.

'So what this basically means is . . .' she heard Raven explain and hastily looked back at the open book in front of her.

There was a knock on the door. The college domestic staff had come to play Holi. Raven nodded at them and stepped out onto the veranda.

Mili watched as some of the staff squatted on the ground on the veranda and commenced singing folk songs. A couple of men stood in a corner playing bagpipes. She was fascinated. She had never seen such a dignified and musical Holi before.

The rest of the group now encircled Raven and started dancing. The dance movements were quite intricate, involving a lot of whirls, jumps, twists and turns. Raven danced with them for some time, accompanied by loud cheering and clapping and laughing.

Mili smiled as she watched him from the door. She had never seen him dancing and letting down his hair before. She had always seen him serious and buried in books. But seeing him like this – dancing, swaying his hips, laughing and drinking some of the local brandy – was like looking at a different person altogether. He gestured to her to join in the dance. She shook her head. He came towards her and pulled her to the centre of the veranda.

'Come on,' he said. 'I know you can dance.'

Biting her thumbnail shyly, Mili joined in.

She blushed as he let out a wolf whistle and said, 'You dance well.'

The music and dancing stopped after a while. The college chef broke a large block of gur into smaller pieces, which was welcomed with a loud 'Whoopee!', and began distributing it to everyone.

Raven took a piece of the jaggery from him and popped it into Mili's mouth even before she could protest. 'Happy Holi, Malvika,' he said with a smile.

'Happy Holi, sir.' Mili gave a muffled reply as the sweet brown gur melted in her mouth.

The Holi revellers finally left after Raven had given them money to buy some more jaggery.

As the last one left, Raven turned to Mili. 'There goes all the money I'd saved to buy a dress for Mother's birthday.'

'You didn't have to give them *all* your money.'

'They need it more than I do.'

'What will you say to your mother?'

'She'll get what she gets every year.'

'And that is?'

Raven laughed. 'A big hug and a kiss. She knows my wallet is always empty.'

'You love her very much, don't you?'

'She's all I've got,' Raven said with a sigh. 'She's had a difficult life. First she was struggling to make her marriage work. Then she was struggling to meet our needs. But luckily, all these struggles have not made her cynical.'

Mili nodded.

'Now, let's get back to our books, shall we? As I was saying, this book has an excellent commentary on how Milton's bitterness on becoming blind and his gradual acceptance of his handicap are reflected in his writings . . .'

Picking up her pen, Mili started scribbling in her notebook. Raven reached out over the desk and touched the back of her hand with his finger. 'Understood? It's more important that you understand what I'm saying, rather than noting down everything I say.'

Mili stared at Raven's finger touching her hand. She felt as though it was a red-hot iron nail and was burning a hole through her hand. An alien tingling sensation ran down her spine. She looked at Raven, perplexed. Unable to understand this new feeling, she hurriedly muttered, 'Yes, sir, thank you, sir. I'm getting late, I've got to go.' She gathered her books hastily and rushed out of the house.

Later that night in her room, as she sat at her desk leafing through the notes, her thoughts flew to Raven. Raven Sir – frowning at her; Raven – smiling indulgently at her; Raven – dancing, laughing, drinking; Raven – touching her hand and awakening feelings in her that hitherto did not exist. Was she falling in love with him? Hey Lord Kishan, was this love?

A flapping sound distracted her and she looked at the

lamp. A moth was fluttering around it, getting closer and closer to the light bulb, as though hypnotised by its glow. Just like she felt drawn towards Raven against her will. And if she dared get closer or fall in love, she'd get singed, destroyed. Just like the moth that now lay still on her table – quite dead.

Chapter Nineteen

Mili looked at all the doors that opened onto the main corridor of Kishangarh Club and frowned. Now, how would she know which one was the billiards room? 'Card Room', the first door read. She walked on to the next door. 'Billiards Room' it said on the door. She listened. She could hear the sound of cue sticks hitting the balls. She heaved a sigh of relief and walked in. There he was – Raven Sir. Bent over the billiards table, concentration furrowing his brow, about to hit a ball with his cue stick.

'Madam,' called out the doorkeeper as she entered the billiards room. Mili turned around to look at him. He was panting. Apparently, he had been running after her. 'I'm afraid I shall have to ask you to leave. This club is exclusively for the English. Indians are not allowed,' he said, pointing to a placard that stood near the door.

'It says Indians are not allowed. But nowhere does it say princesses are not allowed,' Mili coolly replied.

The doorkeeper gaped at her in confusion. Mili brushed past him and looked at Raven. He had straightened up and was looking at her in surprise. Mili realised everyone in the room had stopped playing and was now staring at her.

She watched Raven nod at the others and say, 'She's with me.' He then excused himself from the game, caught hold of Mili's elbow and led her out of the room.

'What's the matter?' he asked as they stepped onto the corridor and the door closed behind them.

'Sir, the warden asked me to meet you, on my way home. Owing to some personal problem, she had to suddenly rush off to Shaampur.'

'Oh no. Thank you for letting me know. I shall go to the hostel right away and make sure all the inmates are fine.'

'Yes, sir, and sorry for barging in on your game like this.'

He looked at her with a crooked smile and a raised brow. 'I noticed someone is becoming cheeky.'

'Sir?' Mili said, puzzled, a frown creasing her forehead.

'I heard what you said to the doorkeeper. But I'm glad you're standing up for yourself these days.'

'I didn't have to, earlier. Vicky used to do it for me . . .' She looked down and chewed her thumbnail. 'It's hard to explain, but when you lose something that means the world to you, it makes you . . . unafraid . . . kind of. Because now you have nothing to lose.'

She looked towards the main door. She knew Raven was regarding her quietly. He raised his right hand. She thought he was going to caress her cheek, but he let it fall limply by his side.

'How did you get here?' he asked.

'My palanquin, sir,' replied Mili.

'Tell them to go. I'll drop you.'

They had reached the gate of the club and Mili sprinted ahead to tell the doli-bearers to call it a night. Then she walked towards Raven's car. Raven was already inside. The driver, Murli, held the back door open for her. After she was comfortably seated, he closed her door and slid behind the steering wheel. But he did not start the engine. Instead, he thrust a box of nukti laddoos in front of her and Raven and the aroma of cardamom filled the car.

'Sahib, my wife gave birth to a boy yesterday,' he gushed.

'Congratulations, Murli,' Raven said, picking up a laddoo and biting into it. 'Mmm . . . very sweet. It looks hard, but when you bite into it, it's actually quite soft.' He turned to Mili. 'Try one, it's delicious,' he said.

Mili swallowed. Then hesitantly picked one.

'Come on, eat it,' said Raven as he took another bite.

'I can't,' she replied in a voice barely audible. 'He belongs to a lower caste.'

'What?' Raven exclaimed.

Mili didn't say anything and tried to bite the laddoo but couldn't. One did not even shake hands with a low caste, let alone eat something given by them.

'I'm disappointed with you, Malvika,' Raven was saying, shaking his head. 'A few minutes back you yourself were the victim of the discrimination between the English and the Indians. And now you're behaving in the same way. What do you call this?'

Mili hung her head. She brought the laddoo to her lips but found herself unable to bite into it. It was as though some invisible chains shackled her, and try as hard as she might, she was unable to break them. Just as she had been unable to enter Lord Kishan's temple all those months ago. Perhaps it was because ever since she was little she had been told that the lower castes were dirty, untouchable, pariahs. Anything touched by them should not be eaten as it was defiled. She knew it was wrong to think in that manner and yet . . .

She sat in silence for the rest of the journey and quietly slid out of the car when they reached Mausi's house. Rushing into her room, she flung herself across the bed and cried into her pillow. She didn't know why she was crying. All she knew was she felt really small. What must Raven Sir think of her? That she was shallow? Narrow-minded? She would never be able to look him in the eye again.

Mili sat outside Mausi's house, watching the little brook gurgling down the mountainside. During the monsoons it was thick and swollen and the waters made a deafening sound. But at the moment it looked like a thin silver line and the waters purred tamely.

Raising her face heavenward, Mili closed her eyes and breathed in the subtle fragrance of spring. She could smell the freshly cut grass, hear the birds chirping. Such a wonderful day it had been. That morning, Raven was taking their attendance as usual and had called out her name.

'Malvika Singh.'

'Present, sir,' she replied.

Raven looked up from the register and raised his brows in surprise. 'You have one hundred per cent attendance this term. I'm glad you're taking your studies seriously. That reminds me – I was browsing through your essay on Milton. It's brilliant. Well done.'

Mili smiled to herself as the words 'it was brilliant, it was brilliant' reverberated through her mind. Raven Sir had actually praised her work. She could scarce believe it. Especially after she had refused to eat the mithai the driver had offered – she'd been convinced Raven despised her. She hugged herself. She had not felt so elated in a long time.

A voice called her from behind – 'Mili.'

She turned around with a start. It was Gurpreet. He waved and walked up to her. 'You know Guruji? Our Congress leader in Kishangarh?'

'Yes, what about him?' Mili asked in a low voice, looking around to make sure Mausi hadn't seen him.

'I spoke to him this morning about you and told him you wanted to meet him. He has agreed to meet us after two days, but he's not free until five in the evening, when we have our meeting.'

'Oh, you mean, I will be able to attend one of your political meetings?'

'Yes. He said his doors are always open for my friends.'

'Why does everyone call him Guruji?'

'Because he's a teacher first, then a politician. He teaches Hindi and Sanskrit in our college. Didn't you know?'

'No, I didn't.'

'He's a very learned man. And not only is he intelligent but he's also a shrewd diplomat like Chanakya.'

'Don't tell me more or I'll be too scared to meet this haloed Guruji of yours.'

Gurpreet grinned. 'But don't mention him to anyone or that I'm taking you to meet him.'

Mili nodded. 'So what's going to happen at this meeting?'

'The party needs more funds, Mili. We're going to discuss how we can raise some money.'

'Wait here,' said Mili as she got up. 'Don't go anywhere.' She went inside the house and emerged ten minutes later with a box encased in red velvet.

'But this is your jewellery. And a lot of it.'

'Take it. I don't need it. Not any more,' she replied. She smiled as she remembered how some freedom fighters had been collecting money on Mohanagar railway station – when she and Vicky were about to board the train to Kishangarh – and how she had hidden her jewellery.

'Guruji will not believe this,' said Gurpreet, still amazed at Mili's generous donation. 'So is five o'clock in the evening all right with you?'

'Of course it is.'

'What about Mausi?'

'I'll make up some excuse about extra classes.'

'That's confirmed, then. After the meeting, we'll go and have supper and then I'll drop you back here.'

'Yes, that sounds fine. Now go before Mausi sees you.'

'It's settled, then. So we have a date in a couple of

days. Be ready. I'll pick you up at four-thirty sharp, from school.'

Date? Now where did that come from? He did say something about going for a meal after the meeting. But she hadn't thought of it as a date. What was she to do? She couldn't go on a date, she thought miserably, as she got up, dusted her clothes and went inside the house.

Raven looked at the doli and the palanquin-bearers waiting near the school gate and wondered who it was for. He walked into the library and was surprised to find Mili there. He had expected the library to be empty by now. 'What are you doing so late? Aren't you supposed to be home by now?' he asked.

'Quiet please,' the librarian said, looking at them sternly.

'Two minutes, Mrs Ferdinand,' Raven pleaded.

Mrs Ferdinand nodded slightly and looked the other way.

'Sir,' Mili whispered, 'I was just finishing some assignments . . .'

'I hope that doli is for you?'

'Yes it is. Sir, what is a date?'

Raven dropped the book he was holding. He looked at Mrs Ferdinand from the corner of his eye. She was watching him over the rim of her glasses, her lips a straight line. He mouthed the word 'sorry', then turned his attention back to Mili.

'I beg your pardon?'

'You know, a date, when a boy and girl go out together?'

'Well, you just answered your own question. That's exactly what a date is. A boy and a girl going out together, for maybe something as simple as a cup of coffee.'

'Just that?' She joined her hands and looked heavenward. 'Oh Lord Kishan, thank you. Thank you.'

'Why, what did you think?' Raven asked with an amused smile.

'Well . . .' Mili shifted uncomfortably and avoided his gaze. 'You know . . . what they show in the talkies . . .'

'What *do* they show in the talkies?'

'The boy goes to drop the girl home after the dinner, and then they kiss, you know, not on the cheek but right on the lips . . .'

Raven tried his best to keep a straight face and not smile. 'Yes, do go on.'

'Then she has to invite him to her house for coffee . . .'

Unable to control himself any longer, Raven burst out laughing. 'So who has asked you out on a date?' he said, still shaking with laughter.

'Gurpreet was taking me to meet someone and then we might have dinner together, but . . .'

'There's no need to worry, little one. You don't have to kiss him or invite him in for coffee if you don't want to.'

Mili looked at him indignantly. 'I'm not little any more. I'm going to be eighteen soon.'

'My, that's big,' said Raven with a broad grin. 'Go home now, before your aunt starts getting worried and sends out a search party.'

'Yes, sir; good day to you, sir.'

'Goodbye, little . . . I mean child-woman.' Then he winked at her and watched her turn red with embarrassment.

It was May. The month when Kishangarh's beauty was at its peak. Her voluptuous body was laden with all kinds of fruit – strawberries, kaafal, plums, peaches and apples – while her garish ghagra choli were resplendent with lilies, blue poppies, roses, anemones and dahlias.

Raven stopped to look at the placard that hung over the main door. 'Vidushi weds Jatin' it said. He entered the wedding hall with Gurpreet and a couple of other students. He spotted Jatin sitting on one of the special red chairs set aside especially for the bride and groom, at the top end of the hall, and walked towards him.

If he were to be frank, Jatin looked like a clown. His clothes – a silk kurta and pyjama – were fine. But the ridiculous pink turban and the jewellery and jasmine flowers hanging all over his face made him look silly.

But he was glad the nuptials were finally taking place. He'd heard that it had taken a lot of cajoling on Gurpreet's part to get Jatin's parents to agree to the wedding. For them, it was an indignity that their only son should be marrying a widow. More so since they were Brahmins, apparently the most revered caste amongst all the Hindus.

All eyes turned towards the entrance as Mili entered the hall slowly, holding Vidushi's arm and leading her towards Jatin.

'O balle balle, you've won the lottery, Jatin,' Gurpreet said. 'Bhabhi's looking like an apsara.'

Jatin turned red.

'Just look at him,' said Gurpreet. 'He's blushing even more than bhabhi.'

'Obviously,' said Jatin's mother. 'After all, this is his first wedding, unlike her.'

But Raven barely heard what was being said around him or noticed the bride; he was so taken in with Mili. Most of the time he saw her in her drab school uniform and here she was in a beautiful peacock-blue sari, all woman. The sari as well as the matching puff–sleeved blouse seemed to shimmer when she walked. A friend whispered something in her ear and she started giggling. Raven smiled. It was such a pleasure seeing her laugh again. She had tied back her hair, which gave her an elegant charm. And she moved so gracefully that she almost seemed ethereal. Raven was spellbound. He could not tear his eyes away from her. She saw him looking at her, blushed and looked away.

They did not get the chance to speak much that evening, but throughout the wedding his eyes sought hers. With great difficulty he tore his eyes away from her and looked at the bride and groom. They were about to exchange garlands.

'Jatin, lower your head, Vidushi can't reach,' Mili was saying.

'No, Jatin, no,' said Gurpreet. 'If you lower your head today, you will be bending to bhabhi's wishes for the rest of your life.'

Raven chuckled as Jatin paid no heed to his friend and bent his head to enable Vidushi to put the garland around his neck. He smiled again as Mili clapped her hands and stuck out her tongue at Gurpreet.

Dinner was soon served. Jatin's mother was still in a sulk. She stood in a corner, a permanent scowl on her face. Raven walked over to her and tried to persuade her to have some food.

Gurpreet handed him a plate and whispered, 'Let her be, sir. She's even more stubborn than that khotta Jatin. Don't worry, she'll eat slyly when no one's looking.'

Raven suppressed his smile and looked around. He could not see Mili anywhere and wondered if she had eaten.

Everyone was now moving towards the sacred fire, where the wedding rites were going to take place. And still no sign of Mili.

'Where are all the girls?' he asked Gurpreet.

'They've gone to help bhabhi change,' replied Gurpreet. 'The bride needs to wear a chundri sari given to her by her mama, for the pheras.'

'Pheras?'

'When the bride and groom go around the sacred fire.'

'I see. But I thought her family was not partaking of the wedding?' said Raven.

'They aren't. My father gave it to her,' replied Gurpreet.

The girls soon arrived, tittering. Mili helped Vidushi sit beside Jatin, before the fire. The priest started reciting the marriage vows. Raven looked at Mili and wondered what she would look like as a bride. What had that girl done to him today? What the hell was wrong with him? He couldn't get her out of his mind. It was as though she had cast a spell on him.

* * *

A few more steps up the steep incline and Raven had reached the summit of Hem Parvat. He turned around to address his students. 'I've brought you all here today because we're studying Wordsworth and, as you know, Wordsworth and nature are synonymous. This place is as beautiful if not better than the Lake District where he wrote much of his poetry. I want you to soak in the beauty of this place and then write an essay or a poem on it. We will meet at this very spot in an hour.'

'Yes, sir,' murmured the students and began to disperse in different directions.

'Malvika,' Raven called out.

Mili turned around and walked up to him. 'Yes, sir?'

'Have you had the chance to meet Vidushi after the wedding?' he asked, walking towards the adjoining chain of mountains. He slowed down as he realised Mili was finding it hard to keep up with him.

'No, sir, but I'm sure she's happy.'

'I hope so,' Raven replied. 'She's my responsibility, Malvika. I took her out of the ashram and antagonised her parents by doing so. And then I encouraged her to remarry and upset Jatin's parents in the pro—' He stopped speaking as he gazed at the spectacular sight before him. For there stood the snow-capped Himalayas – tall, majestic and aloof, like a monk with his long-flowing white beard, who after years of meditation had attained nirvana and now stood calm, cool, elevated.

Raven and Mili stood transfixed, for a long time. Neither of them spoke. It was one of those rare magical moments when time seems to stand still. And in that moment everyone else ceased to exist.

Feeling Mili's eyes on him, he looked at her. As he gazed into her soulful eyes, he felt as though he was drowning in them. He could not look away. He took her hand in his and squeezed it gently.

'Sir.'

The sound seemed to come from another land.

'Sir.'

The spell was broken. Raven tore his gaze from Mili and turned around to see who it was. Jatin was walking towards them. Raven hastily let go of Mili's hand and walked a couple of paces to put some distance between them.

'Isn't it breathtaking?' Jatin asked, pointing to the snow-capped mountains.

'Yes,' Mili whispered. 'Now I understand why they call the Himalayas the abode of the gods . . . They look so beautiful . . . like a string of pearls – pure, untouched . . .'

'A pearl necklace around Mother India's neck,' added Jatin.

Raven laughed. 'I think we'd better start trekking back,' he said and started walking towards Hem Parvat where all the other students were waiting for him.

Chapter Twenty

Gurpreet, Jatin and Mili walked together down the hill, making their way home from Hem Parvat. This part of the hillside was lush with pine trees. Even the air smelt of pine. The ground was covered with pine needles and pine cones.

Gurpreet saw Jatin pick up a closed cone and give it to Mili.

'Hold it over a fire,' he said. 'The cone will open up to reveal tiny pine nuts. You can remove the outer case and eat them.'

Mili looked at the cone with amazement. 'Really?' she said as she stroked the woody cone. 'I didn't know.'

'We should be ashamed of ourselves,' said Gurpreet, grimacing and hitting the bushes by the side of the road with the thin long cane that he was carrying. He looked at Mili and Jatin who were now looking at him in surprise.

Jatin scratched his head. 'Ashamed of ourselves? For picking up a pine cone?'

'Here the entire country is rising up in arms against the Raj,' said Gurpreet. 'And we are admiring nature, writing poetry. If father hadn't insisted, I wouldn't be wasting my time studying English.'

'No, Preeto,' said Jatin. 'To understand our enemy better, it is important to know their language. Only then can we defeat them at their own game.'

'Bravo, Jatin,' said Gurpreet, slapping Jatin across his shoulders. He ignored Jatin's scowl and carried on speaking. 'Always has an answer for everything.'

'Like Lord Kishan,' said Mili, giggling.

'Oye, Lord Kishan's devotee . . . I forgot to ask you because of Jatin's wedding - where were you that day? When we were supposed to meet Guruji?' asked Gurpreet. 'I waited outside your school gate for an hour. And got a scolding from Guruji for being so late.'

'I forgot,' Mili lied.

'You can come with us right now if you wish,' said Jatin.

'Actually, I think I'll stay away from all this. Politics is not really for me.'

'This is not politics,' said Gurpreet. 'This is fighting for our freedom, for our rights.'

'I haven't got Mausi's permission. She gets worried if I stay out after dark,' said Mili.

Gurpreet shrugged his shoulders. 'Ah well, in that case, we'll just see you to your door.'

They trudged along in silence for a while. They could hear a brook nearby. Gurpreet thumped Jatin's back.

Jatin glared at him angrily. 'You're bent upon breaking my back today or what?'

'So tell me, brother, how is married life treating you?' Gurpreet asked, completely ignoring his friend's protest.

'Best thing that happened to me in a long time, Preeto,' Jatin replied with a grin.

'How about a party to celebrate?' asked Gurpreet.

'Yes, do let's have a party. It's been ages,' said Mili.

'Hmm. This Sunday? Lakeview Club in Nainital?' said Jatin. 'I'll work out all the details. I'll invite Raven Sir as well.'

'Are you mad?' exclaimed Gurpreet.

'Why? What's wrong? He's not a stick–in-the-mud like the other teachers,' said Mili.

'Yes, and he's only five years older than me,' said Jatin. He stepped on a loose stone and his right foot skidded. He steadied himself as the stone went hurtling down the hill, before continuing, 'Besides, Vidushi and I wouldn't be together today if it hadn't been for him. We can't have a party to celebrate our wedding and not have him. We owe him this one, Preeto.'

'All right, do what you will. But remember, it's a party and I'm going to smoke and drink, whether he likes it or not.'

Gurpreet and Jatin waved goodbye to Mili and made their way to Guruji's house. A revolutionary whom they called Comrade Jaidev opened the door for them.

'Is Guruji home?' Gurpreet asked.

'Yes,' Jaidev replied. 'Come with me. I will take you to him.' He led them to an anteroom beside the prayer hall which was used as a storeroom for stacking things for the puja. Silver plates for the arti, kumkum powder, agarbatti, dhoop, camphor, some broken statues of gods, lots of diyas and candles.

Comrade Jaidev shifted a small cupboard with their help to reveal a latch.

Gurpreet and Jatin looked at each other as he lifted the latch and started walking down some narrow wooden stairs. He held a lantern in his hands, to show the way. The two friends followed him to the basement. They had never been to this part of the house before. It looked like a mini laboratory. Something was bubbling over the burner. There were lots of beakers, tubes and decanters. Gurpreet was amazed by what he saw before him. So this was where they made their bombs.

'Good day to you, Guruji,' Gurpreet said as he touched Guruji's feet.

'May God always be with you,' said Guruji, holding his shoulders lightly.

Gurpreet looked around to see why Jatin had not touched Guruji's feet. He found him gaping at the bombs curiously.

Guruji picked up one and held it out to Jatin. 'Straight out of the chulha,' he said with a chuckle. 'Want to try it?' He laughed as Jatin shrank back. 'Darta hai saala,' he added as he led them back up the stairs to the living room and ordered the servant to bring some tea.

'What happened to that girl you were going to bring along?' asked Guruji.

'She's not sure whether she wants to join us or not,' replied Gurpreet.

'That's all right,' said Guruji. His voice rose as he spoke again. 'We only want those Indians who are a hundred per cent committed to the cause. We need people who are ready to do or die for their country.'

'Yes, you're right, Guruji.'

Not hearing any response from Guruji, Gurpreet followed his gaze. He was looking out of the open window and pointing to a flag fluttering in the distance. 'See that flag?'

'You mean the Union Jack?' asked Gurpreet.

'The day is not far when the Indian flag will be flying in its stead,' whispered Guruji.

'It seems that day will never come,' Gurpreet said with a cynical smile.

'It will. And soon . . .' said Guruji. 'The Congress is planning something. A nationwide protest against the British to quit India.'

Raven knocked on Principal Perkins' door. Hearing a 'Come in, please' he walked in.

'I have some bad news, I'm afraid,' said Miss Perkins. 'The warden's problem seems to have escalated. It's something to do with her brother–in–law getting wounded in the war and becoming impaired. She will be taking longer to come back than we had previously thought.'

'I'm sorry to hear that,' replied Raven.

'Miss Agatha has kindly offered to take the warden's place until her return. I hope you approve?'

'Yes, of cou—'

Cries of 'Bharat Mata ki Jai; do or die' made him stop

speaking and look out of the window. There were some revolutionaries marching down the street below.

'Those demonstrators look like your students from MP College.'

'So they are,' said Raven as he narrowed his eyes and looked out of the window again.

'In that case you ought to stop the protest.'

'It is a peaceful march, Miss Perkins,' Raven answered slowly, continuing to look out of the window. 'I can hardly object to that.'

'If I were you, I'd keep an eye on them.'

'Really, Miss Perkins, I think they're harmless enough.'

'It seems your sympathies lie with the Indians, rather than the English. Don't fool yourself, Raven. You're a white man, a gora, a foreigner to them. You may think of yourself as an Indian, but they never will. And they will have no qualms throwing you out of their country, given the chance.'

Raven looked at her and saw the mistrust in her eyes. He sighed and got up. 'I should take my leave now. I'll go and meet Miss Agatha and make sure she has been briefed about the rules and regulations governing the hostel.'

Miss Perkins made no move to get up. 'I wanted to ask you about Princess Malvika Singh. Has she settled down? Her friend's death was a bit of a shock for all of us.'

'Bit of a shock?' exclaimed Raven. 'It was a huge shock. But yes . . .' He turned his back to Miss Perkins and looked intently at the painting of the Last Supper that hung on the wall. He touched its cold gilt frame. 'She's much stronger than I'd thought,' he said slowly. He swung back to face Miss Perkins. 'She was extremely upset that no action had been taken against the collector, bu—'

'Well, we don't really know for certain what happened that night,' said Miss Perkins. 'I mean, a frivolous Anglo-Indian girl's words as opposed to a respectable collector's . . .'

Raven stared at her, not quite believing what he had just heard. 'I'm appalled,' he said in a low voice.

'It's the truth, you know,' replied Miss Perkins with a shrug. 'If matters had gone to court, everyone including the judge would have said the same thing.'

'Not everyone,' said Raven. 'I'm sure the Indians would have felt differently.'

'Who would have listened to them? Certainly not the judge. But I'm glad that girl – Malvika – has settled down. So tell me, Raven, is it really necessary to spend so much time with her?'

Raven's mouth fell open and he glared at her. 'I beg your pardon, miss?'

'People talk, Raven, and I've been hearing things. If you're unable to maintain a healthy distance between yourself and your students and these rumours continue to grow, I may have to take the matter to the vice chancellor.'

Pursing his lips, Raven nodded slightly. 'Good day to you, miss,' he mumbled and left the room, banging the door shut.

Raven angrily changed gears and reversed out of the driveway at full speed. Who was Miss Perkins to tell him what he ought to do with his students and what not to? He slowed down as he perceived a palanquin approaching. Was he in love with Malvika? He thought hard. No, he didn't think so. Then why was he always looking out for her? He worried about her; felt sorry for her for all that she had gone through. Yes, that was it. He felt sorry for her, that's all.

He parked his car and made his way towards Lakeview Club, a lovely resort constructed fully with logs and wood, on the edge of the Naini Lake. It had rained all day, so much so that the entire place now looked intoxicated and full of revel. He took a deep breath, inhaling the heady fragrance of moist earth, took off his hat and walked into the club. Normally he did not attend these social gatherings, more so if they were hosted by students. He felt as inconspicuous at such parties as a peacock would in the Himalayas. But one imploring look from Vidushi and he could not say no.

A cheer went up as he entered the room where the party was in full swing. He accepted a glass of whisky from the waiter and looked around. After exchanging a few niceties with his students and congratulating Jatin and Vidushi, he made his way to the door that led to the deck.

Mili sat there alone, at the edge of the deck, her feet dangling in the waters of the lake. Raven went and sat down beside her, his glass in hand.

'Good evening, sir,' she said with a smile.

Raven nodded, raised his glass, then took a sip. 'You seem to be far away,' he said.

Mili looked down. 'I was just reminiscing – the last

time I went to a party, Vicky was with me.'

'Yes, I remember, you almost got expelled from the hostel,' he said, smiling sardonically.

Mili grinned. 'We've been friends ever since we were babies, even before we could talk. Ma used to tell me, whenever we were together as toddlers, we'd sit side by side, holding hands. Always holding hands. She thought it was awfully sweet.'

Raven smiled softly and the two of them fell silent. He looked around. It was twilight. The lake was surrounded with purplish-blue mountains on all sides. A thin veil of mist was descending down the mountains and dipping into the tranquil waters, like the weeping willows. Why had he never come to Nainital before, he wondered? It reminded him of Avalon. There was even a boat on the lake that looked like the barge on which Arthur had lain, after he was mortally wounded.

From the corner of his eye he saw some students about to walk out onto the deck. Then they saw him and walked back inside. He smiled disdainfully. Cowards, all of them. He wondered why they were all so scared of approaching him.

He stole a sideways look at Mili. She was chewing her nails. 'Stop biting your nails,' he said, snatching her hands and looking at them in horror. 'You're a girl. Not just that. You're a princess. And your nails are worse than the washerwoman's.'

Mili pulled her hands out of his grasp and hid them behind her back. 'You're scolding me at a party? You can't scold me about my studies here, so you're picking on my nails,' she grumbled.

Raven put back his head and laughed. He took a long sip and emptied the contents of his glass. He gestured to the waiter to come over and refill it. The waiter walked over with a half-full bottle of whisky and an empty tumbler. Ignoring the glass, Raven picked up the bottle, then shooed the waiter off with a wave of his hand.

He took another sip, then turned to Mili. 'That principal of yours, she's a cow. She says to me, "You're not an Indian." You tell me, Malvika. What makes you an Indian?'

'Sir, I don't understand.'

'Why do you say that you're an Indian and not a German or Russian or Japanese?'

'I was born and brought up in India, that's why, sir,' replied Mili.

'Exactly,' said Raven, taking another long sip of the whisky. 'So was I. I have lived here all my life. I can speak Hindustani. I enjoy Indian food. So does that not make me an Indian?'

Looking slightly baffled, Mili answered, 'I suppose.'

It was getting dark now. Raven looked at the lake again, its waters gently lapping the boats, like a mother rocking her baby to sleep. The boats swayed slightly every now and then, as though stirring in their sleep.

He moved closer to Mili. *Miss Perkins should see me now*, he thought and chuckled. He noticed Mili looking at him curiously and glugged down some more whisky. 'Sod Miss Perkins,' he muttered.

He began tapping his feet in time with the music playing inside. Someone had put on 'Let's Do It'. As the words '*Let's do it . . . let's fall in love . . .*' rang out,

Raven looked at Mili and their eyes met. He gave her a sheepish grin. Mili smiled back shyly, a slight blush creeping up her cheeks. She had a very captivating smile, Raven thought as he stared at her lips, mesmerised. It started with a small twitch of the corners of her lips, spread timidly to the middle, quivered softly, gathered courage, then reached her eyes, giving their depths a greater intensity. He took a swig at his bottle and curbed an insane desire to touch her.

There was something potent about the combination of darkness and drink, he decided. It brought to the surface emotions and desires that stay buried at the bottom of one's heart and never dare surface in broad daylight. He looked again at Mili. Her eyes were glittering in the moonlight and he could not look away. 'Your eyes,' he whispered, 'they're so hypnotic . . . so intense . . . You're the first woman I've met whose eyes speak volumes.'

He looked down at her hands as she looked at him incredulously and said, 'Sir?'

He pulled her right hand into his and caressed her stubby fingernails. 'Poor nails,' he mumbled.

'Oh no, sir, please don't start again,' she groaned.

Raven continued to look down and play with her fingers. 'I feel so calm, so much at peace with myself when I'm with you,' he said. 'I don't feel the need for words. I can be myself when I'm with you.' He lifted her hand to his mouth and kissed it tenderly. 'There are very few people in this world who you can actually talk to, and fewer still with whom you can remain silent and yet communicate.'

He emptied his bottle with a glug and called out to the waiter to get him another drink.

'Sir,' said Mili in a worried tone, 'I don't think you should be drinking any—'

Raven put his fingers on her lips and drawled, 'Shh! I'm your teacher. You're not supposed to interrupt me. Now listen . . .' He lowered his voice and spoke so softly that he was barely audible. 'Do you know why I talk to you so much and not to anybody else?'

'So that I forget my own loss and grief?'

'Umm . . . maybe . . . maybe not . . .' He threw the empty whisky bottle into the lake. He watched the rippling waters for a moment, then looked at Mili. Pushing back a tendril of hair that had fallen over her brow, he tucked it behind her ear. Then ever so gently, he cupped her face in his hands. He watched her as she slowly lifted her eyes to meet his gaze.

'I think I'm falling in love with you,' he said. Then he got up abruptly and went indoors.

Chapter Twenty-One

Mili sat in the library, fiddling with her pigtails and staring at the book in front of her. What happened at the party last night? Did Raven Sir really say he was falling in love with her? Did he mean it? Or was he jesting? Or had he guessed her feelings for him and wanted to see her reaction? She got up and closed her book. She had to know. She went down the stairs and walked to his office. *Oh Lord Kishan, be with me*, she muttered under her breath as she hesitated and looked around. Then gathering her courage, she knocked on the door.

'Come in,' Raven barked.

Mili walked in. She looked at Raven. He was seated at his desk and did not bother to look up. 'Good evening, sir,' she said as she sat down. Was she imagining things, or did he still smell of alcohol?

'What is it, Malvika?' he asked brusquely, without looking up. 'I'm busy. Can it not wait until tomorrow?'

Lowering her eyes, Mili began to chew her thumbnail. Oh Lord Kishan. Someone was in a foul mood today. She cleared her throat. 'Sir, do you remember what you said last night?'

Raven averted his gaze. 'I'm afraid I had a little too much to drink. I don't remember anything.'

'Sir, but you're a teacher. How could you get so drunk? Aren't yo—'

'Yes,' Raven cut in sharply. 'Yes, I'm a teacher. But teachers are also human. I made a mistake . . . like human beings sometimes do.' He continued to leaf through his students' essays.

Mili stared at him. He was behaving as though she had already left the room. Or was invisible. She sat in silence for a long time, then whispered softly, 'Sir, are you sure you don't remember anything? Or are you afraid?'

'Me? Afraid? Of what?'

'Of what people might say?'

'Have I ever cared about such things?'

'Then what is stopping you?'

Looking up from his papers, Raven glanced at her. 'I'm not selfish. That's all I can say.'

'I don't understand.'

'You will, with the passage of time. Go home now, it's getting late. And shut the door behind you.'

'Yes, sir,' Mili replied quietly and left the room. She dragged her feet to the palanquin waiting for her by the school gate. She got in and sat down. The palanquin swayed uncomfortably as the bearers picked it up and started their descent down the hill.

Mili stared ahead into nothingness as tears rolled

down her cheeks. Why was she crying? She had known all along that Raven Sir had not meant a single word of what he said last night. Then why was she upset now? And what did he mean by saying he was not selfish and she would eventually understand? None of what he had said today or last night made any sense. And yet she had hoped against hope . . . that he too would love her as much as she loved him. Maybe not as much, just half – not even half; if only he could reciprocate even one-tenth of what she felt for him.

She got off the palanquin hurriedly when they reached home and ran towards her room. But Mausi had seen her and noticed her swollen eyes and red nose.

'Have you been crying?' she asked tenderly.

'No, Mausi.'

'You're going to lie to me, Mili?' she said, lifting her chin with her fingers. 'Won't you tell me what's upsetting you? Am I not like your mother?'

Mili pulled Mausi's hand away. She sat on the sofa and began taking off her shoes. 'I was reading a sad poem, Mausi, and couldn't control my tears.'

'Then go wash your face and come for your meal,' said Mausi.

'I'm not feeling too good. I think I'll skip supper and go to bed right away.' With that she went to her room and shut the door.

12th August. 1942. Mili was in Gurpreet's house. She had gone to collect some books she had left behind at Uncleji's Tuck Shop the other day, when having lunch with him and Jatin.

She looked at Gurpreet. He had let himself go after Vicky's death. His hair was long and unruly again, beard unkempt. He almost looked like a fakir, except for the haunted look in his eyes. 'What happened to the rest of the litter?' she asked as she stroked Bruzo, Gurpreet's dog, a brown Lhasa apso with an adorable white patch on its forehead.

'My aunt sent them to different homes. Couldn't afford to keep them all. But this one is close to my heart, there was no way I was going to let her give him away,' said Gurpreet as he caressed Bruzo.

'He's the one Vicky wanted to take to Mohanagar?' Mili asked, as she tried to brush Bruzo's hair off her clothes and grimaced. She was going to smell like a dog all day today.

'Yes, the greediest of the lot. When he was a puppy, he used to look so funny when he walked. He'd run two or three paces, then fall flat on his face. I got worried and took him to the hakim, thinking there might be something wrong with his legs. But it turned out he was just a little overweight. Fancy that! An overweight puppy.' He laughed as Bruzo barked at him, looking offended. 'You're an absolute glut, aren't you?' he lisped, as he playfully pulled Bruzo's ears. 'The time when Vicky saw him as a puppy, he used to drink up an entire saucer of milk, while his brothers and sisters barely managed to finish one between the five of them . . .'

'Talking of drinking,' Mili said, 'you shouldn't have worried about Raven Sir objecting to your drinking at the party.'

Gurpreet guffawed. 'True, he was more drunk than I

was.' He stopped playing with Bruzo and looked at her. 'And what's between you two? He was stuck to you like a leech all evening.'

Mili looked away. 'Don't be mad,' she eventually said. 'He's my teacher.'

'Yes, and don't you forget that. A teacher *and* an Angrez. That reminds me – on our way here, we passed the collector's car. Wasn't he our Vicky's Uncle George?'

'Yes,' Mili replied tersely.

'He was looking at you in a funny way . . .'

'That's because I spat in his face the last time I bumped into him.'

'You spat at him?' said Gurpreet, staring at her incredulously.

'You would too, if you knew what he did to Vicky.' Mili bit her lip no sooner the words were out of her mouth. She shouldn't have said that.

'What? What did he do to Vicky?' Gurpreet asked. His Adam's apple moved. He raised his voice. 'Mili, what d'you know about Vicky that I don't?'

'Nothing.'

'You're trying my patience, Mili. Tell me.'

'I can't,' Mili replied. She gulped and bit her thumbnail. She had never seen Gurpreet so angry before.

He now grabbed her by her shoulders and shook her hard. 'Don't play games with me, Mili; tell me.'

'I can't,' Mili sobbed. 'I have sworn not to tell anyone.'

Walking over to his desk, Gurpreet picked up the holy book of the Sikhs. He put his right hand on the book. 'I swear on the holy Guru Granth Sahib that I will not breathe a word to a single soul. Now tell me.'

Bruzo padded up to Mili and began licking her hand. Mili looked down at him and stroked his back. 'He raped her,' she whispered.

Gurpreet's eyes blazed as he stared at her. She shrank back, afraid he might strike her. He finally spoke. 'I'll destroy that man,' he said through clenched teeth. 'I'll drink his blood.'

The door flung open and Jatin barged into the room. 'Preeto,' he said. 'All the Congress leaders including Gandhi and Nehru have been arrested.'

'Why? What happened?' asked Mili.

'It was because of their Quit India movement against the British. The Congress, why, all of Hindustan, is enraged. You can't put people behind bars for carrying out a peaceful demonstration. Trouble has erupted all over the country now.'

Mili looked at Gurpreet. He was facing the window, his back towards them. He was trying to get a hold on himself. His hands were shaking slightly as he lit his cigarette.

'How do you know all this?' he asked, taking a puff and turning around to face them.

'I was at Guruji's house,' replied Jatin. 'He himself said so. And he wants to see all of us urgently tomorrow.'

Gurpreet's Adam's apple moved. 'We'll fight the bloody goras,' he said in a quiet voice. 'Draw blood for blood.'

Mili noticed his forehead had tautened, his hands were curled into fists and his eyes were incensed. And a numbing fear ran down her spine.

* * *

The next day dawned crisp and clear. The monsoon rains had packed and left, promising to be back the following year.

Gurpreet entered Guruji's house nodding at comrade Jaidev, who had opened the door for him. He looked around the prayer hall. It was packed. There were about seventy-eighty people in there. Maybe even a hundred. It was difficult to say. More than half of them were students from MP College.

Once they were all seated, Guruji proceeded to address them. 'As you all know, the British Raj has once again acted unjustly. They have put our leaders behind bars for carrying out a peaceful demonstration. Are we going to sit at home and watch them languish in prison?'

A shout went up. 'No!'

'Then we must act, and act fast. All of you present here, especially the students – you are the future of this country. It is you who will herald in a free Hindustan . . .'

A shout of 'Vande Mataram!' rent the air.

Guruji raised his right hand to quieten the crowd. Once everyone had stopped shouting, he continued speaking. 'I'm going to select some of you to aid me in cutting off the British lines of communication. Our aim is not to hurt anyone, but merely to protest against the unfair imprisonment of our leaders.' He took off his cap, raked his fingers through his hair, then put it back on again and recommenced speaking. 'We want to make them realise the strength of our power. Simply because we follow the path of ahimsa does not mean we'll take everything lying down. We have done till now. But not any more. And by blowing up the post office and the telegraph office, we will be demonstrating to them that we can also rise up in arms if required.' Guruji raised his voice. 'It is a warning to the British Raj that if they do not release our leaders, there is more to follow. And we are not afraid.'

The students began cheering and clapping, and shouting, 'Do or Die!' Guruji again waited for them to become quiet. 'The rest of you will join me in carrying out a peaceful demonstration across town this evening,' he said. 'Are all the banners and placards for the march ready?'

Jaidev pointed to a heap at the front of the hall.

Walking over to the pile, Guruji read the banner right on top. FREE OUR COMRADES, it said. He picked up the next one and read it aloud – 'DO OR DIE'. He put them back on the pile and said, 'Good.' Then he walked over to the corner of the room where lots of sticks and wooden torches had been piled up. Turning around to face his audience, he said, 'These are to be used only for self-defence. You are not to beat or kill anyone. It is against the principles of the Congress . . . Gurpreet . . .'

'Yes, Guruji?' answered Gurpreet, upon hearing his name.

'Come here, my son,' said Guruji.

Gurpreet went up to him and touched his feet.

Guruji gave him his blessings and, turning his attention back to the audience, began calling out twenty-five other names.

The rest of the party members started talking, coughing, shuffling.

Having finished calling out the names, Guruji clapped

his hands to have everyone's attention. 'The rest of you, take these sticks, torches, banners and flags and leave quietly two by two. We will collect in the town square at four this evening. And if you have nowhere to hide them, collect them on your way to the town square. Vande Mataram.'

Everyone echoed 'Vande Mataram' and began leaving the house gradually.

Gurpreet and the other twenty-five boys now followed Guruji to the anteroom, which smelled strongly of incense and camphor. They watched as Guruji opened a couple of the many boxes that filled the room. Under the incense sticks in one box were revolvers, and in the other, which had a top layer of cotton wool battis, there were bombs.

'You lot will not take part in the procession,' said Guruji as he divided the boys into two groups. 'You will keep low until 9 p.m.' Touching Gurpreet's shoulder lightly, he said, 'You're going to lead your group and blow up the telegraph office. But mind you, no one should be hurt, unless it's a must. And the rest of you are to follow Chirag and destroy the post office. Is that clear?'

'Yes, Guruji,' chorused all of them.

Gurpreet did not say anything but his eyes shone. Yes, this was his chance.

It was pitch dark as it was a moonless night and the street lamp wasn't working either, which was just as well, thought Gurpreet as he lit another cigarette. He had already smoked twenty since morning and his clothes reeked of tobacco. But with each puff he took, his anger grew. All he could see in front of him was the collector's face, his big, pale, grotesque face. That man did not deserve to live.

He walked purposefully to the park in the neighbourhood. Standing before the bushes at the end of the green, he lit a match and held it high above his head. That was the agreed signal. About a dozen boys came out from behind the bushes, just as Jatin and Shivam sprinted towards them, across the park.

'Jatin, Shivam and Devashish, come with me,' whispered Gurpreet. 'The rest of you, proceed to the telegraph office and do exactly as you've been instructed.'

'But what about you fo—' asked Mukul.

'Don't ask questions,' Gurpreet cut in. 'Just do as you've been told. We don't have time to waste. Move on, now.'

He then led the others down the hill, towards the Mall. Kishangarh seemed unusually quiet that night. Just a faint shout of 'Quit India, Jai Hind' could be heard in the distance, which soon died down.

From the corner of his eye, he noticed the look of bewilderment on Jatin's face. Gurpreet stared at him, his chin set in a firm line. He was not going to let even his dearest friend stop him today. Jatin withered under his incensed glare, mumbled something and began following him up the dirt track.

'I heard the procession this evening turned violent when some firangis started hurling abuse at them,' said Jatin. 'A lot of arrests have been made.'

Gurpreet did not reply but carried on walking.

A few paces away from the collector's cottage, Jatin looked at him again and asked, 'Preeto, why are we heading towards the collector's house?'

'Because he has committed a heinous crime and must pay for it,' ground Gurpreet through clenched teeth.

'But Guruji said—'

'To hell with Guruji, Jatin. Are you with me or not?' asked Gurpreet.

Jatin looked at him aghast. Then he spoke quietly. 'I've always been with you, Preeto. How can I desert you now? But I'll not kill anyone.'

Gurpreet's face softened and he slapped his friend across his back. This time Jatin did not protest. They quietly walked up to the collector's gate.

'Where to, young men?' asked the gatekeeper.

'We need to meet the collector,' said Gurpreet.

'He gone to bed. Come some other day,' replied the gatekeeper, waving his hand to shoo them off.

'What? Gone to bed already?' Gurpreet narrowed his eyes at the gatekeeper, not quite believing what he had said.

'Yes, gone to bed,' repeated the gatekeeper. 'He having headache. So sleep early.'

Gurpreet scowled. Bloody paleface. Had robbed him of his sleep and was now sleeping peacefully himself! He had no right to.

'Go and wake your sahib, we need to see him now,' ordered Gurpreet.

The gatekeeper stood his ground. 'I can't do that,' he said.

Opening the gate, Gurpreet tried to push past him.

The gatekeeper attempted to stop him. In the scuffle that followed, Gurpreet took out his handkerchief soaked in chloroform and held it over the gatekeeper's nose until he became unconscious. As soon as he passed out, Gurpreet shoved him aside and stormed towards the house, followed by the other three.

'Not the front door, the side door,' he hissed at Jatin, who had started walking in that direction. Mili had told him the side door only had a single bolt on the top. Gurpreet threw himself against the door. Again. And again, until the bolt loosened and the door flung open.

The four of them listened. They couldn't hear anything. So the noise hadn't woken the servants. So far so good. Mili was right. The house did look like a railway carriage, with several doors opening onto a single corridor. Gurpreet entered the first room. It was the living room and was empty. The next room was the dining room. The third one, the study. Still no sign of life. The fourth door was shut. Gurpreet gestured to the others to be quiet. He pushed the door slightly. It wasn't bolted. He pushed it further ajar.

There on the four-poster bed was the collector, – spreadeagled and snoring like an engine. Gurpreet stared at him with venom and then kicked him hard. George woke up with a start. Before he could say or do anything, Gurpreet hit him with his stick. Shivam and Devashish too began raining lathis on him.

'Tie him to the bed and gag him,' Gurpreet ordered his boys. He smiled bitterly as the collector tried to struggle. Once he had been securely tied, Gurpreet asked the others to step back. He then tore off the collector's clothes. He smiled cruelly as George looked at him in alarm. He looked like a scared skinned rhinoceros, without his clothes. 'You remember what happened to your niece, don't you?' Gurpreet asked as he began sprinkling kerosene all around the bed. He watched George dart a frightened look at each of the boys and then at his shackles. And struggle once more to free himself.

Gurpreet lighted a match and lit his cigarette. He drew a long puff. Then without putting out the matchstick, he threw it on the ground. It immediately burst into flames. As the flames engulfed the bed, he shot one last look at the collector, then strode out of the room.

The four of them ran towards the gate. A couple of servants had woken up by now. They could hear them shouting 'Fire!' and running helter-skelter trying to put it out. Gurpreet paused at the gate and looked at the gatekeeper. He was still unconscious. He hastily drew his gun and shot him.

'Why did you do that?' asked Jatin.

'He'd seen us. We don't want to leave behind any witnesses,' replied Gurpreet. Then he looked heavenward. He had avenged his Vicky's death. He did not care what happened to him now.

Chapter Twenty-Two

It was twenty-six hours since George had been killed. There had been pandemonium in Kishangarh that morning. The people had woken up to the horrifying news that the telegraph office had been burnt down, the post office destroyed and the collector set alight in his own home.

Gurpreet walked towards Jatin's house. He and Vidushi lived by themselves in a small house, not very far from Guruji's. He knocked on the door and waited.

Vidushi opened the door. 'Oh, come in please,' she said smiling nervously.

Gurpreet and Jatin looked at one another but said nothing.

Vidushi looked anxiously from one face to the other. 'Is something the matter, Bhaisaheb?' she asked. 'He has not been himself since yesterday.'

'We killed the collector,' Gurpreet replied.

'What? Have you gone insane?' exclaimed Vidushi.

'I had my reasons,' said Gurpreet lowering his eyes.

'Why did you tell her?' Jatin asked, clearly upset.

'It's better she knows,' said Gurpreet, lighting a cigarette.

There was a knock on the door. Gurpreet looked at Jatin and then at Vidushi, then again at Jatin. He slowly opened the window an inch and peered out, careful not to be seen. It was Shivam. He heaved a sigh of relief and opened the door.

Shivam hastily bolted the door as soon as he was inside. 'The police have been questioning the collector's servants. They said that by the time they woke up, the culprits had escaped and the collector's house was on fire. They got busy putting it out and trying to save barre sahib and did not notice anyone.'

Gurpreet watched him as he sank down on a chair, and lowering his head, held it between his hands.

'But one servant saw a Sikh in a maroon turban shooting the gatekeeper and then fleeing,' said Shivam, shaking his head from side to side.

A deathly silence fell on the room.

Gurpreet's Adam's apple moved. Lighting another cigarette, he walked over to Jatin's desk and fiddled with his typewriter. Then he turned around to face the others. He spoke with deathly calm. 'I want all three of you and Devashish to run away.'

'And what about you?' Jatin asked.

'Nothing will happen to me,' replied Gurpreet. 'I'm a sardar.'

'I'm not going anywhere without you,' said Jatin.

'And why do we need to run away? Shivam just said they did not see the rest of us. Isn't it, Shivam?'

Shivam nodded.

'No, I don't want you to take any chances,' said Gurpreet. 'You want to make my bhabhi a widow again?'

'Then come with us,' said Jatin.

'If I come with you, we'll surely get caught,' said Gurpreet.

'Why don't you cut your hair and get rid of your turban?' said Vidushi. 'No one will recognise you then.'

'Bhabhi, I've killed an Englishman and that too a collector,' replied Gurpreet. 'Sooner or later, they *will* find me. And when they do, I want to go with dignity, proud to be a Sikh.' He stopped speaking and looked at Jatin – at his ashen face, his downcast eyes brimming with unshed tears. He went and embraced him. 'Don't be sad, yaara. I've no regrets. That man deserves to rot in hell.'

Without looking up, Jatin wiped his eyes with the back of his hand.

Gurpreet spread out a map on the little cane table in front of him. Moving his fingers over it, he said, 'Go through the forest here and keep moving towards Pithoragarh. From there you can easily escape to Nepal without attracting any attention.' He looked at Jatin. 'Take Shivam and Devashish with you. Once you're safe, ask bhabhi to join you. And don't tell a single soul where you're headed, not even your parents. Even when you speak to bhabhi, speak in codes. Don't mention the place or your names, ever.'

Pursing his lips, Gurpreet folded the map and gave it to Jatin. What a mess. He did not regret killing the collector, not even for a moment. But he was damned if he did not feel awful about bringing his friends to this. Why did he have to drag them into this? Why, oh why, didn't he go it alone? He would never be able to forgive himself if something should happen to them.

Mili sat on her bed, her pillow propped up behind her, reading the Bhagavad Gita. *Death is certain for the one who is born, and birth is certain for the one who dies. Therefore, you should not lament over the inevitable. All beings, O Arjuna, are unmanifest before birth and after death. They are manifest only between birth and death. So what is there to grieve about?* She put down the book and frowned. But grieving over the death of dear ones was inevitable as well. She wondered what the purpose of Vicky's life had been. For that matter, her own life. What was the purpose of *her* life?

She should be happy. Gurpreet had avenged Vicky's death. Finally justice had been done. But she wasn't. An unknown fear gnawed at her heart and filled her with dread. She had read about the collector's death in the newspaper. She knew who the Sikh in the maroon turban and his accomplices were. She feared for their safety. Even the slightest sound or knock on the door made her jump up in fright.

'Your friend's here to see you, Mili,' called Mausi from the prayer room.

She looked up as the maidservant Ramdulari led Vidushi to her room. As soon as Ramdulari left, Vidushi darted a quick glance down the corridor, then shut and bolted the door. She hastened over to Mili's bed and sat down at the edge.

'Gurpreet bhaisaheb has been arrested,' she whispered.

'What? When?'

'Yesterday. One of the collector's servants identified him,' said Vidushi, wiping her forehead with the edge of her sari.

'Where are the others? Where's Jatin?' Mili asked.

Vidushi looked around to make sure all the doors and windows were closed. Then she whispered, 'Don't tell anyone. Jatin has escaped to Pithoragarh. The other two are in Garampani.' Vidushi got up and walked over to the dressing table mirror. She pressed the red bindi on her forehead lightly, then stared at the sindoor in her hair. 'I'm worried, Mili.'

'Don't worry,' Mili tried to sound reassuring, 'I'm sure he'll never be caught.'

'Yes, and I owe his life to Gurpreet bhaisaheb.'

'How so?'

'They flogged him all day yesterday. Perhaps all night even; who knows? And when that didn't work, they hit him with whips dipped in salt water to increase the pain.'

Mili's eyes narrowed and her forehead creased at the thought of what he must have had to endure.

'But he would not tell them who the others were and where they were hiding.'

She stood up. 'I won't be seeing you again, Mili. Maybe never again.'

Mili looked at her questioningly.

'I'm taking the bus today to Pithoragarh. From there we plan to escape to Nepal.'

Walking over to Vidushi, Mili clutched her hands. She pursed her lips and wiped the tears that were rolling down Vidushi's cheeks with her fingers.

'They're going to hang Gurpreet bhaisaheb,' Vidushi sobbed.

After making her sit down on the stool in front of the dressing table, Mili went to the kitchen to fetch a glass of water. Now she understood why she did not feel elated at the collector's death. Gurpreet was going to be hanged. She remembered what Gandhiji often said: 'An eye for an eye makes the whole world blind.' Gurpreet had killed the collector to avenge Vicky's death. But now he himself was going to die. It all seemed so futile.

Mili walked slowly towards the town centre where the public execution of Gurpreet was to take place. A huge crowd was already there. It seemed the whole of Kishangarh was there today. Mili pushed her way through the throng, until she was right in front. She looked around as she bit her thumbnail.

A sudden hush fell on the square as Gurpreet was led towards the gallows, flanked on either side by a dozen policemen carrying rifles. His hands had been tied behind his back. He had been stripped down to the waist and the marks of the flogging could be seen as angry, oozing welts, criss-crossing his entire back. He was ordered to stand on a wooden stool, just below the noose. Mili looked at his face. It was expressionless, his beard matted with blood, the tip of his nose glistening with sweat.

Mili looked around, feeling an overwhelming sense of helplessness. She wanted to scream, but no sound came out of her mouth. She felt a sense of déjà vu. Was she to watch another friend die in a similar fashion and not be able to do anything about it? Lord Kishan, why? Why were you making her go through all this?

The mayor arrived and the policemen stood to attention. Mili stared at Gurpreet with terrified eyes. His Adam's apple moved as the noose was put around his neck. His eyes were vacant. Just like Vicky's had been, the day she ended her life. They lit up for a second as they alighted on Mili. Tears ran down her cheeks as their eyes met. He looked heavenward, then smiled at her.

She understood. Vicky will be happy that her death had been avenged, he was saying. She made the V sign with her middle and forefinger, pointed heavenward, then pulled the edges of her lips with her fingers to make a mock smile.

Gurpreet nodded slowly, closed his eyes, looked heavenward and smiled.

Mili smiled back. Yes, she was sure his soul would meet hers, up there. Perhaps she was waiting for him to join her and together they would be reborn again.

The mob had begun to shout, 'Vande Mataram. Bharat Mata ki Jai.'

Closing her eyes, Mili said a fervent prayer to her Lord Kishan. 'Hey Kishan,' she prayed. 'You are known for your miracles. Please spare my friend his life.' Maybe

Lord Kishan would suddenly appear out of nowhere and save Gurpreet. Just like he had come to Drapaudi's aid when the Pandavas had lost her in a game of dice and she was subjected to humiliation in front of the whole court. Her Lord Kishan had saved her. He would save Gurpreet too. He had to.

Mili opened her eyes slowly.

'Hang him,' the mayor barked.

The crowd went silent again.

The stool, on which Gurpreet stood, was kicked off from beneath his feet. His legs thrashed about for a while as the noose tightened around his neck.

Covering her mouth with the edge of her dupatta, Mili sank to her feet, her body racked with sobs. No, there had been no miracle and no Kishan Bhagwan had appeared. The crowd had begun to disperse, leaving her alone with the lifeless body of her friend, swinging from the rope.

That night Mili had a fitful sleep. She dreamt of a puppy she had once seen dying, as a little girl. The puppy had been attacked by a stray dog. Its skin had been so badly torn that its ribs could be seen. It lay whimpering until it died the next day. Every few minutes it would let out a chilling, heart-rending cry, followed by a long whimpering. Suddenly, it was not the puppy's body that was being torn apart by the stray dog. It was a human body, her own body which was being molested. A pair of stubby white hands with cracked fingernails were pawing it, maligning it, tearing her clothes away. And now the same hands were putting a noose around her neck. Mili screamed. Her scream woke her up. She sat up, sobbing. Soon her sobbing turned into a low, whimpering sound similar to that of the puppy's.

Mili looked around Prof. Raven's room. She had been summoned to this room so many times before. Sometimes with Vicky, sometimes without. But this might be the last time she was here.

'Good evening, Malvika,' said Raven, looking up from his papers and gesturing to her to sit down. 'What brings you here today?'

'Sir, I'm leaving STH and going back to Mohanagar,' she said as she sat down. 'I can't stay here any more, after all that has happened.' She paused to take in a deep breath. Looking down, she said in a low voice, 'It was all my fault, sir. If I hadn't left Vicky alone soon after her rape, if I had not blurted to Gurpreet about the collector, both of them would be alive today.'

'Listen to me, Malvika,' said Raven, leaning forward. 'No one can change what is to happen. Vicky would have committed suicide no matter what you did and Gurpreet was a revolutionary; he would have got killed sooner or later. Stop blaming yourself.' He rested the palms of his hands on the desk before adding slowly, 'Wait for three more months. Sit your Senior Cambridge exams and then go.'

'No, sir, I have to go. I've lost two friends, in a way no one should ever have to. I'm confused. I need to work some things out for myself.'

'I understand.'

Mili looked at him, her eyes beseeching. 'What do I do, sir?' she whispered.

Raven got up, walked over to the window and rubbed the back of his neck. Turning back to her he said, 'That is for you to decide, Malvika.'

'I'm so confused,' Mili replied, in a defeated voice.

Raven walked around the desk to where she was sitting. Pulling up a chair beside her, he sat down, his face just a few inches away from hers. His eyes twinkled as he said, 'Well, you can now fulfil your lifelong ambition of marrying your Prince Charming.'

'Sir, that's not my ambition any more,' she said, smiling slightly. She knew he was trying to distract her.

Raven raised his brows. 'It isn't?' he asked with mock horror.

'When are *you* planning to get married?' Mili asked, her smile widening.

'I don't believe in the institution of marriage,' he said, taking Mili's hand in his and stroking her fingers. 'Not after what it did to Mother.'

Mili looked down. Her hands looked so small in his. Getting distracted by a sound, she listened carefully. 'Is it raining?' she asked.

'It seems so,' replied Raven, looking out of the window. He got up and pulled something from his coat stand. 'Here,' he said, handing it to her. 'You can borrow my mackintosh.'

'That won't be necessary, sir. My brother is waiting for me in the car, just outside the school gates.'

'It's raining too hard. You'll be drenched by the time you reach it.'

'But sir . . .'

'I insist.'

Reluctantly, Mili put on the raincoat, conscious of his eyes looking at her with amusement.

She turned red as Raven threw back his head and laughed. 'You're drowning in it,' he said. He lowered his voice and brought his face close to hers. 'You look cute,' he said with a smile. 'Like a penguin.'

'I may not see you again. I'll ask Mausi to have it sent back to you.'

She realised Raven wasn't listening. His eyes lingered on her lips before reaching her eyes. 'Go, my child-woman,' he finally whispered, wrapping his arms tightly around her. 'Whatever you decide, soar high, do me proud,' he whispered hoarsely.

Mili's eyes glittered with unshed tears. She swallowed. 'I promise,' she said in a choked voice. She raised her eyes to his. What she saw in them frightened her. There was passion and something else that she did not wish to read.

Then before she realised what he was doing, his rough lips were crushing hers. She clung to him as he kissed her long and hard, and wished it would never end.

Just as abruptly, he let go of her. Roughly pushing her aside, he went back to his desk, sat down and opened a file. 'Go now,' he said with a wave of his hand. 'I've work to do.'

Mili lowered her eyes, nodded and left the room.

She knew Uday was waiting for her in the car. But she had to go there – one last time. She sprinted round the back of the hostel building to the mound. She remembered how happy and excited she and Vicky had been when they had got admission to study here. She sat down on the mound. Like she used to with Vicky. And wept. For Vicky. For all that they had shared. And then she cried for herself. For a love that would never know fulfilment. Because she would never see Raven again.

Chapter Twenty-Three

It was Janamashtami. Her Lord Kishan's birthday. There had been a lot of hustle and bustle in the palace since morning. The priest and his helpers were busy decorating the family temple. They were recreating the scene of Kishan's birth – a prison cell where Lord Kishan's mother and father sat huddled and shackled. Across the inner courtyard of the temple ran a zigzag piece of blue silk – the River Yamuna. And on the river a statue of Kishan's father, Vasudev, carrying baby Kishan on his head in a basket and the snake god forming a hood over baby Kishan, to protect him from the torrential rains.

Mili sniffed the air as the smell of sweetmeats and savouries emanated from the kitchen. She usually partook of the preparations with full enthusiasm, but this year she watched from afar. She was at home, in her room, in her palace in Mohanagar, but her thoughts were elsewhere. Why had Raven not tried to stop her when she had gone to say goodbye? Or said that he loved her? She would have never left Kishangarh if he had.

It was foolish of her to have such expectations. She loved him with every part of her being, she thought of him every waking moment and perhaps even when asleep. But for him, she was just another student. It was time she woke up to that fact and stopped yearning for something that was never there in the first place.

But why did he kiss her, then? If he didn't have any feelings for her? Why? Why? Would her questions ever be answered? It didn't matter. Like hell it didn't. All she knew was, even though her love would never be reciprocated, she would always hold him close to her heart. Always.

So then, was this really the end? Would she never see him again? The thought filled her with despair and a longing so deep . . .

She looked at her dolls that sat glumly, piled up in a corner of her room, at her bright-blue rocking horse, at her wooden toy utensils. She was back from Kishangarh, back to where she had lived all her life. But it did not feel like home any more. She felt a strange kind of detachment. Nothing felt good, nothing felt right. Would she ever know happiness again?

Ma walked into the room. 'You're not yet dressed? Your cousins will be here any minute.'

Mili hid her face in her mother's bosom. And as the soft folds of her sari engulfed her, she burst into tears.

'Mili?' Ma said tenderly. 'What happened, my child?'

'Nothing, Ma,' sniffed Mili, swiping at her tears. 'I just feel like howling. No reason . . . at all.'

Ma held her close. She caressed her head, then gently kissed her on the forehead. 'Hush, my child,' she whispered. 'Everything will be all right. Now that you're back home, it's all going to work out fine.'

Mili nodded. 'Where's Mrs Nunes?' she asked, wiping her eyes with a handkerchief that Bhoomi had timidly handed her.

'She's gone to Kerala to finalise the date for her daughter's wedding.'

'I want to meet her when she gets back.'

'Yes, do that. And now put on that lovely smile of yours . . . That's better. And wear some jewellery. It doesn't bode well for a princess to have a bare neck and bare arms on a festival.'

So saying, she began rummaging through Mili's jewellery box. 'Here, wear this,' she said, holding up a rainbow-coloured necklace.

Mili smiled. One day when she was little it had been raining hard. And the sun was also shining – that's the time, they say, when jackals get married and rainbows appear in the sky. It was the first rainbow Mili had ever seen and it was beautiful. She wanted it. Ma summoned the jeweller and ordered a special necklace for her. It had rubies, amethysts, panna, sapphire . . . all the colours of the rainbow.

And Mili used to love it. She wore it even to bed for a month. She smiled again and ran her fingers over the jewels. She'd keep this one, yes, but she'd give the rest of her jewellery away. Just as she had given some of it to Gurpreet, in Kishangarh. She had no need for it now.

*   *   *

It was almost a month since Mili had come back home from Kishangarh. She sat on her bed as Bhoomi brushed her long hair. There was a faint scent of moist soil seeping into the room from outside. The rain was beating down on the window in gentle sprays. The leaves of the rhododendron tree and the amaltas were a brilliant green. A little sparrow sat on the window sill, preening itself. It was the same window that Vicky always used to come into her room.

She looked at Vicky's photograph that stood on her bedside table and smiled. Vicky had been trying to act the clown when that picture was taken. She had scrunched up her nose and was trying to look at its tip. The outcome had been hilarious. She looked like a cross-eyed joker in the picture.

She picked up Vicky's glasses, which were always kept in front of her picture, and put them on. They were too powerful and everything looked blurred. Or was it because of the tears that had suddenly sprung up? She quickly blinked her eyelids to push them back, then turned her attention to Bhoomi. 'My hair looks fine now,' she said. 'Go and tell Ma and Bauji that I wish to speak to them.'

'What about the jewellery?' Bhoomi asked.

'No, I don't feel like wearing any.'

Mili noticed the look of disappointment on Bhoomi's face. Previously, getting dressed, choosing what jewellery to wear used to be the highlight of her day. Sadly, not any more.

She got up and adjusted her dupatta. Her mind was made up. She would go and live in Gandhi Ashram and join him in his struggle for India's freedom. She remembered when she had her first glimpse of him. It must have been about seven years ago, when she was at Nani's house. Everyone was whispering 'Gandhiji . . .' and rushing to the terrace or onto the streets to have a glimpse of him. Just like they did whenever a baraat was passing through the streets.

She was extremely disappointed when she saw him. A scrawny, bald man in a white dhoti. People were pouring out of their homes and joining him. What was so great about him? He was so shabbily dressed and wasn't even handsome. Plus he needed a walking stick. She had looked uncomprehendingly at the excited crowd and wondered why they were making such a fuss over him.

But now, the more she read about him in the papers or heard about him on the radio, the more fascinating she found him.

Maybe immersing herself in the freedom movement would fill the void in her life that had been left by Vicky and then Gurpreet. And help her forget Raven.

Thanks to the sudden showers that morning, a lovely cool breeze was coming into the room through the windows. Bauji sat on the sofa, poring over the newspaper. Ma sat beside him, going over the guest list for dinner that night and discussing the menu with the chef.

Mili rubbed the tigerskin rug on which she stood with her big toe. 'Bauji,' she said, 'Can I speak to you and Ma in private?'

'Of course, my child,' replied Bauji. He waved to the servants to leave the room.

The chef as well as the two servants who stood near the door bowed low and backed out of the room.

'We too wanted to speak to you, Mili,' said Ma, as she adjusted the pleats of her sari. She looked up and smiled at her indulgently. 'Mausi has found an excellent match for you. He's the Prince—'

'Ma, I don't want to marry,' said Mili in a soft voice, chewing her thumbnail. She hesitated. Just like she had at the entrance to the inner sanctum of the temple . . . or when Raven's driver had offered her mithai. Would she finally have the courage to break free of age-old customs and traditions and leave home? To pursue a life which none in her family had ever done before? All the girls in their dynasty had been good little princesses who had married the man of their parents' choice and become good little wives. Would she be able to break off this tradition? She took a deep breath and said, 'I wish to serve my country. Go and live in Gandhi Ashram.'

Bauji stared at her with an open mouth. He looked as though he had been struck with a bolt of thunder.

'What did you say, my child?' he asked softly.

Lowering her eyes, Mili repeated. 'I want to live in Gandhi Ashram.'

'Have you lost your mind?' said Bauji. 'Our troops are fighting for the British in Burma and you want to join the movement against them? Are you crazy?'

'They lead a simple and austere life at the ashram,' said Ma. 'You won't be able to cope.'

'Maybe not,' said Mili. 'But I want to see it for myself.'

There was silence for a long time. Mili listened to the tick-tocking of the grandfather clock that had been presented to Bauji by one of his English friends.

Bauji finally spoke. 'We're afraid we cannot give you permission to go,' he said.

'I haven't come here to seek your consent, Bauji,' Mili said in a defiant tone. 'I've merely come to inform you.'

Bauji's nostrils flared and he was about to lash out at her when Ma put a restraining hand on his arm.

Mili sighed with relief and looked at Ma gratefully.

'Let her go,' said Ma. 'We think she wants to be on her own for some time. We're sure she'll be back soon.'

Bauji sighed. Mili looked at him from the corner of her eyes. He was growing old and age seemed to have mellowed him. She was sorry she had spoken to him so sharply. She had never talked to him in that manner before. She used to be so scared of him. With downcast eyes she left the room.

As soon as she stepped into the inner courtyard, a dozen pigeons that had been cooing and pecking at some grain took flight. She watched them soar high into the azure. She remembered Raven's words – 'Soar high, do me proud' – and felt strangely uplifted.

Raven was looking for a book on the bookshelf in his study when his eyes fell on *Sons and Lovers*. He smiled as he remembered Mili and Vicky browsing through the book in the library. They'd read a bit, then cover their mouths with their hands and snigger. His thoughts flew to Mili. He recalled how she used to bite her thumbnail whenever sad, excited or nervous. And how he had scolded her for not taking care of her nails.

He remembered the last time he saw her. It had been

raining hard. He watched her leave, becoming smaller and smaller gradually, until the rain-shrouded world swallowed her up completely. She had looked so lost, so adorable in his oversized mackintosh, that he had felt like running after her, hugging her tightly from behind and never letting her go.

And why the hell had he kissed her? Had he no sense? He ought to have controlled himself. She was a princess, for crying out loud, and he . . . a poor teacher. Moreover, she was his student. Whatever was he thinking?

. . . But her eyes. They were so intense. And the way they looked at him when he kissed her. He had been staggered by what he saw in them. They were frank and vulnerable and asked him questions to which he had no answers.

Raven shook his head slowly from side to side, as though trying to rid himself of thoughts of her. Was he missing her? Maybe he was. Why else would life seem so desolate, so incomplete ever since she had left? *Don't be silly, Raven*, he chided himself. He had a life before he met her, didn't he? Like hell he did. And he'd forget her. Soon. It was just a matter of time. Her face had already begun to blur. Well, not really. Even so. Life did not stop for anyone. It went on and on and on.

March. 1947. Kishangarh. Raven sat in his living room, drumming the centre table with his fingers.

Yes, he'd be fine, absolutely fine. So what if he hadn't spoken to her in four and a half years? He just had to take it slowly, one step at a time.

Would she come? Raven looked at his watch. He

284

couldn't believe only five minutes had passed since he had last looked at it.

'Your tea, sahib,' said Digachand, placing a cup of tea before him. 'Anything else, sahib?'

'That'll be all for the moment,' replied Raven. His hands shook ever so slightly as he picked up the cup and took a sip. He wondered if he had done the right thing – getting in touch with her again, after such a long time. But then he remembered everything so clearly, as though it was yesterday.

He patted his hair as he glanced towards the door. He had been shocked when he saw her that morning, in a starched cotton sari, her hair piled on top of her head. She looked so elegant, and oh so mature. He wouldn't have recognised her, had it not been for her smile.

She was here. He could hear voices in the hall. He got up and smiled as she entered the room. She smiled back as she sat down. Raven fumbled, not knowing what to say. There was so much he wanted to talk to her about. But would he be able to say them? Much had changed in the intervening years. She had changed. She not only looked different, she even behaved differently. She was not the child he used to know. She had blossomed into a beautiful woman and he simply could not take his eyes off her.

He kicked himself mentally. C'mon, she was his student once upon a time. Yes, once upon a time. Not any more.

'What brings you to Kishangarh?' he finally asked.

'I was invited to come and present a paper and also to speak about our organisation. We are trying to make people aware of the work we are doing in order to gain more support and funds . . .'

Raven could only stare at her and blink. Who was she? This was not his child-woman, Malvika. But she smelt the same – like a baby. She had stopped speaking and was waiting for him to say something. He ran a hand over his face and tried to collect himself. Clearing his throat he asked, 'So what exactly does your organisation do?'

'It takes care of women who have been raped, beaten or abused in any way. We give them a place to live, teach them how to read and write, embroider, weave and help them become independent . . .' She paused and looked at the ribbon tying her hair. A thread was coming loose. She pulled at it and spoke again. 'And you know what, sir? I'm finally at peace with myself. Whenever I see a smile on the face of a woman who was at the edge of despair, or even suicide, I feel I have saved another Vicky.'

Raven watched her – how zealously she spoke. She had done him proud. Very proud. 'So is this what you've been doing since you left Kishangarh?' he asked.

'Oh no, sir . . .'

Sir. She still called him 'sir'. He grinned and tried to pay attention to what she was saying.

'Initially, I went to Gandhi Ashram and tried to get involved in the freedom move—'

'So you joined the party that wants to throw me out of the country? And here I was thinking . . .' Raven pulled a face and sighed deeply.

Mili laughed. 'Not you, sir,' she said.

'I was so surprised when I saw you this morning. Couldn't believe it was you.'

'I wasn't sure you were still here, else I would have informed you. You never did reply to any of my letters,' she complained.

Digachand knocked on the door. 'You and your guest wanting anything, sahib?'

'What would you like to drink, Malvika?' asked Raven.

'Any juice, sir,' Mili replied.

'Two orange juices,' said Raven.

'Very well, sahib,' muttered Digachand and left the room.

'Still teaching?' Mili asked.

'Yes, still teaching.'

'Why did you choose to be a teacher? You would have made an excellent politician . . . or . . . or a civil servant.'

'No, Malvika! The satisfaction of shaping and chiselling young minds that come to me like tabula rasa into something I can one day be proud of – like I am of you – is so great that no other job could have given me as much pleasure.'

'I remember,' said Mili, blushing at his compliment. 'You used to teach us with a Rasputin-like fervour.'

'Rasputin-like?' Raven threw back his head and laughed. 'I'll think of it as praise.'

'Is that why you didn't . . . you didn't . . . stop me? Because I was your student and it would jeopardise your vocation as a teacher?'

'Surely you know me better than that?' said Raven, gazing into her eyes. 'Have I ever cared for such things?'

'Then why?' she asked, her eyes looking wounded.

'Well, to be honest, I did care a little about losing my job. But that wasn't the reason I let you go.' He smiled as he remembered his old Malvika – in her grey school skirt and ladders running up her socks, with pigtails all messy and coming undone. 'You were too young and I was too old – eleven years older than you. I had to let you go, grow up, spread your wings.'

He stopped speaking as he heard the rustling of skirts. A moment later Mother was in the living room.

'Oh,' she exclaimed, as she stared at Mili. 'I had no idea my son was entertaining guests in my absence.'

Mili got up. 'I really should be leaving.' She smiled at Mother. 'It was nice meeting you.'

Raven hastily grabbed Mili's elbow and turned to Mother. 'I shall see her to the door.'

They walked together to her waiting car in silence. Once she was inside the car, he asked, 'Can I see you again?'

'Sir, I'm leaving tomorrow morning.'

'Malvika?'

'Yes, sir?'

Raven shot an irritated look at Mili's chauffeur who was listening to every word they were saying with great interest.

'I'll write to you,' he finally said. 'Take care of yourself, Malvika.'

'I will, sir. Goodbye.'

Raven waved slowly as the car pulled away. He felt a great sense of loss. Yes, it was clear. He loved her. Loved her so much that it hurt to see her go.

* * *

It had been snowing hard all day. Raven brushed the snow off his coat as he handed it to the waiter. Taking his seat beside the window, he looked out. The snow under the street lamp was sparkling, as though it had been sprinkled with fairy dust.

Mother had been surly all day. She now sat across him, not saying a word. She was studying the menu as though she had to sit an exam on it.

Raven caught hold of her hand. 'Mother, come on, talk to me.'

'Why have you brought me here?' she asked.

Raven fidgeted nervously with his cuffs as she narrowed her eyes and studied his face.

'What do you want, Raven?' she asked.

'Sir, what would you like to drink?' enquired a voice from behind.

Raven looked around. It was the waitress. She looked as cheerful as a constipated bulldog. She was not in uniform, but a pretty floral dress with a small apron at the waist. Too haughty to be a waitress, Raven decided. Must be the owner's wife, filling in. After all, the restaurant was heaving that night.

He looked back at Mother who sat staring gloomily at the menu. She looked as sour as a cat that has lost its bowl of cream. Surely, this must be his worst nightmare.

'What would you like to drink, Mother?' he asked.

'Nothing,' came Mother's precise reply.

Raven sighed. 'Two orange sherbets, please,' he said to the waitress.

'Cheapskates,' the waitress muttered.

'You said something?' Raven asked sharply but the waitress was already out of earshot.

'Mother, why didn't you go back to England?' Raven asked carefully. He noticed the startled look on her face as he asked the question.

She answered slowly. 'Who would I have gone back to? I married your father against my parents' wishes. They did not think it was a good match. How right they were.'

'What if you think the same about the girl I wish to marry?'

'It's that Indian girl, isn't it?'

'Her name is Malvika. And she's no ordinary girl. She's a princess.'

'I knew it. I saw it in your eyes – the way you looked at her. You're just like your father.'

'How can you say that, Mother? He left the girl he loved. While I want to marry the girl I love. Surely there's a difference?'

'This is no time to marry an Indian girl, Raven,' Mother said, shaking a finger at him. 'Can you not see what is happening around us?' Her voice had risen and become shrill. 'The Indians don't want us here. They hate us.'

Raven's ears turned red with embarrassment. Everyone in the restaurant was staring at them. 'Mother, let's have our meal. We'll talk about this at home,' he said in a low voice. He smiled gratefully as the waitress approached them with their drinks.

Raven looked at his sherbet absent-mindedly and took a sip. He wasn't sure what he felt about the political unrest in the country. It was true that a lot of people from his community were going back to England or had already left. But he saw no reason why he should leave. His students loved him and he loved his job. He would just have to convince Mother that all would be well. There was no need for her to feel insecure. He looked at her as she sat there, her lips set in a grim line. Yes, it wasn't going to be easy. He would need all his persuasive skills.

Chapter Twenty-Four

14th August. 1947. Mili looked wistfully at the clock. Eleven o'clock at night. But sleep eluded her. She had received her first missive from Raven that day. He had written that he was coming to meet her soon. How could she sleep after reading that?

It was so warm and humid. She fanned herself for a while, then twisted her hair and tied it into a bun on top of her head. She smiled softly as she remembered how her untidy hair used to annoy Raven. Once when they were alone together in his office and he was explaining how she could improve her essay, out of the blue he had remarked, 'Why is your hair always such a mess? Didn't your mother teach you how to braid your hair properly?'

Mili had said, 'No, she didn't. I'm sure she herself doesn't know how. We have servants at home to do our hair.'

'Come here,' he said, rummaging through his drawer. He gathered her hair clumsily and tied it up with a bit of lace he had just found.

'How come you had lace in there?' Mili asked.

'Mother must have left it.'

'Your mother comes to your office to put lace in your drawer?' Mili asked, biting her lip mischievously.

Raven frowned. 'I don't know how it got there. Look, I'm your teacher; I'm the one who asks the questions, not you.'

'Yes, sir; sorry, sir,' said Mili, standing at attention and giving him a mock salute.

Mili lifted her pillow to reveal a bit of lace. She smiled as she picked it up. She ran her fingers slowly over it, feeling its silky smoothness, the little holes, then kissed it. She hurriedly put it back under the pillow as she heard knocking on the door.

Now who could it be at this hour? She looked at her watch. It was almost midnight. 'I hope it's not an emergency,' she muttered as she opened the door. There were a handful of inmates of the ashram. 'All of you are still awake?' she asked.

'Malvikaji,' said the one right in front. 'India has just become independent. How can anyone sleep tonight?'

'Nehruji is going to give a speech soon,' said another inmate. 'You got a radio. Can we listen to it?'

'Yes, of course,' replied Mili. She stepped aside to let them enter the room.

The inmates came and sat down on the rug, talking excitedly in high-pitched voices as she turned the radio on and tried to tune it. Some more inmates came along.

Soon Mili's hut was packed with the women who lived at the ashram.

'Shhhh,' hissed somebody as the disturbance cleared and Nehru's voice rang out over the radio. Silence fell over the room as everybody listened. 'Long years ago we made a tryst with destiny . . .' he was saying.

A loud cheer went up from the inmates as they heard him say, 'At the stroke of the midnight hour, when the world sleeps, India will awake to life and freedom.'

Mili wondered if Gandhi and Nehru had really been instrumental in gaining India's independence. Was it really the triumph of ahimsa? After all, India's struggle for independence in 1942 had been far from non-violent. Or had they simply screwed in the last bolt?

She looked around at the jubilant inmates, ecstatic at the birth of a new nation. A nation that had bled to death in 1857 and then again in 1942 had now been reborn, like a phoenix.

She peered at herself in a mirror. How plain and simple she looked in her cotton sari. So different from the Princess Malvika who was always clad in georgettes and silks and laden with jewellery. She looked around the hut, at her scant belongings, and thought of all the luxuries that had surrounded her in the palace in Mohanagar. And yet, she had never been more happy or at peace with herself. It was as though – here, in the ashram, amidst all these women who looked up to her as their saviour – she had been born again. Reborn from the ashes of her past . . .

Raven ran up the steps of the Billiards Club. He had had a long day. Miss Perkins too had decided to go back to England. He had been helping her with all the paperwork with regard to the handing over of charge to the new Indian principal.

He now looked forward to a relaxing evening and a few good games. And a couple of pegs, he decided, as he passed the bar. The future looked promising. Mother had finally given him her consent, albeit reluctantly, to marry Mili.

A rasping voice with an Indian accent called him from behind. Raven turned around to see who it was. He was an Indian gentleman dressed in a weird combination of a suit jacket and a dhoti.

'Yes?' said Raven.

'I beg your pardon, sir, but I need to draw your attention to this noticeboard,' said the Indian, pointing to a sheet of paper.

Raven glanced at him and then at the board. The notice used to say 'dogs and natives not allowed'. The words 'dogs' and 'natives' had been struck off and replaced with the word 'Angrez'. He looked at the Indian again. By now a small crowd of waiters and other members of staff had gathered in the corridors and were listening to their exchange with keen interest.

'I'm sorry, sir, but I shall have to ask you to leave,' the Indian said, trying to hide his gloating smile.

'And you are?'

'The new owner and manager, sir.'

Nodding briefly, Raven left the premises. He felt saddened. And humiliated. It had finally hit him that he was not wanted in this country. The country where he had been born, where he had lived all his life, the only home he had ever known, did not want him any more.

Mother had been right all along. They had to go back – to England. Somehow, he did not blame the Indians. The British had a lot to answer for. There was much they had done that Raven was ashamed of. Leaving India would not be so difficult for Mother. After all, she had not been born and brought up here. But for him it would be different. He would be devastated.

Raven knocked on the door and waited. He looked around. Naari Shakti Ashram looked like a mini hamlet, with lots of little huts close to one another. Mili's hut as well as a couple of others looked slightly bigger than the rest. He sniffed appreciatively as the wind blowing from the east brought with it the fragrance of jasmine. He spotted the jasmine plant, close to the edge of the veranda. He scooped up a handful of blossoms from under the plant, just as Mili opened the door. 'For you, my love,' he said with a grin as he poured them into her surprised hands.

Mili stood still for a moment, not knowing what to do.

Pointing to the table in the centre of the room, he said, 'Put the blossoms on the table there and ask me to sit down here.' And he pulled up a chair and sat down.

'Yes,' mumbled Mili and put the flowers down.

Raven stole a glance at her. How beautiful she looked. And so peaceful. In her starched pink sari and a white blouse with lace around the edges. Her hair was tied neatly into two plaits. He looked around the simple hut. It had a cane table, some cane chairs, a small bed, a cupboard and some bookshelves in the name of furniture.

'You mean to say, you have given up all that jewellery that you so loved, the palace, the luxuries, for this?'

'I have indeed.'

'Hmm . . .' He propped his chin on the palms of his hands 'I also heard Gandhi's wife has to clean her own toilet in the ashram?'

'I'm not that noble, sir. I refuse to clean the toilet and I still can't accept sweets from a driver. But—'

Raven put a finger on her lips. 'But you have blossomed into a fine young lady and I'm proud to have taught you.'

'Just proud?'

'So does that mean that if I asked you to eat some beef to prove your love for me, you wouldn't?'

'Certainly not, sir.'

Chuckling, Raven got up and took her hands in his. 'Call me Raven,' he whispered.

Looking down, Mili answered, 'How can I call you that, sir? It feels incomplete.'

'You didn't have any qualms calling me Rav*an*.'

'Sir, it was Vicky . . . I called you that just once – when I made that drawing on the blackboard. It was Vicky who used to call you Ravan all the time.'

'You want me to believe that?'

'Yes, sir,' she said wringing her hands in the air. 'I swear on Lord Kishan. I never called you that.'

Raven chuckled again. 'All right, I'll believe you, if you get me some water.'

'Of course, sir,' said Mili. 'That ought to have been

the first thing I asked. You must think I'm a rotten hostess.'

She came back from the kitchen with a glass of water. 'Sir, how about some aloo-poori?'

'Aren't you supposed to eat simple, live simple, in the ashram?'

'Once in a while is all right, sir,' she said with a grin as she made her way to the kitchen, with Raven close on her heels. 'It's not every day that I have a guest,' she said as she took out some flour and prepared the dough.

'Look at you now. You even know how to cook. Whoever would have thought? There was a time when you couldn't even do your hair by yourself. Did you know, before I saw you for the first time, I'd been told you were a princess. But when I saw you – with your hair like Medusa's I said to myself, 'Princess? No way. She's too shabby to be a princess.'

Mili laughed as she rolled out the pooris.

Raven kept speaking.

'You used to be such a girl back then. Twittering over silly things . . .'

'So, I'm not a girl now?' Mili asked, trying to tuck a stray lock of hair behind her ear with the back of her hand.

'No, you aren't,' he replied, curbing the desire to hug her from behind. 'You're a woman now and a beautiful one at that . . .' He pointed to the pooris she had rolled out. 'I can't say the same for these, though. Aren't they supposed to be round?'

Mili sniggered. 'I was just trying to show you the new map of India.' She picked up some potatoes and washed them under the tap. Then wiping her hands on a kitchen towel, she began to peel and dice them.

'That's not how you dice potatoes,' said Raven. He snatched the knife from her hand. 'Let me show you.' Within seconds he had chopped up the potatoes into perfect one-inch-by-one-inch pieces.

'I didn't know you were so "at home" in the kitchen.'

This time Raven did hug her from behind. 'My dear child-woman, what you know about me is just the tip of the iceberg. Come with me to England and you'll learn a lot more about me.'

Shrugging out of his embrace, Mili turned around to face him.

'You're going back to England?'

Raven looked away. 'I have no choice.'

'But why?'

'I know I'm hated in this country, Mili.'

'Because of your father?'

'No. Because of the colour of my skin.'

'I don't.'

'Others do. I regard myself an Indian, but they don't. I can't change the colour of my skin, can I?'

Mili did not answer. He watched her quietly serve the food. They ate in an uncomfortable silence, the buzzing of mosquitoes the only sound that could be heard. Raven sought her eyes across the table but she refused to look at him.

After they had finished eating, he walked over to where she was sitting. He lifted her chin with his finger and forced her to look into his eyes.

'I'm leaving in two days. Will you at least come to the station to see me off?'

'No.'

'Then this is – goodbye?'

She did not reply.

Raven sighed and shrugged his shoulders. He opened the door and left the ashram as quietly as he had come. He felt shattered. He had hoped to propose to her, ask her to come with him to England. But alas! An evening that had started so well had gone all wrong. What was he to do now? Not a single day went by when he did not think about her or miss her. How was he going to live his entire life without her? Mother was unwilling to stay in India any more. And he was reluctant to leave his heart behind.

Chapter Twenty-Five

'Thank you, thank you, thank you, Lord Kishan,' Mili muttered as she reached the platform. The train was still there. But where was Raven? Biting her lower lip, she looked around. She smiled with relief as she finally spotted him. She should have known. Where else could he be, but at the bookstall?

'Sir,' she said, running up to him.

'I knew you'd come,' said Raven with a smile. 'But the train is about to leave.' As he said so, the train blew the whistle. He ran towards his compartment, followed by Mili.

She wanted to stop him, persuade him not to go, but then, did she really have the right to do that? After all, she wasn't even sure what he felt for her. He had not said he loved her. Not even once. And the only relationship that ever existed between them – that of student and teacher – was no more.

Raven stopped at the door, turned to face her and handed her a long-stemmed red rose, just as the guard blew the whistle.

'I'll write to you,' he promised.

She watched him as he climbed into the train, then turned around and waved to her from the door. 'Sir, don't go,' she finally shouted. But the train had started pulling away.

He put his hand next to his ear to indicate he could not hear her.

Running on the platform to keep up with the moving train, Mili cupped her hands over her mouth and shouted, 'Don't go, sir!' But the train had gathered speed. She had left it too late. She stood there for a long time, waving slowly, as the train chugged out of sight, brushing the petals of the rose against her cheek, her eyes shining with unshed tears. A similar train had taken her to Kishangarh, just six years ago, and her life had changed for ever. And now another train was taking her life away from her.

It shouldn't have left so soon. She felt cheated. There was so much she wanted to speak to Raven about, to persuade him not to go to England. But now, it was too late. She walked slowly out of the station, a long, lonely life stretching ahead of her. She stopped at the main entrance. She felt as though she had left something behind. She looked around, then checked her belongings. Her purse, her hanky, her money, they were all there. The only thing missing was her heart. And she had given it to someone whom she may never see again.

'Memsahib.'

It was her driver.

'What is it, Bhootnath?' she asked.

'Rumours of Hindu–Muslim riots again. We better get out fast.'

Mili hurried to the car. Riots had indeed broken out. As the car drove through the city, she saw hundreds of Hindus carrying sticks, torches and tridents attacking Muslim homes. Shouts of 'Jai Shri Ram' rent the air. The car was now moving at a snail's pace. She cringed as she saw half-burnt houses, courtyards strewn with split grain, broken crockery, burnt wood, torn photographs and bits and pieces of other personal belongings. She watched in horror as some rioters looted a shop. They threw out all the furniture from the shop and made a bonfire of it in the middle of the road.

'I think we better abandon car and hide, memsahib. I scared they might set it alight.'

Mili nodded and ran out of the car. Keeping low, they made their way through the crowd to a by-lane. They kept running till they reached a small park and hid behind some thick bushes and hedges.

'We wait here till dark,' said Bhootnath. 'Then we escape to ashram.'

Nodding again, Mili looked around. It looked like a quiet residential area. The park, which must fill up with children on a normal evening, was empty today. Just then, a mob rounded the corner and approached the house opposite the park. They were Muslims. Mili held her breath. She watched in terror from behind the bushes as they banged on the door.

A postman came along. 'Why are you bothering them?' he asked the throng.

'We were told a wealthy Hindu family lives here,' said someone from the crowd.

'No they aren't. They're Muslims like you and me,' said the postman.

The crowd hesitated as they debated whether to believe the postman or not. They decided not to and broke down the door.

'Bloody liar,' shouted one of the men at the postman who was trying to slink away. He held him by his collar and kicked him hard. Mili gasped as the crowd then broke into the house and dragged a boy of about twelve and his father out. The boy was trembling and crying while his father was pleading with the irate Muslims to spare his son. But it was in vain. Mili covered her mouth with both her hands to stop herself from screaming as a dagger slit the boy's throat. She closed her eyes, keeping her hands tightly clasped over her mouth, and sobbed silently. After what seemed like a very long time, there was silence. She listened carefully. All the voices had died away. Opening her eyes, she peered through the bushes. She could see the slashed bodies of the boy and his father covered in blood on the parapet in front of the house, under the peepul tree. They seemed to have been cut into pieces. Mili swallowed and closed her eyes again. She felt numb. And cold. As though a block of ice had been placed on her forehead.

Much later that night, as Mili sat on a mat in her kitchen, holding a comforting cup of tea in her hands, she thought back on the happenings of that day. It seemed like one long nightmare. First the hasty goodbye to Raven, which left her feeling bereft, then the orgy of looting and bloodshed. And then the never-ending flight back to the ashram under cover of darkness. She had never run so much or so fast in her entire life.

She felt a deep sadness. Like she had felt at the time of Gurpreet's hanging. He had avenged Vicky's death, but at what cost . . . ? India was now free. But was this the price she was to pay for her freedom? 'Our country has been reborn,' she had heard people say. But was this hatred and killing what she and the rest of the country had been waiting for? Rejoicing for? Was this the new India that all the leaders had fought for, laid down their lives for?

Maybe Raven was right to leave the country. How could anyone live in a place so wrought with hatred? She felt angry, drained. Today the Hindus and Muslims were at each other. Who knows? What if tomorrow they turned their hatred to the handful of English who had stayed behind? No, she would write to him. Tell him he mustn't tarry and must leave this country as soon as possible.

She got up and put away the cup. Sitting down at her desk, she tore a sheet of paper from her notebook. '*Dear Raven Sir,*' she wrote. Then crumpled the paper and took out another sheet. '*Dear Raven,*' she wrote again. Shaking her head shyly, she tore it up. '*Dear sir . . .*' she finally wrote.

It was the first week of January and cold winds had been sweeping from the north for almost a week. Mili wrapped her shawl tightly as she sat on the rug on the veranda, teaching a group of girls how to use the spinning wheel. She glanced at the gate for the tenth time that morning, to see if the postman was coming. No sign of him yet.

It had been four months since Raven had left and four months since she had posted her letter to him. She hoped he had reached England safely by now. She tried to forget him, but she couldn't. Eating, sleeping, working, drinking tea – he was constantly on her mind. If only he hadn't come to her hut in the ashram. If only he had not touched her, held her, kissed her, it might have been easier to forget him. If only . . .

'Sister, letter for you.'

Mili looked up. It was the postman. Finally. She snatched both the letters that he held out to her and ran indoors. Bolting the door, she tore open one envelope. It was from Vidushi. She and Jatin had settled down in a small village in Nepal, it said. They had a two-year-old son. Now that India was free, she felt it was safe to finally get in touch with her again. Mili looked at the other envelope. It was from Mausi. Her heart sank.

'Didi, come fast,' called out one of the girls from the veranda.

Leaving Vidushi and Mausi's letters on the desk, Mili scurried outside. She was needed in the office. A badly beaten woman, found by the side of a road, had been brought in. She was too scared to tell anyone who had hit her. 'Must be her useless husband,' Mili muttered as she examined her. She gave instructions to the girls to take her to one of the huts and to call the nurse.

Much later, as she came back to her hut and sat

down to eat, her eyes fell on the unopened envelope from Mausi. Mili chuckled. She was sure she must have written, 'I hope you're reading the Ramayana everyday and not forgetting to wash your hands before meals.'

She opened the envelope and began to read. *My dear child-woman* . . . This did not sound like Mausi. With a thumping heart, Mili quickly turned the sheets over. It was signed – *Raven.* But the letter had come from Kishangarh. That's why she had thought it was from Mausi. She looked at the envelope. Yes, the stamp on it clearly said Kishangarh. Puzzled, she started reading the letter again.

My dear child-woman,

You will be surprised to see the postmark. Most of the English students have left Kishangarh, as also a large number of the English teachers. I ought to have left as well, but after much deliberation, I decided not to. How could I? At least not until the doctors have devised a way of staying alive in one country while one's heart resides in another. Until such a day, I have decided to continue staying in Kishangarh . . .

I know this is the coward's way, but I don't think I will ever be able to say this to you face to face. Maybe because I was your teacher once upon a time or maybe it is my ego . . .

I don't know where to begin. Do you remember what I said to you at the party in Lakeview Club that night? That I was falling in love with you? I meant it then, just as I mean it now . . . It killed

*me when you came to me the next day and I had to
lie to you. And the look on your face when I said
I didn't remember anything – it cut me to pieces. I
felt like a worm . . .*

*But what could I do? I was your teacher. I
was eleven years older than you. I had to let you
go . . . grow . . . blossom . . .*

*And after you left Kishangarh and the years flew
past, I thought I had got over my feelings for you.
But the truth is, when I saw you last year again in
Kishangarh, I found myself falling in love with you
all over again.*

*When you came to my house that evening, you
were this woman who spoke so zealously about
her work, her organisation, her paper, her dreams
– so different from the child-woman I had kissed
goodbye some years ago. And yet the same smile,
though not that shy any more, just a little, perhaps.
And the same laughter, the same dark, intense eyes.
Do you know how beautiful your eyes look when
they flash with anger or excitement? I knew then
that this was the woman I wished to have and hold
for the rest of my life.*

*There is one image of you that I can never get
out of my mind. Do you know which one? When
we had gone to Hem Parvat and you had quietly
slipped your little hand into my large calloused
hand so trustingly, so innocently, so confidently,
that I had almost lost control . . .*

*We will have a wonderful life together,
Malvika . . . Cooking together, like we did at the*

ashram, reading together, setting up our home together. I am waiting eagerly for you to say yes and be mine.

Yours truly,
Raven.

P.S. By the way, will you marry me?
P.P.S. I forgot to mention, in the last letter that you wrote to me, there were three grammatical errors and four spelling mistakes. The comma was also missing on two occasions.

'Oh sir, I'm not your student any more,' Mili muttered with a grin. She kissed the letter, held it close to her bosom with both her hands and swirled around, doing a little jig.

Mili was sitting at her desk, looking through some papers, when one of the inmates of the ashram announced that there was an English gentleman here to see her. Mili looked up. Raven? 'Send him to my hut,' she replied. Her heart began to beat erratically. She took a deep breath. 'Relax, Mili, relax,' she told herself.

Five minutes later, Raven lifted the khus mat hanging over the door and walked in. He wore a white shirt with sleeves rolled back carelessly and a pair of khaki trousers. He looked like that Greek god he had taught them about in the English class. What was his name? Adonis?

She hid a mischievous grin as a thought flashed across

her mind. Looking sombre, she pointed to a cane chair next to her desk and said, 'Kindly be seated.'

Raven sat down.

'And what brings you here, sir?' she said, leafing through the papers on her desk. She suppressed her smile as Raven scrunched up his eyes and studied her face.

He then gave her a lopsided smile and cleared his throat. 'Ma'am, I'd sent an application for marriage some time back. I was wondering if you have been able to find the time to consider it.'

Mili pointed to the pile of papers on her desk. 'I've had so much to do, I haven't yet had the time to look at it.'

'I'm sorry to have wasted your time. Good day to you, ma'am.' He got up and turned to leave.

Mili could control herself no longer. She burst out laughing and flung her arms around his neck. 'Of course I will marry you,' she whispered.

Raven smiled and held her in a tight embrace. 'I love you so much, my child-woman.'

'I love you too, Raven S—' But before she could say 'sir', he had covered her mouth with his.

And as they kissed, the rays of the setting sun filled the room with a warm glow. The day was about to end, only to be reborn the next day.

Author's Note

As a child, I spent nine glorious years of my life in the hill stations of Kumaon, now a part of Uttarakhand. I have drawn upon my childhood memories of places like Almora, Nainital, Pithoragarh – to create this idyllic village-town called Kishangarh.

The other two fictional places in the novel are Mohanagar and Shaampur, as also the river Bhoori. I chose these names as Mili, the protagonist of the novel is a devotee of Lord Krishna, who is also known by a number of other names including Kishan, Mohan and Shaam.

Glossary

Agarbatti	incense stick
Ahimsa	non-violence
Aloo	potato
Amaltas	the golden shower tree
Apsara	angel
Arti	a Hindu ritual or prayer
Ashram	hermitage
Baba	baby; also used to address someone respectfully; father
Badam	almond
Baksheesh	tip
Balle balle	an expression of happiness
Baraat	wedding procession
Baisakhi	a Sikh/Punjabi festival
Barfi	an Indian sweet in the shape of a diamond
Barre	big
Batti	wick
Bauji	father
Bhabhi	brother's wife
Bhagavad Gita/ Gita	a 700-verse Hindu scripture
Bhagwan	God
Bhai/Bhaisaheb	elder brother

Bharat Mata ki Jai	Long Live Mother India
Bhutia	of Tibetan origin
Bindi	a small, usually round, forehead decoration
Brinjal	aubergine
Chachi	aunt
Chai	tea
Chinar	poplar tree
Chulha	mud stove
Chundri sari	a type of sari
Dadaji	grandfather
Dahi	yogurt
Darta hai saala	he's scared
Dhoop	frankincense
Didi	elder sister
Doli	palanquin
Dupatta	stole (clothes)
Firangis	foreigners
Gamcha	piece of cloth
Ganesh	the Hindu elephant god
Ghagra choli	skirt and blouse
Gujjia	an Indian sweet
Gulal	coloured powder used during Holi
Gur	jaggery
Gora	fair-skinned
Haiyo Rabba	oh God
Harijan	Gandhiji referred to the untouchables as Harijans or children of God
Holi	Hindu festival of colours

Hyderabadi	from Hyderabad
Jai Hind	Hail India
Jalebis	an Indian sweet
Kaafal	a fruit found on the hills of Uttarakhand
Kadi	a curry made out of gram flour
Khadi	homespun cotton
Khotta	donkey
Khus	type of grass
Kishan/Krishna/ Kanha	a Hindu god
Kumaoni	of Kumaon
Kumkum	a red powder used for social religious purposes
Kurta	long tunic-like shirt
Laddoos	round Indian sweets
Lassi	a drink made from milk or yoghurt
Lahenga	long skirt
Langar	free food offered in a Gurdwara
Lathis	sticks
Lohri	a Punjabi/Sikh festival
Lol biwi's kotha	home of the prostitutes
Mahabharata	an Indian epic
Maji	mother
Marjaaneyaa	a swear word
Masala	spice
Mausi	mother's sister
Mem	madam
Milap	meeting
Mithai	Indian sweets

Murg	chicken
Nani	grandmother
Nukti laddoo	Indian sweets
Paan	betel leaf
Pahari	of the mountains
Pakora	bhajji
Parathas	Indian bread
Parvat	mountain
Peepul	fig tree
Phaag	songs sung during Holi
Pheriwala	hawker
Pitaras	metal box
Prasad	offering from god
Preet/Preeto	beloved
Puja	prayer
Rajasthani	from Rajasthan
Rakshas	demon
Roti	Indian bread
Salwar kameez	long tunic-like shirt worn over pyjama-like trousers
Sardar	a male Sikh
Sasural	in-laws' house
Sat Sri Akal	a Punjabi greeting
Sepoys	soldiers
Sindoor	vermilion powder worn by married Hindu women
Sitaphal	custard apple
Siyappa	a Punjabi swear word
Swaraj	self-rule
Swayamvar	the practice of choosing a husband

Syce	groom
Tadka daal	tempered lentils
Tandor	clay oven
Thelewala	a hawker selling his wares on a cart
Upanishads	Hindu philosophical texts
Vande Mataram	I bow to thee, Mother India
Yaara	friend

Acknowledgements

My heartfelt thanks to:

Mr Hem Pandey for patiently answering all my questions about schools and colleges in Uttarakhand.

Shilpi for conceptualising the character of Gurpreet and a couple of scenes in the book.

Harmeet, my Punjabi dictionary.

Susie, Chiara, Sara and Lesley for all the hard work and attention to detail.

Jane for her support, guidance, insight and positive energy.

My parents for their encouragement and pride in everything I do, however small or insignificant.

My children, Karn and Diya, my inspiration, my reason for being, my all.

My husband Bhaskar, as always, to whom I have dedicated this book.

When I wrote the acknowledgements for *The World*

Beyond, I was told that at least it wasn't as long as the glossary. This time, it threatens to be longer than the novel itself. So I'm afraid I will have to confine myself to a collective thank you to my dear family and friends. Each and every one of you, who has touched my life, has contributed to this novel, either directly or indirectly and for that I am eternally grateful.